THE
MOTORCYCLIST

THE
MOTORCYCLIST

GEORGE ELLIOTT CLARKE

HarperCollins*PublishersLtd*

Published by HarperCollins Publishers Ltd

HarperCollins books may be purchased for educational, business, or sales promotional use through our Special Markets Department.

HarperCollins Publishers Ltd
2 Bloor Street East, 20th Floor
Toronto, Ontario, Canada
M4W 1A8

www.harpercollins.ca

Library and Archives Canada Cataloguing in Publication information is available upon request

ISBN 978-1-44344-513-9

Printed and bound in the United States
RRD 9 8 7 6 5 4 3 2 1

For William Lloyd Clarke (1935–2005),
artist and motorcyclist

Not only pain
There was beauty and longing.
—Lorenzo Thomas, "Historiography"

Muore per metà chi lascia un' immagine di se stesso nei figli.
—Carlo Goldoni, *Pamela*

PROVISO

Tell him Mr. Clarke sent you there—
Mr. William Clarke—
He'll fix you up all right.

    —STEPHEN VINCENT BENÉT, *JOHN BROWN'S BODY*

The unpublished 1959–60 *Diary* of my father, William Lloyd Clarke (1935–2005), informs this novel. Because his *Diary* chronicles the year of my conception, it is the catalyst for my story. Moreover, the *Diary* relates my father's endeavours to secure *Love* and a sustaining and satisfying wage. Still, his *Diary* only *hints* at my novel: I have rendered the *Diary*'s subtleties explicit and fleshed out its abbreviated episodes. I have also guessed at some motivations and invented others, just as I have wilfully altered names and redacted characters. I have also exaggerated or minimized real-life flaws and virtues. The story reflects upon *Race* and *Romance* in an era when *Chance* governed family planning and *Prejudice* determined social status. I describe, then, the quandaries of courtship pertinent to a Cold War generation. So, the novel is faithful to the truths in W.L.C.'s *Diary* (and his *Trip Diary*, a chronicle of his 1959 U.S. Eastern Seaboard tour)—such as street names, movie titles, girls' initials, weather conditions, world events, and, crucially, the motorcyclist's *actual* life. This novel is neither biography nor history, but it does sketch the he-said, she-said, *black* comedies of coupling and their *personal* consequences. All open to *Interpretation*. As usual . . .

George Elliott Clarke (X. States)
Toronto, Ontario
Nisan XV

DETERMINATION

And before I'd be a slave,
I'll be buried in my grave . . .
— Africadian Anthem, "O Freedom"

A most honest thing is pavement. It doesn't go wrong, even when it curves. It's always taking you somewhere, even if you are clueless about a destination or just insouciant, letting miles lap and lapse, lap and lapse, so long as the road is always more highway and freeway than it's ever a strict street or—worse—a blankety-blank dead end.

And pavement is hard, serious; it doesn't let you down. If you spill, then rub and smear your face against it, scraping even your teeth. You know the incident is fact; there is no fakery. It slaps you awake brutally. You can't daydream when it comes to navigating a motorcycle over the potholes and the busted bits of truck tires and even broken parts of cars or dead creatures, their bodies pierced and exploded by tons of chrome simultaneously battering and skewering, or simply smashing and splattering such unlucky critters.

(It be sad *Art*: the ruddy incineration of fur, skin, and bone upon collision with chrome, so living blood becomes tarnish, and chrome looks muddied once blood dries.)

You need a cold eye, a clear eye, to avoid the random annihilations that pavement permits. You need a steady hand, an iron grip, to steer yourself over that tough surface: to intact arrive, wherever. *Stately*, prancing, *stately*.

Pavement will never let you take it for granted. It is what you've always wanted, in launching yourself, Coloured chap, out a harsh burgh, that East Coast city prospering most when at war, embarking sailors to preserve the English King and Queen, keeping the world "safe" for Empire, if not "democracy." Eh?

It's not pavement that throws you for a curve, a loop, but the cemetery at the end of it all, all that racing and passing. Or it's the traffic jam that troubles: it's always as long and as hard to sit through as a pregnancy.

Good thing that the wind is almost a spectral femininity, caressing and mollycoddling as it slips across helmet or open face, nipping and tucking, kissing and enfolding. The wind cradles and nurses. It touches intimately, even whistling about your crotch, for no denim or leather can resist its fluid penetration.

And that's what an engine is good for: to greet and pet the wind, to move in tandem with it as suavely as a beau and a beaut. There is a marriage of sorts, or, a flirtation. Man and machine hurtle forward in a non-stop attack that is also surrender, a yielding to the atmosphere about, the sumptuous tang of cow shit and apple blossoms, gasoline and engine oil.

Yes, pavement is terminal—somewhere, sometime—but the deferment is vertiginous. You think you can reach an end, but there are reversals, switchbacks; or you stop short, while still steering forward.

But as you look out over the pavement, or dismount and stand upon it, it is both ephemeral *Possibility*—just like the horizon—and as solidly factual as answered prayer, or, maybe, as arrival. Fascinatingly, even a humdrum alley, an oasis of garbage and rancid smoke, bleeds into the higher order of the street, its curbs and gutters and sidewalks, controlling and facilitating the movements of vehicles and pedestrians, and then bleeds yet farther into the ascetic aristocracy of freeway and highway, where advertising almost vanishes and whole cities and towns appear as exits or rest stops, utterly vacant of *Glamour*.

The cars—always sleek, stretching, capacious, built to carry a brood of oral-oriented consumers (babes at teats, men chomping cigars, women sucking candies)—represent every income paid out, from wheezing jitney to bounding Jaguar. Indeed, this year, 1959, cars are so spacious that meals are served in them, movies are watched from them, and babies are conceived—and even delivered—in them.

One hears, at times, the backfire of a cut-rate auto, half-rust and half-paid-for, lurching down a street: a sad-sack *Looney Tune* come to *Li'l Abner* life.

A vehicle's leather seats prove the triumph of the industrial city over the church-and-cattle countryside. The city doesn't see a cow, only comfy fashion. Headlights show off secular transcendence, an incandescent halo that transforms autos into godly chariots come down to earth.

Of course, the motorcycle's an impractical machine, compared to the automobile: Detroit bodies and Hollywood interiors, chrome and dream. But the cycle means purity—of one-man or one-duo transpo. Cars imply—usually—family or the whole gang tuckin in.

Intriguingly, a weird democracy governs the highway: every destination is as valid as any other. New York City has more exits, more on- and off-ramps, than does, say, Halifax, Nova Scotia. Yet, each is a terminal capillary of a road that skirts it, bypassing it, leaving it to shrink in a rear-view mirror, and either city—whatever its magnitude and vitality—will shrink until it is only a blur, a haze, a map dot.

But the long-distance highway—turnpikes, interstates, the

Trans-Canada, etc.—are also working-class in mood, so brazenly Stalin-ist, for they are controlled by truckers and trolled by police. All other drivers and vehicles are second-class and third-class interlopers—in contrast to the true lords of the freeways, and all the pit stops, rest stops, and garages built for their benefit and to attract their largesse.

No wonder Rébecca Nul, the *bourgeoise*, adulteress heroine of *La Motocyclette*, dies trying to pass a transport truck. The act of passing, of overtaking another vehicle, is class warfare, a bit of Marxism-Leninism that the overtaken *never* take in stride.

All roads lead to Rome, but a few shunt to Damascus. Before you, always, in whatever direction, lies *Perdition* or *Salvation*. Just start your engine. Go.

TOUR I

'Perhaps we could look each other up.'
'It's a date. 1959.'
    —John Glassco, *Memoirs of Montparnasse*

Saturday, May 9

Carl thrusts back bedclothes—a bristling surf—and leaps up, ascendant, urgent to start motorcycling afresh: to get from Easter to Christmas, astraddle. He dabs Brylcreem on his Negro curls; he slaps Snap on his hands, to scour off even invisible grit. Quick, he sheathes himself in black leather chic, from boots to jacket. The boots are so polished that sunlight, enmeshed in that dark dazzle, mirrors a solar eclipse. He's had the toggery ready weeks now. He picks up his black helmet that he's painted so edgily, flames fringing the face area. *Apollo Negro*, he audits his flash in a full-length mirror, then strides—no, struts—out the door, awaiting, expecting, plaudits. Practically jogs to the Halifax Motorcycle Shoppe. Motorcycle man is slick; just sharp style—like Lee Van Cleef, only more coppery, less devious, in look. *Rough trade*, he could be, forwarding such svelte, sporty black, a blackness that radiates—he posits—both immaculate macho and charismatic charity.

• • •

9 a.m.: Punctual, pale, reedy, spectacled, jet-haired Corkum enters the backroom and flicks on the lights. He whooshes open the front door to his sable-leather patron; exchange of hands. Bamming a screen door, Corkum leads Carl through the shop and out back. Primed to go is "Liz II," as Carl has named his motorcycle, out of fealty to the Queen. An act of sweet, beatnik *Irony*.

Carl doth got royalist predilections: He likes Nat King Cole, just for the middle name of the crooner. He's no jazz fan, but lauds the monikers of Duke Ellington and Count Basie. Why not? His natty aunt Pretty, the worldwide-famed contralto, has scored the hat trick of serenading Edward VIII (thus becoming the only Canuck and only Negro to have an audience with the ephemeral monarch), then George VI (though he coughed throughout her performance, due to his royal prerogative of lung cancer), and, most recently, Queen Liz II herself, whose tiara boogie-woogied when she heard Pretty's show-stopping aria as Carmen.

The bike's fresh polish is transparent silver. Liz II blazes; Carl beams. Offset by chrome parts and black rubber tires and grips, her purple shade flares gloriously, shaming the dull light of morn. Carl walks her down the driveway—like a groom takin his bride down the aisle. *Boy oh boy*, he thinks as he straddles the bike. *Mine—and does it ever feel good to be back on her.*

So pertinent is the machine to his being, his bearing, his antipathy for *Ennui* and *Ignorance*, that he's told some friends that he got to Bavaria, *personally*, to oversee the final tinkering in the crafting of this motorcycle. Carl don't care that he's turned to German engineering to realize *Excellence* at a time when the propaganda adjective *jerry-built* presupposes poor construction. His purchase flouts *Prejudice*; his profile, astride the machine and gliding black leather and purple metal, through Halifax streets must give whites-only segregationists serious heart attacks. Or so he grins to himself, imagining such a scene.

Liz II gleams gorgeous, in that violet paint and loud, spanking chrome. The *Big Marvellous Wonder* (BMW) boasts huge black fenders, with *C.A.B.*—Carl's initials—flagged atop the front fender. No mistaking that she's *his*. Like Aladdin rubbing the genie-laden lamp, Carl will hand-scour Liz II until her sheen slashes every stray eye. The machine is lean power; Carl is now bluntly male. Buffed. Not to be *rebuffed*.

And don't the world look better—sliding, guying, giddy—mirrored in chrome? Kids love to see their faces stretched or squashed, depending on how near or distant they are to this wondrous element—a silvery mirror—that proves that shapes are never as steady as geometry alleges. The machine's chrome whirls and swirls the surrounding vista as Carl leans forward, projecting himself into wind; but the bike's silvery, mercurial finish also lends the world a fanfare of colour: a rainbow fringes all.

Carl steers the sporty R69 model Bayerische Motoren Werke (600 cc), a first-class bike that seats two superbly. The two-cylinder, four-stroke engine, plus four-speed gears, lets a solo rider, scrunched low, in snug clothing, attain 102 mph. Add a passenger, and the top speed drops to 90 mph. The R69 BMW is *Beautiful Motorcycle Work*. This majestic bolt of aluminum darts through streets that got no choice but to yield.

After scrimping, scraping, and scavenging for railway-job tips, Carl motors—masters—the first brand new BMW in Nova Scotia. A shining, purring thing! The machine enthrones him: black prince of the roads. He attains that great object: *Majesty!*

Hotly, the trim machine glitters. The tail lights, bunched together, offer a cornucopia of potential directions. Yet, the R69 is sleek, clear of unnecessary ornament, save for the saddlebags, which Carl has decorated to accent the aerodynamic aesthetic of her suspension, engine, and exhaust. Liz II is as intricate as a lithe, nimble insect, but far gaudier, as if animated da Vinci–drawn musculature. Carl relishes the ingenious poise of pistons and gears, the innumerable Eiffel Towers figured in the wheel spokes.

The ignition key is in the centre position and the neutral indicator shows a green-for-go glow. Exultant, Carl leaps up, thrusts down, kick-starts the engine that now roars and snorts, born again, bawling, and ready for brawling. He buckles on the helmet; the red, yellow, and white painted flames, licking back from the black face opening, look as proud and as incendiary as the flag of any new African state. Yep: here be liberated Ghana, a one-man motorcade.

Carlyle—a.k.a. Carl—Black whistles as he manoeuvres his machine over the gullies of this dirt driveway in which every rainstorm gouges new furrows. He nods at all who pass, all who eye him, handsome, with a lean, iron-dark frame, fierce eyes, and a steel-jaw look. His speech sounds *suave*; his wardrobe models *dapper*.

The man be Coloured, but not *colonized*, not *totally*. Unlike his buddies, he can escape, temporarily, the *Drudgery* that traps so many "Nofaskosha" Negroes: from the red-uniformed man with a flashlight, ushering kids into a cinema (the closest a dark dude can get to being a cop), to the shoeshine boy, or waitress, whose tips are the reward of a sultry smile, to the folks aching in *Labour* that shatters souls. In contrast, Carl can be a cavalier, a "cat" privy to cathouses.

This Year of the Pig, Carl be twenty-three (and soon twenty-four), a Grade Ten dropout (at age eighteen), and a linen-and-equipment checker for the Canadian National Railway. He seems a helluva hail-fellow-well-met, a guy who whistles as he totes baggage and bedding to and fro night-train sleeping cars. But *Discontent* nudges him to leaf through Ian Fleming at lunch and warble Sibelius when he's grooming the sleepers, preparing them for the next outing to Montreal or the Boston States.

So he desires Coloured chicks *and* white dolls (the *Playboy* school of *Integration*). He loves Beethoven, Bach, and his BMW. He classifies himself as the most incongruous—most conspicuously debonair—Negro in all of Nova Scotia.

Carl suspects: to advance is to recreate the *Self*—in a chrome mirror.

• • •

Wavin at Corkum, Carl rumbles—*Hurrah!*—down the H.M.S. driveway and onto the easy slope of Cunard Strcct, blasting cast (the machine rattles like a Gatling gun, but much less so than other bikes) two blocks to Gottingen—that German-branded—Street, and then executes a right turn that dashes him south to Cogswell. Now, Carl takes a left that dips him east again, downhill toward the deadliest naval harbour on the North Atlantic. (Halifax berths a hundred warships easy.) At Brunswick Street, with the wind bawling—banshee—in his ears, Carl veers south, then flies east down Buckingham Street, straight to harbour-hugging Water Street. (Because the wood-frame houses are painted a kaleidoscope of colours, each Haligonian *rue* is a Red Baron–style flying circus, albeit grounded.) Carl streams south again, all along the waterfront, following the zigzag promenade, with its sail-and-rigging shops and Red Ensign–flagged government edifices on his right.

To his left, Carl spies the harbour piers, docks, wharves, storage tanks (here oil, there molasses), and multifarious vessels, some flapping sails and others belching smoke. The smell is rousing, too: fresh-caught mackerel vies with the Moirs Chocolates factory aroma; and there's the salt-water-laden gusts off the Atlantic, plus the diesel fumes of some cargo ships and the oily odours of other vehicles. At the water's edge, Halifax feels like Istanbul: Dartmouth's minaret is the Imperoyal gas flare.

Sensual scents inundate downtown. Streets reek of mussels and lobster; smells of salt water, tobacco, beer, fish—mackerel, trout, perch, cod, and eel—and bread abound; and then whiffs of sidewalk-side perfume.

A brick smells like apple blossoms; a leather coat decants burgundy.

The burgh is a city of fumes—and of nylons that can be oil, so sheer as to be liquid. A guy hugs on a dame, and she either writhes away like smoke, or slips away like wet glass. Halifax is, say sailors, Babylon on the Atlantic: any *Vice* at any price. But the city pretends to be Salem, jailing fly-by-night whores the way the Massachusetts town hanged witches.

The elongation of Carl's arms to the handlebars, the pistoning of his feet (when required), the instinctive, adept agility of his body, torquing to the needs of speed and grace-in-space, jitters him with ecstasy. Liz II connects him to the world: his feet are bare inches from pavement or soil or grass; the wind licks him with rain and peppers him with bugs; the sun heats even as the breeze cools. So much is he an articulate extension of the muscular machine (or *vice versa*), Carl feels his driving merges boxing and ballet. How he anticipates gliding brazenly—black in black on black—through a city whose billboards and posters glorify pallid London and alabaster Hollywood. Carl will hurtle into view—a dark flash, a glimmering figure—seizing a corner, loping a boulevard, hovering above a hill, his wheels taking briefly to air.

Other vehicles are hindrances and obstacles, but they also vanish in the wake of his gleaming, "Johnny Angel" passage. His lungs seem to enlarge, engorged by the oxygen of speedy flight. The exhilaration is hearty, bullish—like how Lazarus felt when he limbo'd up from his grave.

A pose? Sure: a (white) woman turns her head; she sees Carl—the "lug"—his mahogany visage flaring dark shades, and she feels a twinge of arousal. So he hopes. And, yes, he's flattered. But Liz II is just a prop: the machine props him up. Something has to.

His good news? *Wage Slavery* and *Light Deficiency* end—if only for *today*. Carl seeks *Pleasure* now—just sheer, reflex *Happiness*—like a Greenwich Village in-crowd type or a Harlem bebop player. The Maritime air—salty, fishy, chocolatey—thrills his lungs. The BMW is an airship, uplifting him—from other cars, other folks' creeds, and the dullard crowd. Carl wheels about like a slick hero. He could be one of Hemingway's matadors, one of Hannibal's mountain-striding generals. All winter, until now, his life has been humdrum walking or trolleying among the same set of city blocks (and trolling through the same gals). Until *today*. *Ta-da!*

"Now is the time," to quote Dr. King (from, yes, a more enlightened context), for Carl to indulge—to be all man for all women in all seasons, to make up for make-believe *Equality* by making love. He suspects that his behaviour is bankrupt, but he can't help it. He has seen too many photos of Negroes put on trial—or lynched—because of their lust for love.

Only now doth Carl expect women's heads to swivel as he U-turns or pivots, one black-booted, blue-jeaned leg extended for careful balance. Finely, from his mounted vantage, women seem to step with sweetened energy, dancing or bouncing their way along each sidewalk, each concrete panel suddenly flaunting a catwalk.

Carl's aviator-style sunglasses, like black chrome, make onlookers' visages expand, contract, and assume a slick of colour. The white-marble city buildings swim and swirl over his black shades, only to be dismissed.

Carl zips past the Central Wharf, the Imperial Oil Company dock, the Market Wharf, the Dartmouth ferry, the City Wharf, the Irving Oil slip, A.J.M. Smith Limited (famous for its gifts of *vers libre*, i.e., "Free Worms," to anglers), Bliss Bissett & Walter Whitman & Co. (relatives of the Yankee bard), National Seafoods Products Limited, Boutelier's Wharf, Robert Burns Fisheries, North Atlantic Fisheries, Nova Scotia Light and Power Company, and the Halifax Harbour Commission. The government buildings and the Keith's brewery come clad in as much beautifying ivy as do Harvard and Yale.

Abruptly, Carl ascends from Water to Lower Water Street (which is actually *uphill*) and meets with Terminal Road. Directly before him looms the north side of the red-brick facade of the Nova Scotia Hotel.

Rolling west to Hollis Street, Carl turns again to prance directly in front of the CNR station, the railway building. Now he gotta stop. *Tarnation!*

His ride has taken only ten minutes. It seemed longer because Carl just had to—just had to—relish this indisputably fine sunlight.

Down in America, the white Beats and white bikers pout like James Dean, slouch like Marlon Brando. Carl differs; he digs James Baldwin. Yet, he admires Brando—despite the soupçon of homosexuality in his slumping posture, his kissable sneer, his T-shirt-and-blue-jeans lingerie, his hard-candy ass. Carl likes to vogue—to appear sweet, juicy, intolerably spicy; to garb in black like Kid Hamlet; to astonish dainty, plaster faces; to inspire oohs and ahhs. What he'd like: to be a Lone Ranger type, cutting through a landscape, or loping away—lickety-split—from a *Catastrophe*. To lone-range into a bedroom, then mosey off at dawn.

What a thrill, now, to conquer the train station—like Miles Davis taking Paris. Nothing's out of place on Carl or his machine.

Still, he's never dreamt the coffee shop waitresses—blond, ponytailed Una, sixteen; brunette and blue-eyed Mona, nineteen; and Violette, twenty-five (homely enough to be an old maid, but whose violet eyes are as hypnotic as a vampire's)—would rub up against him so, laurel him with their perfume, press their tits against his arm or chest. Their fuss makes Carl blush invisibly; he feels unambiguously cocky.

But *Joy* is perilous: His bosses got jealous, in January, when they green-eyed that newspaper photo of Carl, a bow-tied and spiffy Baptist, standing behind *two* white girls, also Baptist, bent over a table before him. The bosses' lyncher imaginations could easily picture sodomy. Here's one more reason for Carl to get out of Dodge as frequently as he can: to dodge backward men spitting *Spite* between puffs on their reeking stogies.

Carl's work shift—a long four hours—just drags. Too many sheets to launder; too many suitcases to tote. Not enough tips to make the bother worthwhile. No wonder he's itchin to jump back on Liz II and earn the debut saddle sores of the season.

• • •

2 p.m.: White-marble, white-breasted Britannia looks on in profile as Carl roars from the station, throttles west up South Street, then north at Robie, then farther north to Kempt Road, thus bisecting the upside-down Tyrannosaurus rex–skull shape of Halifax. Passing Fairview Lawn Cemetery (graced with corpses from two disasters, the *Titanic* sinking of 1912 and the even-more-titanic Halifax Explosion of 1917), Carl skirts the Coloured village of Africville—invisibly northeast of him (though 150 years old, it's struck from city maps)—the city dump, swamped by squawking seagulls, directly before him, and heads north-west to Rockingham and the Bedford Highway, girding Bedford Basin's west shore.

Carl aims for Sunnyside, just past the north reach of Bedford Basin. En route, he ogles Prince's Lodge, the breast-shaped love nest that Prince Edward, Duke of Kent, had built for fucking his French mistress, Madame de Saint-Laurent: heaven for the hell of it.

Carl holds Liz II steady at 50 mph. It's also windy going, but the vision of scads of other bikes, pitching against wind and traffic, helps him pitch forward too.

(Speedsters cut corners to get ahead. They treat speed limits as no better than a Manufacturer's Suggested Retail Price: prone to inflation.)

Carl scoots past aquiline, two-toned cars that, with their thick fins, look like flat-bodied rockets. Cinnamon odours bless the air. Apple blossoms erupt from bush.

Admittedly, Liz II's an individualist—or monopoly—form of loco-motion. She, the machine, says, "There's room in my life for only one other person, and *she* must sit behind me, following my lead, my map, my directions, my interests." A car is practically a church-picnic bus, suggesting the driver is a minister in search of a "flock." A motorcycle is about *going*; a car is about *arrival*. Or so Carl sees. Then again, a man's gotta have guts to forego a car's economical advantage (an extra roof over his head) and offer himself to the mercy of the elements, to favour BMW or Harley-Davidson or Indian over Ford, Dodge, and DeSoto. Cars are ships. Carl prefers to be a clipper, blending with the wind, the sun, the rain.

At the Chickenburger, Carl's late lunch is a jumbo chicken burger, plus brown-gravy-slathered fries, plus a chocolate shake. He hangs round an hour, studying other bikes (see that 1953 sky-blue Harley-Davidson FL Hydra-Glide) and lookin o'er da ladies.

Too soon, Carl dashes back to downtown Halifax. Here he can see—and be seen by—the neighbourhood beauts, in long, tight skirts and sharp heels or blue jeans, or white bobby socks and black loafers. Whatever they wear, black women accent upthrust, outthrust backsides, just as white women highlight their busts.

Carl makes a beeline to the Sunrise Café, where he claims many sweet-eyed glances and phone numbers (digits of *Desire*). Donna and Deanna (sisters) and Susan and Sally (best friends)—an entire sorority—tired of being pedestrian, crowd about Carl, clamouring for, and claiming, rides. Carl will provide—he tells himself—*fairly: share and share alike.*

Muriel, a Coloured maid, eyes him. When he exits the Sunrise, she demands a ride, right-this-minute: "Those other girls are just kids. I'm a woman, Carl." *Verily*: every curvaceous inch.

Carl grins as he hefts Muriel aboard the BMW. Damn happy, he watches her long, taut, dark chocolate legs grip the sides of the bike; now, he feels her tits indent his upper back as she leans her head against his neck and shoulder; her arms snake about his waist, grappling hard. Bumps and sharp turns jostle and crumple Muriel and him together. The bike's swerving and shaking sets the lady squirming deliciously against Carl's back and upper pelvis. The drive is nigh conjugal. The rumble of Carl's engine percolates in Muriel's heart. Carl tells her, "Lean when I lean. We'll lean together." The bike is clean; his heart's a machine.

He's had *Delight* before in having Muriel. *Truth*: he likes a hussy—a nice-size, pretty slut. (Heed the Italian proverb: "Nothing pulls stronger than cunt hairs.") But no complications, please—yeah, oh yeah—pretty, pretty, pretty please!

• • •

This association didn't begin auspiciously. Carl recalls his pre-Christmas entrée to Miss Muriel Dixon's dirty, spicy premises. He'd met her down by Point Pleasant Park (the southern tip, boutique forest of the municipal peninsula) in a nervous position: She was scrambling, dishevelled and distressed, from a white car parked facing Black Rock Beach, while a ghostly voice chirped, "Cocksucker! Cocksucker!" A squat, sallow man then opened the driver's door and emerged, shadowy in moonlight, plashing one dark shoe into the slushy grey snow, his fedora dark-fudging his face into anonymity, and he stood upright, to pursue the fleet woman. However, the urge died once he saw Carl, who happened to be present because of his penchant for long strolls, day or night—his preferred exercise and his imaginative means of possessing, *stealthily*, Caucasian-bossed Halifax. (In 1959, Coloureds don't really live in, but only *infiltrate*, the city.) The *oaf*—as Carl dubbed the john—valuing his reputation more than an orgasm, slunk down behind his steering wheel and slid his '58 Ford Edsel backward and then about-face, and surfed through the slush, careening away. After rearranging her blouse and skirt, cardigan and scarf, coat and hat, and smiling through two glistening jets of tears, Muriel hunkered in Carl's enfolding arms, to get warm and get warmth.

Carl's known her since Sunday school—and grade school. At twenty-seven, she's four years his senior, but her failures in some grades meant that she occupied the same classes as he, though she'd been too mature to mingle much with his junior set. A maid in the leafy South

End, Muriel dwells, like most Negroes, in Halifax's rat-infested North End. Carl had guessed that, either by her own hook—or by the gent's crook—she'd found herself in the crisis from which she had now, only by luck and pluck, slipped. A licorice-coloured woman, with a jutting, horizontal bosom, straight black hair, violet lips, and mocha-sweet eyes, Muriel defines *Femininity*. Carl had been glad to wrap her in his arms that December night, just as he is glad now to feel her vigorous clutch. *Voluptuity* presses him; sweat prickles his back. Muriel herself feels empowered, that Carl is answering her wish to be transported some-where, anywhere, *better*.

The December '58 eve had ended two times *ably*—i.e., enjoy*ably* and memor*ably*. Muriel had thanked God for Carl's chivalrous rescue, and then she had tucked her arm into his, as he'd led her, not strid-ing, but pacing easily northward again. At Cornwallis (*rue* of priests—Anglican, Baptist, Catholic, United, plus a clerical-collar'd pedophile or two), they'd turned right, or east, toward the harbour, and walked two blocks to Maynard Street to Muriel's abode near the northwest corner. Her Victorian-era rooming house, with the Schwartz spice warehouse at its back, cascaded odours, from the decay of rats—a nostril-piercing stench—behind the wallpaper to the pungent, black pepper reek from the savoury enterprise itself.

During the half-silent, half-joking, half-hour-long trek, Muriel had said that it was the first time for her to see, by night, some of the streets they strolled along. *True*: fearing they'd be mistaken for prowlers or prostitutes, Coloureds avoided the South End at night. Most *lawful* Negro faces in Dixie-side Halifax belonged to either daytime chimney sweeps or sleepover maids—figures from Disney's *Song of the South* reconfigured for Disney's *Mary Poppins*.

Reaching Muriel's building, Carl had to inhale, gamely, a gross stench of dank newspapers, dog piss, rat droppings, fried mackerel, stove oil, cat feces, boiled cabbage and vinegary sauerkraut, and the rank odours of people who have little reason to wash, and so don't. (He had to recall, in part, his own boyhood barn lodgings.) The common, if desolate, perfumes of the penniless, the acrid bile of hunger and drunkenness, got spiced up by the Schwartz commercial scents that misted fine-ground pepper over some smells or, here and there, allowed a sweetening dollop of cinnamon. A special torture: to be starving and then get a whiff of the spices. The aromas would conjure up an invisible feast, thus stoking hunger to the point that a deluded wretch could slice off his nose.

Despite the twitching of his nostrils—or, maybe, because they were flaring like a bull's—Carl had traipsed close after Muriel. He'd trotted up the creaking, old-wood stairs and sidled into her cramped rooms, reeking of kerosene and long-downed greased-cardboard-plate meals of fish 'n' chips, expecting that, soon, he'd be nosing her pungent woman scent. *Sho nuff*: clothes began to smell steamy—as if in a laundry—and then hot—as if under an iron. Carl ended up prone, on her bed, licking her where it was fine to lick. The circumstances legitimized her dirtiest dreams but suited the filth of the premises. (*Pornography* is autobiography, sometimes.) Yet, once climaxes subsided, Carl hurled himself from Muriel's clasp, hauled on trousers and galoshes and sweater and coat, and then leapt down—two steps at a bound—the rancid staircase, back into the sharply clean night, praying that he and Muriel hadn't just become Mom and Pop.

(In 1959, *Conception* is a matter of numeracy—periods. Eves of courtship: sixty minutes of "hittin," then a split-second of quittance before the generous, dangerous, male emission. In this era, a man lets fly while gambling that his seed don't catch. One prays an instant of coitus don't lead to nine months of anxiety and decades of regret.)

Carl don't want his sex odysseying to end with his being hog-tied to an unlettered maid. Though he's a railway serf, he don't wanna settle for a scullion. For Muriel. He's gotta have someone—anyone—*better*.

Someone like Marina White, the student nurse. She's sinuous as a dollar sign, the secular side of a caduceus. Carl'd love to get her wine-sozzled, wobbly, so he can nail her ass to his bed like Luther hammering home his Ninety-Five Theses. To show the hoity-toity how to be hoochie-coochie *nuff* to please a truly gritty man. He want to grant her a "Ph.D."—penis hard and deep—ASAP, never mind that B.Sc.!

Certes: Marina's university studies—in *Nursing*—will make her middle-class, if not an intellectual. In contrast, Carl's broadsheet schoolin has made him an intellectual, but one who got grime—sometimes—on his face and calluses always on his hands.

Carl guesses that if he can persuade Marina to have him, their children will be middle-class thanks to her pay, but high achievers thanks to his prodding (or so he thinks). Let her earn more than he: he'll always be on top—*if* he can get her down—in bed.

Too bad all these calculations make *Love* so unromantic, and so make it much more like a combo of sombre economics *and* foolhardy gambling. Yep, too bad. But not Carl's fault.

• • •

That Point Pleasant December night, out parking with "Allowishus"—what's-his-face, whatever his dummy moniker (phony as Canadian Tire script)—Muriel was willing to see how far she could get ahead by tumbling, sprawling, in the humongous back seat. How much could her compliance, her kisses, her strokes and squeezes, "Golly gees," wrench from a white man's wallet? *True*: the hawk-nosed palooka had come off more as bungling rapist than big-spending Romeo. So, she'd been glad for Carl's accidental rescue of her bod, and had been thrilled to see a white man falter in his arrogance toward a Coloured gal, and skedaddle in fright, but first plant his argyle socks and leather shoes in salty, corrosive slush.

Exciting also was it to step through the chilly, smarting night, the Christmas-illuminated South End, Santa Claus–visited streets, with Carl, the beanpole, the straight-ties-and-narrow-thighs lad from school, always smart, always in the right grade and at the head of his class (*The Head Boy*, she thinks). Their breaths, jointly penetrating the night with personable white mist, were almost marital in their mingling. Too, Carl knew his way around, knew the city far better than she, though a South End–oriented maid. Muriel is proud that she doesn't have to live "in service" with a white family, nursing the very babes that the head of the household might have made her bear so that he could then adopt them as a sign of his social-work benevolence, his tax-deductible, phil-anthropic, liberal *Humanitarianism*.

So, even though Carl experiences Muriel's scent-accented quar-ters as miasmic, swampy, pestilential, or as squeezed and constricted as tubercular lungs, for Muriel, it is that best of places: *hers*. Her kitchen, kitchen table, sink, window overlooking Cornwallis Street, bathroom adjacent to the kitchen, and bedroom off the kitchen, is a refuge—a redoubt—from the posh South End mansion where she must dress as a maid, clean and cook as a maid, kowtow as a maid, bend like a maid, stoop like a maid, and be furtively pinched and fondled as a maid. But here, in her own few rooms, with a hot plate and a squat fridge, a radio and a record player, a set of drawers and a laundry hamper, a closet stuffed with always-fashionable clothes and shoes, every inch is hers—albeit rented—and her bed is her palace. Outside her doors, a man might be a pig; but if she lets him into her quarters, he edges toward princely.

Muriel's actual *Elegance* don't impress Carl. Following their love-making back then, he'd scrammed as if he'd been rusty-nail lacerated. Muriel had felt insult, even as his spunk had sunk deep into her, for she thought he ought to have felt *blessed* by her yielding of herself and her bed to him. After all, all that he had received had been her—*hers*. But she'd repressed *Spite* at being slighted, at Carl's own scrambling, cockroach-like, from her lamplight into the cold, sordid darkness of the staircase to the street, for she knew—had always known—that he'd be back.

• • •

After Carl'd interrupted Muriel's near-rape (or an act sloppily, criminally similar) in a pasty fellow's jalopy down Point Pleasant Park in December 1958, they'd got naked and noodled in her peppery quarters. It took his next bout with Muriel, back on February 3 (the same night Buddy Holly had his swan song, then swan dive), for Carl to learn that the gal could be extra elastic in her mores—in her amours. As flexible as is he, in his.

He'd had no date for the Queen Elizabeth High School Symphony Swing, but chose to go anyway. *Yep, might as well.* Come seven p.m., *hell or high water*, then, Carl joined two-hundred-plus souls crowding the bleachers in the steamy gymnasium. Situated in the north end, the orchestra left lots of southern space for swingers to jump and jitterbug. The musicians tuned up, then gyred into gear. One guy hammered drums; others fingered horns or plucked strings. A Royal Canuck Navy pianist tried his hand at Ellington, but it was as if he were wearing handcuffs. Still, music swooped and looped.

Carl ogled *les danseuses*. Was happy to spy Lola Brown and Muriel Dixon, both dateless, both lookin *supoib*. Made him forget the railway all the way. *True*: Lola holds a diploma in all branches of *Beauty* culture, including hair design. She's chunky, funky, and spunky. Her red dress twirled and swirled; Carl glimpsed two smooth—yes, stout—legs. But Muriel was a one-woman debutante ball in V-neck white dress and red pumps.

Limber steps loosened all, so good spirits prevailed as of nine p.m. *Porgy and Bess* started to sound like Bessie Smith; Billy Eckstine started to sound like Billie Holiday.

Then, fisticuffs spread contagious among the musicians: the trombonist brained a violinist with his slide, and the pianist kicked the drummer in the crotch, and the latter stabbed the conductor with his sticks. Memorable mayhem. The swing concert degenerated into wildly swinging fists. A trumpet swallowed a drumstick; the pianist got pied in the face with a cymbal; the second fiddle had a clarinet chip a front tooth; another violinist gave the trombonist a black eye. The ruckus made for raucous, discordant sounds, as if the musicians were just beginning to play, instead of ending up bruised and battered and their instruments splintered and bashed or dented and smashed.

Carl invited Lola and Muriel to vamoose from the *Chaos* and grab some real spirits—not the bubbly emptiness of soda pop. Agreeably, he escorted the young ladies back to 1½ Belle Aire Terrace, where snacks and honest-to-God booze awaited. Six feet tramped past six-foot-high snowdrifts; their black-comic laughter stamped the air; their white breaths swamped the stars.

By nine-thirty p.m., the women's feet—lithe, plump—slipped easily out of boots. Coats hung up, the gals ensconced on his couch, Carl incarnated *Goodness Gracious*. He brought the fireplace to roaring, warming life; he lit candles to bless the room with light as soft as heat. He set out red wine for sipping.

Lola: "I still feel a bit cold. Warm us up, Carl."

Muriel chimed in: "I like dark rum." She stretched out, leaning herself against Lola.

Carl "broke the ice" by breaking open ice cubes and a bottle of Mount Gay Barbadian rum. (He didn't recognize this accidental salute to his long-vanished naval father, Mr. Locksley Black.)

He fixed up solid drinks—so dark, they were black. Carl set Johnny Mathis's *Warm* to work on the hi-fi: Percy Faith's strings quivered, kissing. Three mouths sucked dark rum.

The drinks equalled aphrodisiacs. Rum tasted kinky after the red wine. Both gals joked, teased: Time for three to waltz. They do.

Cuddled up on the sofa, two houris—black-eyed nymphs—looked two candies. Carl sat near them in his big-ass, Mao-style armchair. Buttery candlelight suited this *troika*, waxing and buffing copper, iron, and golden skin. Carl just observed, noting it would be awfully equitable to kiss two moist mouths, feel four dark-fudge-sweet arms. Two cigarettes fired smoke incandescently. Carl's talk was jokes, gossip, movies, LPs, everything easy and mellow.

Then, Lola said, "I dare ya to kiss Muriel, Carl." Titters. Giggles. Both looked damn delectable. Carl rose and kissed Muriel.

Lola laughed softly, not nervously. "Don't ya both look sweet. Oh, look at Muriel blush. Kiss her again, Carl—and me too."

Lips smacked three faces. Six lips: a sextet if there ever was.

Carl relished each lavish labial. Lola, the bigger gal, granted largesse. Carl took it. Well-matched mouths met everywhere. Raw heat wafted musk.

Various mountings and configurations seemed nigh. You could count (on) em: a *folie* à *deux*, a *ménage* à *trois*, a *soixante-neuf*, etc. The New Math minus nothing; or the French *Nouvelle Vague* translated into bossa nova.

Lola and Muriel were kissing and fondling each other: no scruples or qualms or inhibitions. Tongues gobbled sloppily; rum was gulped down. Six hands undid belts, buttons, snaps, zippers. Belts slithered and clasps jangled; buttons, peeling from slits, subtly squeaked; snaps popped; zippers zinged down. This discordant music was an overture to no-doubt harmony. Candlelight was yellow with fire, not caution.

Soon, Lola's panties, once as wide as her hips but cut low, were off, and, snapped back, shrunk down to brand new size. An irresistible circumstance. Carl was set to shut his eyes and pretend Lola was Marina.

Before matters could escalate to low-down lovin, came several bitter, gloved thuds—interfering, disturbing—upon Carl's front door. Clothes hastily reassembled, as if for a full-dress review.

But Lola's panties ended up in her hat; Muriel's scarf became her panties; Carl's sweater clothed Lola; her blouse ballooned over Muriel's chest. No time to coordinate the dressing. The trio had to mix and match as best the three dishevelled could.

Then Carl cracked his door to Muriel's paramour, Frederickson Dent, off *The Sunflower*, a boat from Bridgetown, Barbados, ferrying sugar to Nova Scotia and bearing gypsum back. (Dent always looks like sugar-frosted or sugar-dusted chocolate cake. He be that *sweet*.) His hands, clenched at his sides, were ready sledgehammers. The man was a smokestack: the sorta guy to tear off your testicles if ya try to reason—or tussle—with the taut-muscled hominid.

"Muriel!" Fred's voice hissed like a scythe.

Carl said, "Take it easy, fella. Want a drink?"

"I want Muriel!"

Behind Carl, Lola and Muriel hustled into their coats and boots. Above Fred's head, oily clouds scudded across the charcoal sky. Two coal-black eyes stared out from a smoky face. Again, Carl asked the smouldering man indoors.

Fred retorted, "Ain't steppin in your stinkin shit." He shouted, "Muriel, you Carlyle bitch? You fuckin him?"

Carl shushed the man sharply: "You want the cops here? Shut up!"

Muriel shied through the door. She swished by Carl and took Fred's gorilla-size hand. "Thanks, Carl." As she and her fella left, he threw Carl a look that was merely a substitute for a knife through his jugular. Gay frost cackled under four stepping feet.

Now, Lola murmured, "Thanks," as she went too. Her eyes were dark meteors. She pressed Carl's hand meaningfully, as if she were reluctant to leave.

Outside, the dark night flew up like a cape from the back of a black horse. Carl had turned back to his dark quarters to brood: He'd had two women primed for whatever he desired, one supine, one on all fours.

But he'd let a Tar interrupt. In fact, the night was an ironic revisiting of his first night with Muriel. Chagrined, irritated, peeved, and pissed off: his mood.

As for Freddy Dent, Carl classed him as a typical Bajan: taking a Scotian woman as a dockside doxy, while his real, Bajan *fiancée* or spouse rotted at home, sucking in rum and coconut milk while suckling babes, at both teats, on alcoholized mama's milk. A double damnation!

But Fred viewed Carl as a local yokel; a displaced Canuck Negro, lacking the original black culture of the Caribbean and the strong Negro culture of the U.S. He got nothin to give a Scotiner lady. *Sheeeeit!* To Fred, the incipient independence of Barbados, becoming more effectively independent than be Anglo-Saxon-ass-kissing Canada, is a godsend for Coloured *ladies* marooned in the backward, backslid, back-o-God province that be Nova Scotia: too close to the U.S. for its own good, too far from the B.W.I. to be improved. *Day-o! Day-o!*

• • •

Carl deposits Muriel at her digs. He expects a kiss, but not the very long kiss that it becomes. (But the gas tank, between her legs, felt as thick and hot as a bull—as Carl, *Taurus*, had embodied, thrusting, Muriel remembers, last December.)

Carl hankers to ask the gal back to his rooms; instead, he says, "*Ciao*," and revels in the pleasure (as in James Bond tales) of a chap's being able to coolly kiss off a chippy. He vrooms away, relishing the thought that Muriel is watching him leave her, his "*Ciao*" disintegrating in the breeze as much as her dreams of wedding bells.

Fine, Carl thinks. Since November '58 (when he last rode Liz II) until today, May 9, 1959, his life has been circumscribed. He's had to tramp about the same sixteen square miles of *terra firma*, from the South Street and Hollis Street–situated train station to North Street and

Belle Aire Terrace. Until today, for the last six months, his best adventures (save for a few *wham-bam-ma'am* trysts) have been siphoned from cinema or imagined from books. Life as a pedestrian is, well, damnably *pedestrian*. Today, his purviews widen and his perquisites increase. Instead of whistling to Sinatra, he can howl with Ginsberg. The motorcycle casts him in *On the Road*; or, he's a swashbuckler like *The Wild One*. Liz II—gleam and smoke—is a moving picture. Carl can pretend he's T.E. Lawrence and Joe Louis, all in one dapper package. He wants to be able always to kick-start his machine, zoom to the horizon, and find there a woman—*ideally* with an open mind, an open bottle, and open legs.

Back in his bachelor rooms, Carl tosses back rum to toast this year's debut rides. He thinks about Muriel, how he could've bedded her again this evening. He don't think he's soulless or callous to regard Muriel—or any woman—as a conduit to *Pleasure*. She leaves him panting, gasping, as if on the verge of death when, well, this is when he's most defiantly alive.

He's had a brilliant day, and now a cascade of potential lady conquests (or re-conquests), traipses through his skull as the syrupy rum summons sleep. He dreams, and, as he later thinks, *It is awful (prophetic): a friend of mine looked quite ill with child.* In this dream, he is standing in an apple orchard with a woman whose face he cannot see. Her abdomen is swollen. He plucks an apple to hand to her, but she will not turn to accept it. Next, his motorcycle becomes a bull; its hooves kick and stamp.

Carl awakes. Must he become a *piskijker*—a piss-watcher—to tell who is pregnant, and by whom?

• • •

If he watch his p's and q's—is stealthy—there's no reason why Carl— *he thinks*—can't go "stepping in, step-stepping in, his shoes kicked off, step-stepping in." To bend recalcitrant Marina White to his will, to take her from back of his motorbike and take her backside to bed. *Mmmmmmm.* Define BMW as *Beautiful Marina White.* Muriel is fine, but Marina is *finesse.*

Regard her waist—willowy—see her bust—as pillowy as that of Carmen Jones (Miss Dorothy Dandridge herself). Lawd, have mercy! Mar's *Beauty* just don't quit. Her eyes scorch; her lips rear a rosebud; her skin is coffee. Her perfume arrives like good news, lingers like salvation.

Her kisses prove satisfying, but unsatisfying; promising, but uncompromising: she won't let Carl "take advantage."

• • •

Mar gotta favour *Chastity.* Her mom was—well—*too* open to men. Mar's siblings share her mama, but none her papa. Too, she's grown up hungry; cash could bring home fire, enough for crusts and crumbs, but not enough to always stay warm or to stave off sickness.

So, Mar figures an open-legs policy mandates a closed-door future. *She* won't succumb to some sweet-talker, some haberdashery-fine, dashing fellow. As Carl fronts.

It's 1959; prophylactics come crude and flimsy; condoms slip off; they split open. The *Pill* will only be approved for sale in the United States—and then for wives only—in December: too late to allow Mar a nothin-to-it, no-fuss deflowering.

In grade school, if a boy smiled at her, Marina'd dig her fingernails in his arm. Later, to ward off any Don Juan, she donned glasses that masked her as a severe librarian. Now, her glasses distinguish her from the bobby soxer, hula-hoop-hipped gals, too many of whom view seventeen as a perfect age to don maternity wear.

Bespectacled in visage, respectable in demeanour, Marina got ignored at dances. Most of the greasy, bad-teeth cowboys in Three Mile

Plains only had Grade Three—just nuff schoolin to know they'd never amount to anything but gypsum-quarryin, black-phlegm-spittin drunks and kitchen-table tyrants. So, they chase dumb "broads"; they plan to boss their shacks, get shit-faced, and thrash the ol lady. *Problem*: a schooled wife won't let hubby mistake baby formula pennies for beer money.

So, Mar's teen solitude suited her fine. She favoured suicidal Sylvia Plath and slutty Colette over smarmy rags like *Confidential*. She chose to analyze Jane Austen's acerbic studies of courtship, not gloat over Jayne Mansfield's marital woes and weight gains.

In sum, Marina believes she'll slip outta *Peonage* and into the middle class *if* she keeps Matthew-Mark-Luke-John in mind, and models herself on The Virgin Mary, spurning Mary Magdalene. Leathered-down charmers like Carl are fun, but not guys to fall for, unless a gal wanna be left in the lurch, a papa-less *bambino* at her breast.

Nor does Mar forget how her once-upon-a-time best friend (in grade school) perished ignobly, up Panuke Road, in winter 1958: May Croxen had gone drivin with Joe Jackson in his patchwork jalopy. They'd parked up the lake in frigid Fahrenheit, so tried to get warmth by joinin amiable organs together while keepin th'engine puffin. However, their every gasp of *Delight* saw them ingest—ignorantly—much carbon monoxide. Clutchin madly at each other, they climaxed in an atmosphere of poison gas, and died, stuck together by conjunctive spasms. For decent burial, the coroner had to slice the bodies apart. Still, young Mr. Jackson's proudest appendage must remain engorged in Miss Croxen's friendliest cavity—until dust do they part.

To avoid such *louche* fatalism, Mar intends to don a nurse's habit and then—and only *maybe*—a bridal gown. A B.Sc. first, please, *then* a "Mrs."

She must symbolize *Negress Rectitude*. She must be the school-marm lady with cinnamon in her complexion, peppermints in her purse, and good grammar in her lungs, plus straight-back posture, and lavender toiletries and a lemon-juice diet.

Carl don't understand Marina's discriminations. He's graceful in style; she's gracious in personality. Ain't it natural that she, a student nurse at Dalhousie University, who loves straddling his BMW, should want to straddle *him*? Yet, he ain't blunt in his *Lust*. He's intricate, delicate, sly: Br'er Rabbit out to "Tar Baby" Elizabeth Bennet.

So, Carl plots to ply churchgoing Marina into his sheets. Strategically, then, he's accepted the presidency of the Baptist Youth Fellowship, just so he can appear a right dapper chaplain-in-training to Marina's Bible-readin eyes.

That he has booze in his fridge and girly mags under his pillow just proves that he takes *Temptation* seriously. That's what he'd tell Marina: he's like Christ in the desert, accepting to be tempted because he can (smartly) resist . . .

Once, the two were kissing at a trolley stop, pretty chastely. Then a trolley arrived, and a girl in a swishin pleated skirt got off, smiled at Carl. Still kissing Mar, he waved back. Marina broke off the kiss: "You know her?"

Carl say he was just bein sociable. But Mar *knows* her beau is a Romeo, that his eyes will roam if, or when, ever hers are shut.

For Carl, then, Liz II is a godsend: while dating Mar in Halifax, Carl can fuck a gal in another town. He believes his deceptive practice is not uncommon, merely instrumentalized, somewhat unusually, *via* the motorcycle.

Carl knows other Coloured men—like porters (if enterprisingly lustful)—hold a wife and kids in Halifax and a mirror family in Montreal. They're fanatical, then, about never letting one wife holiday in the city of the other. A prudential puritanism preserves bigamy. Nor do they ever booze enough to confuse one wife or child with another of the sister family. (Their fear of discovery even wards off dementia.) They also strive to prevent inadvertent incest. These men can tell stories about diverting a son by one wife from courting the daughter by another.

They strive to secure a Dominion Atlantic Railway—or Canadian National Railway—*Harem*, while swearing they love only one woman, whom they'd like to be buried beside, to share the warm tears of the bereaved and the cool worms of their grave. They hold on to parallel wives because they have—and need—a lot of love, or because they are heavy-natured, thus negating the European artifice—farce—of *Monogamy*, the household version of *Monopoly*.

But the dilemma for Carl and Marina is not only his impenitent *Lust* or her impenetrable sex, it is also the reality of Coloured Halifax this year. The unmarried young must practise a Russian roulette: they sleep about, trying on—thus—as many genial, unwed genitals as *Health* and *Chance* allow. The communal morality is: Have sex frequently with likeable partners, but marry the one with whom a child is conceived. *Fuck and pray* is the folk theology on *Procreation*, with babies born miraculously—prematurely—within the nine-month purview of gestation, but also within nine months of the discovery of the pregnancy and the swift arrangement of a wedding. African Baptist marriages often get paired with newborns' christenings. And no one protests. Everyone smiles. *For the camera.*

Being a student nurse, Marina is cognizant of these traditions and expectations. She approves: a fixed-up marriage eliminates *Disgrace* and *Bastardy*.

Marina also knows—if Carl does not—that local Negroes feel threatened by a black woman who has more education than they, and will resort to *Rape*—to force motherhood upon their victim—to shame her into "keeping her place." Bluenose whites also perpetrate such assaults, again to teach a "molasses lassie" that she's fit to be a scullion, not a scholar.

Knowing these atrocious truths, Mar resents Carl's irresponsible gallivanting. He should understand, thinks Mar, that her delay of *Coitus* serves to advance *The Race*. He should champion her becoming a nurse; he should palliate her loneliness as a black woman from a poor family, now competing against well-off white girls for decent marks and a chance at a respectable salary.

But Carl and Mar have grown up within a culture thinkin book-learnin equals bein an Aunt Jemima or an Uncle Tom, a white wannabe, an "Oreo." Negroes are supposed to be unsophisticated, earthy, plain folk, who don't speak but spit; who pummel the piano as opposed to playing it; and who are cut-ups in razor-keen comedy or who cut each other up in Sat'day-night razor-blade tragicomedy.

So, Marina has faced jeopardy in exercising her access to letters. Her Uncle Texas, who'd been railroaded into a New York jail for trumped-up thievery, once tried to throw her books in his stove because, he said, "Why a nigger wench wanna mess with white folks' words?" He'd clawed one of her *Biology* texts—illustrated with full-colour anatomical images—and held it just above the grasping flames of the wood stove. He'd sneered, "White folks lynch us as quick as fire swallows these pretty pictures." She'd wept and snatched at the book, grabbing it back even as it had begun to catch fire: her illustrated human bodies—singed, seared, and burnt—looked like the Invisible Man and Snow White, presented as lynchees.

If Marina had stayed in Three Mile Plains, some yahoo might have smashed a beer bottle, cut her, and then wrenched her panties down. So, for her to be accepted at Dalhousie University, and assigned a dorm at shale-stone-and-ivy Miramar Residence, was a gesture supporting racial equality—*Integration*—even up north in Nova Scotia. But Marina is also shadowing the arc of Carl's aunt Pretty, who, a generation ago, had been the first Negress ever permitted to bunk with the Caucasianesses at the Miramar, the edifice boasting Virginia creeper vines, that hardy ivy.

Campus life offers one more advantage: Mar can meet male students—mainly the black West Indian dudes, intent on becoming professionals, now registered at Haligonian universities. These men do court local Coloured women, partly cos they can hook em Canuck citizenship if taken to wife. *Certes*: when the Dominion government relaxed the Negro-immigration ban in 1955, it was to let Carib women disembark as maids and Carib men land as students.

While Marina is pursuing nursing, then, so are West Indian gents becoming doctors. She can't be blamed for wondering, *Am I better off with a doctor, or with a motorcyclist* cum *baggage handler?*

To Carl's chagrin, the answer to the question is his obliteration. So, he is Othello-furious whenever Marina dates a British West Indian—B.W.I.—for that acronym trumps his BMW.

Though lawyerly eloquent, Carl holds no high school diploma; he just holds down a joe job. Can he compete with a man who will have—just as Marina will have—letters chasing his name? Who'll be Mr. So-and-So, LLB, or B.Ed., or B.Sc., with a framed degree on his wall and a sugar-plantation pedigree, with an upper-class accent, spiffy duds, swanky accoutrements, *plus* Sidney Poitier as a cousin? Can he?

Ironically, Carl is part-Wessindian himself, but he can't match the Island Negroes now ensconced at Dal: They're as spanking chocolate as he is; some are gloriously darker. But they're relatively rich—and they'll soon be professionals. And he? He only got Belafonte on his turntable, *not* as a neighbour.

Carl solves his felt lack of status thus: (1) he'll be *the* extra-suave *motorcyclist*; (2) he'll be a stalwart African Baptist—to the extent that his *Saved* status looks legit.

Naturally, Carl's Bible-quoting and gentlemanly comportment deteriorates soon as he has a woman on his couch. Then, he's unhooking a bra and tugging down panties, not quoting erection-shrinking Scriptures. It's just sweeter to kneel before a woman than to kneel in prayer. *Correct!*

• • •

As Baptist Youth president, Carl succeeded in seducing Marina over to 1½ Belle Aire Terrace back in March. She'd knocked; they'd kissed; she'd passed him a brown bag full of goodies: two homemade pumpkin pies, two pound cakes, and some peanut butter cookies, all fabulous stuff, baked by her hand. Thus, the lustrous, incorruptible virgin of the Dalhousie School of Nursing entered Carl's umber quarters. She took his right hand and settled onto the sofa. Accompanying her wool coat, that beige sheath, light white silk scarf, and brown leather gloves and black leather boots, delicately swished off, was Chanel No. 5, a fragrance redolent of Coco Chanel's delirium for Igor Stravinsky. Mar looked as slinky as a mink. Her auburn hand swished back her coppery strands. Her coppery shoulders showed through her white silk top.

Carl attacked a pastry. He took a bite of one peanut butter cookie but, soon, every bite was beautiful. The texture was buttery-smooth and rum-moist. He just loved the crumbly sweet taste of Mar's cookies. He wanted her "barefoot and pregnant." She even said so, laughing as she read his mind.

They were supposed to discuss reviving the Baptist Youth Fellowship. Instead, that cold night, kissing the icicle-thin Marina—she "frigid" perhaps—Carl vowed to thaw her out, even volcanically. Under the insinuating effect of the rum he'd served her in coffee "to cut the chill in the air," Marina stretched out on the sofa, her head upturned on Carl's lap. He bent to kiss Mar's lips, and found he was sipping sugar, butter, chocolate, in any mixture, with cream or whipped cream, as two tongues began to taste each other, French style. Carl roved his lips over Marina's. Two tongues, turning pepper, made honey. As his *Pleasure* surged, urgent, Carl tried lightly—slyly—to rest his left hand upon Mar's left breast; he found the tip nicely hard, and he did begin to stroke her nipple, hoping to have her top up, her bra cups off, and two sweet, hard nubs in his lips. But Mar was too much a nursing student—and too disciplined a Baptist—to let happy petting turn hazardous hanky-panky. She withdrew her tongue; her right hand deftly wiped drool from her lips and brushed Carl's hand from her pointed, heaving tit. Suddenly again genteel, but with strange fierceness, she looked down at her dishevelled waist, and then looked up at Carl and said, "Help me resist . . . my own . . . needs . . . Let's pray . . ."

Carl did want to take Mar just then; *damn* her scruples. *Besides,* he thought, *if I do, maybe she'll finally be mine; no more nonsense about dating B.W.I. Negroes.* But, no, Carl couldn't just screw this *lady* he'd like for his wife. It'd not be kosher to pierce through her still-girlish *Femininity,* so she'd know him as a man, herself as a woman, and *then* tie tin cans to the rear of Liz II in that rattling, raucous, working-class mockery of highfalutin wedding chimes.

Though his frustration was palpable, Carl told himself that he'd have Mar *next time.* He played nonchalant, but his heart throbbed, machine-gun rapid: "I answer to your needs. I care for you. No one else means as much to me as—"

Marina'd stopped his lips with a quick, noncommittal kiss. Then, ballerina-belligerent, dismissive, she'd twirled fleetly from Carl's embrace, his hot-and-bothered lap, swirled into her outdoors clothes, blew him a sultry, but airy, kiss, and then, gone, gone-with-the-blizzarding-wind, was *his* auburn Scarlett O'Hara.

• • •

Carl nominates himself the acme of Negro (Scotianer) masculinity, for he ripples through white Halifax, upright on his machine, a black-leathered, magenta-ridin daddy-o—a violet pimpernel. But his symbolism, *per se,* is selfish. In contrast, Mar's entrée to the ivory tower is that of a Trojan mare, to allow other Coloured women to void postmodern slavery, the imposed nursery, and vile *Discourtesy.* If she were to bear a child instead of taking a degree *cum laude,* her private fault would fail *every* black girl.

She'd need shotgun marriage, or she'd have to hightail it to Montreal, she fears, to be a nightclub floozy, to hide *Humiliation*.

Too lusty to value Mar's devotion to decorum, Carl's felt stymied, checkmated: he'd had sugar, not *sweetness*. *Tragically*. He thinks, *I'm a damn sap to expect Mar to pay me more attention, although she must study so hard. Besides, Mar's* incomparably *superior—to all others*.

Maybe. But a winking slut is—sometimes—more desirable than a mincing lady, whether she's under a man or atop him. And Mar can only flirt, only trifle. *Only*.

To assuage his broke heart and broke-down dick, Carl picks up his contraband copy of *Lady Chatterley's Lover*—a cheapo version on bad, beige paper. Smutty writing in sooty ink. But haunting and arousing too. He could be Mellors, a rustic intellectual seducer of a Lady-Chatterley-like Marina. Carl thinks of Mellors and mistress in their dreamy cottage, a fusion of Thomas Hardy and Laurel and Hardy, and he fantasizes of his belly and Mar's, coupled, chafing.

Yep: Carl wants a Greenwich Village, not Africville, existence; to have more than one woman—in more than one colour; to enjoy "Turkish delights" and French ticklers, plus Greek positions—to take Sappho the way that Plato took a lad.

But, luckily, there is the highway; there is Liz II. There is room to roam and rove, if not to Rome, then at least to Rome, New York. Lovers can be frustrating and the railway job revolting. But the motorcycle attracts fresh, new candidates and delivers Carl always the possibility of fresh, new destinations.

Neither *Freedom* nor *Love* is a given. They must be taken!

But this proviso can also be taken the wrong way. Too easy it is to make a wrong turn . . . *Un virage!*

DETERMINATIONS I

Even one's crimes, one's neuroses, have possibilities of Beauty.
—ANAÏS NIN, *INCEST*

I taly Cross still haunts Carl. What went down, down there, in 1950. Not to him. But to someone he could be—if unlucky: a Sambo mid a snow-face mob.

Having been a paper boy, aged nine as World War II was climaxing, Carl tracked lustily the Red Army's Rape of Berlin, the pistol-to-mouth fellatio of Hitler, and then Truman's atomic wasting of Hiroshima. Impressive also was the May 8, 1945, Victory-in-Europe riot, when soldiers and sailors, revolted by the dumb-ass decision to padlock liquor stores, had gangwayed into Halifax, to booze and vandalize and buss upper-crust ladies as if they were bare-ass whores. Survivor troops—in memory of slain comrades—torched trams and paddy wagons. In the Sack of "Slackers" (as mariners dub Halifax), Carl was amazed to see Gottingen Street blazing as much as had Allied-bombed *Göttingen,* Germany.

Though his mother, Mrs. Victoria Black, had feared for her son's safety, to be out and about the boozed-up streets during such a repulsion of *Law and Order*, Carl found tips showering down upon him, for tipsy troops had spare coin to toss up, now that they needn't any for alcohol. (Just as their comrades-in-arms had liberated the Netherlands and northern Italy from Axis sovereignty, so had the local soldiery liberated liquor from local—prudish—suzerainty.) And all the coloured glass in the streets, from broken bottles and smashed windows, turned alleys and gutters into desecrated, flattened, cathedral ruins. Instructive was it for Carl to experience lucrative (for him) *Chaos* one day and then eye it, in cold print, hot off the press, the next.

The Morning Herald newspaper was also illuminating when it came to "race." As Negro Yanks trooped back to Dixie, fresh from saving too few Jews and Gypsies from Nazi machine-guns and crematoria, they were themselves, still in uniform, frequently shot down in gullies or strung up from magnolias. Carl did feel grateful that he was in Canada, in Nova Scotia, and not in the Ku Klux Klan–crabby South, where Negroes could be bludgeoned for sport or railroaded—to electric chairs or gas chambers—for the crime of their descent from African slaves whose forced labour had transformed European peasants into U.S. plutocrats. The broadsheet daily also carried stories and pics that clarified that Coloured folks were either comic minstrels—as in ads for Aunt Jemima pancake mix—or mad-dog criminals—as in the case of the wanton hanging of Daniel Sampson, in Halifax, just prior to Carl's 1935 birth.

By about fifteen, in 1950, Carl discovered the violent emotions of some white men when contemplating the threat—or visceral treat—of Negro lads lying with Caucasian "lookers." Often, he'd be asked, "Sonny, ya wanna marry a white girl?" It was safest to shake his head no and exit, lickety-split. Occasionally, he'd hear rumours: so-and-so's daughter ran off with a Negro, so now she's disowned; or so-and-so's daughter had a brown baby and got shipped to Boston. Carl soon realized, thanks to backyard scuttlebutt plus brutal photos in *Life* magazine—and the coverage of the Italy Cross affair in *The Morning Herald*—his dark sex was—is—perilously seductive, an enchanting, life-enhancing organ that jeopardizes his life.

• • •

To Carl, delivering *The Morning Herald* door to working-class, North End door, the star of the front-page Italy Cross tragedy was, amid the drab dots of newsprint, tauntingly lovely. The Germanic, Gothic brunette boasted a sharp-tip nose and phosphorescent eyes that defied the constraints of the newspaper page. Next to the black and white snap of the fisherman's daughter, as lovely as any one of those provincial-tourism postcard Nova Scotian belles in leotards, heels, and skirts, there was framed a Boston black boxer–type, muscled enough to be a stevedore. Under nappy head and sleepy eyes, his hands dangled gargantuan. Easy to imagine those gigantic hands hurling the lady down onto a bed of slickers in a fish shed. Carl's own ebony-copper hands trembled as he held the broadsheet open, like a giant hymnal, and surveyed the headline: "Negro Faces Noose for Shotgun Slaying of White Husband."

The village of Italy Cross, on South Shore, Atlantic-side Nova Scotia, was outraged: *Lusts* had been satisfied among fish heads in a shed and maggots in a garbage truck. The black-ass Othello guilty—Peter Paris, eighteen—had to hang. Carl quivered to read this story, not only because he recognized that it could be his neck stretched in that legal noose, but also because he felt pangs of desire for the milk-faced adulteress, Darlene Naas, twenty-five.

To wit, Paris, the hamlet's garbageman, had gotten used to exploring the fishwife's wares while her hubby was at sea with his mates, pitching upon the Atlantic, trying to haul in weighty, surging cod. While

Darlene's husband had been tossing on the water, she'd been tossing under Peter, all the while ignoring the stench of drying cod and the sight of fish eyes avidly ogling their conjunction. The pair'd kept their tryst secret—a deft act in a minuscule fishing village where Peter was a giant six feet tall and looking broad and dark as a Christmas pine. That he had no woman was the belief, for Coloured women were either up north in Halifax or down south in Yarmouth or even farther south in the Boston States. But Darlin (as he called her playfully) and he had found coitus a fit extension to the courtesies they'd exchange when he'd stop his rickety truck to retrieve her household offal—potato peels, carrot tops, newspapers, fish bones. The fish shed proved nice shelter for their jigging jags, for the cod no longer had tongues to speak of, just gaping mouths and bulging eyes, observing the lovers' exertions with astonished gossips' looks. (Now and then, they also made use of his truck, as the reek of garbage and the congressing of maggots proved unusual—if awkward—aphrodisiacs.)

To keep her true love—and true love-life—secret, Darlene'd kept up a pretense of marital *Joy*. Her act enraged Peter when he was sober and outraged him when drunk. Thus, after sloshing his mouth and throat and almost his lungs with the brightest rum, he'd gotten to thinkin hotly of his white-hot, white-lightnin woman, and how much he had to stick his dick in her, *immédiatement*, and how her husband had no right to the lusciousness (*Luxury*) that he had cultivated through bouts of strenuous—if dextrously muffled—congress.

So, fuelled by *Frustration* and *Jealousy* and liquor, Peter'd grabbed his shotgun and barged into Darlin's home. He crashed into the bedroom of the shack, found his beloved writhing under her sworn groom, and discharged his smoking, steely gun into the man's chalky back, while Darlene just screamed and screamed.

Peter knew he'd murdered; the blood was irrefutable. He staggered himself over to the Mountie detachment, surrendered his ass, and X'd a statement, given lawyerless, that was pretty much a death warrant. Although Peter was clapped instantly into a tiny, stone gaol, the dead man's fishermen pals still rigged up a posse to demand the "nigger" be freed to get his comeuppance, a noose to lasso him from a pine.

Carl trembled to read these facts because Darlene's visage reminded him of the schoolgirl that he'd liked from afar, Liz Publicover. At fourteen, Liz and he had been Head Girl and Head Boy at their junior high school, in the smokestack-smoky north half of Halifax, and their his-and-her snaps had unfolded in a newspaper. They'd posed together for the Waterman picture, and Carl had inhaled enough of Liz's Sunlight-soap scent, and seen enough of her apple-blush cheeks and the Bauhaus curves of her brassiered tits, that he knew arousal, if not—quite—yet the danger of arousal.

Then again, *Innocence* was no longer, for him, now fifteen, a reasonable prerogative. A month before, in April 1950, Carl'd been riding the trolley, heading uptown from a movie he'd seen on Barrington Street (just steps uphill from Halifax Harbour), when a white woman—wild, fiery red hair and lips—sitting across from him, began shouting, "You black ape! Close your legs! All you gorillas want is to jump on white ladies! You just want to dock your big dicks in us." Carl had looked about wildly; he couldn't imagine this crazy—but pixie-cute—lady was addressing *him*. Then the woman stood, tumbled onto Carl, and began to fumble between his legs. She screeched, "You black bastards are the same! You just wanna bang white women!" Other passengers intervened; brusque white men dragged the crazed lady from Carl's lap, where she had throned herself, despite his efforts to shove her off and protect his privates from her groping, octopus hands. Irritated, the trolley driver yelled, "Hey, get your diarrhea mouth off my bus! You two wanna fool aroun, take a long walk off a short pier!" Carl was miffed that the bus driver blamed both *him* and the woman for *her* lewd and crude shenanigans. Another man told the girly gruffly, "Ya must be drunk. Siddown, lush!" But the doxy cursed Carl again: "Black bastard! Baboon! Bet ya wanna fuck me!" She then flipped up her short black skirt to show her pink panties. Now a tall, silver-haired white man barked, "You're in Nova Scotia, not Mississippi!" Other passengers applauded this geography lesson. The redhead retorted, "Nigger boys'll stuff their johnsons into any white hole." Now, the trolley operator stopped the vehicle and twisted round in his seat as he levered open the front door and shouted, "You two: get your scruffy, dirty butts off my trolley. Now!" Carl protested: "I didn't do anything!" The redhead chortled, "Yeah, but y'all know he wanted to." The driver snapped, "Trollop, get your big mouth and big ass off my trolley!" As Carl watched, the woman glared at him, sucked her teeth, then sashayed her skirted bottom off the bus, sunlight shimmering on her black silk stockings. As she left, shaking her red head in angry negativization of the universe, the other passengers, though all white, surprisingly clapped and cheered. The trolley driver lurched the vehicle forward again. When Carl reached his stop, at Agricola Street and North Street, he turned and said "Thank you" to the driver, who glared at him as if *he* were also the guilty party.

Though bizarre and destabilizing, the event had also been undeniably *stimulating*. When the tart had yanked on his manhood, Carl'd felt a curious *frisson*. Too, she was sweet to eye—brief skirt, long legs, and tits that'd heaved in his face as her fisting, ivory hand rooted between his thighs. Despite Carl's exact grammar and rigid posture, his guessed-at sexual prowess had been, briefly, everyone's interest on a public trolley. From that instant, he knew himself as a *Negro man*, desirable to dark-complected *and* light-complected females. But he also now saw that he was a clear-and-present threat to the albino racialists who controlled Halifax, Nova Scotia, Canada, the British Empire, and the larger Caucasian European world, which, this 1950 A.D., bossed 99 per cent of Africa and 100 per cent of the Caribbean and the American South. He understood now, even as a Coloured youth, that he had to negotiate the

Gehennas of moneyed Caucasian privilege and the traumas of chalk-faced Christian fear.

Carl could realize one feeble relief: Halifax generates endless Negro versus Caucasian slugging bouts, but lynch mobs are rare.

• • •

Carl did early encounter *White Mischief.* At four, he'd been playing with his younger brother, Huckabuck, in front of their barn—or manger—on Belle Aire Terrace. They'd been horsing around, in dust and dirt, or using twigs to divert ants from one bizarre destination to another, or using shards of glass to concentrate the sun so as to cremate tiny ant heads or thoraxes. (Fascinating it was to see whiffs of blue smoke waft from a thrashing red ant head or body.)

In late spring, 1939, just as chalkboards were being nixed by swimming pools, three older white boys had darkened the paths of the playful Coloureds. The schoolboys stooped to pick up stones and fling em at the "Niggers!" Thanks to comic books, Carl knew that he should pick up whatever pebbles his small hands could carry and fire them back at the kids, and he did so, naming them "Niggers" too. The volleyed imprecation startled the pale lads as much as did Carl's puny missiles. But their assault—their insults—only ended when Mrs. Black appeared and commanded the abrasive kids to abscond. The junior thugs scrammed, and Victoria Black, the work-at-home laundress, bore, at her hips, her two youngest sons indoors.

Carl feared his mom would whip him for using a word he sensed was foul. Instead, as she'd done with their three older siblings, his mom propped Carl and Huckabuck on pillows before a mirror. Next, she set down two china sugar bowls: one held brown sugar; the other boasted white. Mom then told her sons, "Look at the mirror and look at yourselves: you are brown like the brown sugar; those boys who were shouting that ugly word are white like the white sugar. Some white-sugar people do not like brown-sugar people, and they use that evil word to try to shame us." Carl digested the news as if it were a sugared poison pill.

• • •

How could Carl know, only aged four, how nasty some Nova Scotians could be toward Scotianers, as the Coloureds now dub themselves? Yes, they're a unique people. Some descend from slaves that New England Yanks had carted north in 1760 when they scrambled to grab the plush pastures of the kicked-out Acadians ("Cajuns," y'all). But most are the offspring of True-Blue Blacks who sided with the Crown during the American Revolution, and, having lost, were granted empty pockets and stony land in Nova Scarcity. Still others look back to ancestor slaves that British Marines had freed at gunpoint during the War of 1812 and then packed north to the peninsular (or penal) colony, whose beaches were ice-fringed half the year.

Sad to say, but . . . By the time that teen Carl began to fantasize, pantingly, about bedding pink ladies, Scotianers had survived two centuries as either dirt-cheap, dirt-poor labour for condescending whites, or they'd vamoosed—smartly—to the Boston States. Cos their N.S. lives were pinched. They could be servants, maids, and handymen; they could rake pebbles in a pretense of farming. Their static mobility was to shuttle daily from black warrens to white burghs (where they could own no property nor travel after sundown) and perform heart-crushing toil for minuscule coins.

That snapshot captures the whole province: in 1959, Nova Scotia is white towns serviced by slapped-together black villages, while each white-ruled city fields a black shantytown. New Scotland is just a frosty, salt-spray South.

Every day, Negroes exit rude shacks to pick up garbage or shine shoes, while Negresses go into homes and clean toilets and cook meals and pop their dark nipples into pale infants' avid mouths. A regal few men porter on the railway, but they're "on the road," tending to whites, more than they're home, caring for their own families. Others wanna bear arms for King and Queen but are ordered to peel potatoes and scrub latrines. In Nova Scotia, Coloureds have the right to vote, the right to marry whites (and face disgust if they do), and the right to starve—or to sweat to eat a peck of bread, a splash of rotgut, some maggot-polished bone.

So, Halifax hosts a lost African civilization—a populace lost at sea, swamped like Atlantis. Coloured Haligonians waft scents of Coca-Cola and pipe tobacco, rum and ale, coffee and cigarettes, chocolates and crisp Bible pages. Machetes of laughter rip open their faces and their hovels' matchstick walls. (The North End needs a *marché nocturne*, peddling coffee, chocolate, dark rum, molasses, blood pudding, tar, iron, black tea, licorice—only black goods).

Their African Baptist Church got no choice but to espouse a people's gospel: You get born in sin; you suffer disappointments; you die in pain; and, if you have not, in life, cried out to Christ for *Deliverance*, you burn forever, while fully conscious of your living wrongs. Heaven is as distant a promise as Hell is an ever-present threat.

(*Theology* be no damned good: we're defined by what we defile.)

Carl gleaned these beliefs from the sailors who brought their dirty drawers and soiled shirts to Mrs. Black to scour; he gleaned this sociology from the Tars who stayed on, after picking up their laundry, to pour a taste of this and take a sip of that; he got to know all about the harshness of Negro Scotland as he chased titanic rats about the homely abode, the barn to which her bookish preacher pa sentenced Victoria for whelping too many fatherless sons and so—in his mind—soiling her original surname. So, Carl had to outwit rats, catch em by the tail, screeching, flailing, and brain em dead with a bible. *Justice!*

(Always too much black and white in that once-stable with the Dutch doors: rats, coal, hair, ink, iron, rubber, Bible, LPs, char, pencils, pepper, polish, tea, belts, licorice, shoes, coffee, smoke, gangrene, June bugs, tar, molasses, typewriter ribbons, ants, nails, and hats *versus* cotton, skirts, milk, paper, sheets, worms, salt, pus, uniforms, pine, candles, starch, china, soap, lye, bleach, suds, flour, nail clippings, cobwebs, wine, dresses, cigarettes, porridge, shirts, chalk, bread, piss, and sugar. Sometimes snow and soot got miscegenated.)

Carl's roots suck Sargasso Sea routes: houses no better than dressed-up kindling or painted-over splinters; cats curled atop tombstones and shitting upon graves; a gaunt white dog dashing from an alley, a giant, fleshy chicken leg clamped in its jaws; gulls plastering everything with *guano* nougat. Haligonian whores' coos conjuring more pleasure than love ballads. The poor—barking like dogs, squealing like rats, squawking like gulls, clucking like pigeons, caterwauling like cats. Brothels multiplying, furtive, hidden among churches; sailors rasslin a hefty lass, a chunky-bottomed and sassy gal. Say they, "Thank ya, *mamzelle*, most kindly." Doff cap, drop drawers.

• • •

North End Halifax schoolin was red eyes gogglin dirty pictures, plus black eyes winning in sports. A hockey stick could slice open a throat or wreck a tooth; a baseball bat could bash a prodigy into an imbecile—by accident; the gymnasium was where hateful weaklings strove to become idiots-with-badges-and-guns. The schoolyard was, itself, more boxing ring than playground. Snotty noses became bloody noses; cocksuckers got sucker-punched. Tears trickled like blood; blood spurted like semen. Some lads got beat so bad, shit *was* their underpants. Girls'd grab each other's hair and yank, and scratch, and bite. (In Primary, angered by Carl's teasing, a Coloured girl raked his short-pants-bared legs with fingernails that felt like ten razors. *Gee-zus!*)

Because Halifax is a naval base, bristling white power and whistling black servitude, boxing counts as *Anger Management* and a grab-
moolah-quick scheme. Lookit: Some Negroes just gotta hit others. If
they're good-fisted, they can brawl a room empty. So, "Nofaskosha"
spawns champ upon champ. White chimps and chump blacks tussle
for everything. Grade-school graduations feature a beat cop warning
pupils that brawn is better than brain, that they should toss away books
and pick up boxing gloves. "Forget about Doctor Dolittle, that smarty-
pants who can chat with dogs. Ha! Darwin is tops." For statements like
this, the uniformed dropout won lavish applause, even while students
intelligent enough to win good test scores had to shrink in their seats,
ashamed to know how to read, write, and rithmetic.

Carl had been one of those schoolboys made to sweat for
knowing that numbers were for things other than baseball innings or
shots on goal. Still, like all Scotianers, he took pride in Molasses Jones,
that ex-bouncer at The Black Bear Tavern in wax-face, red-brick
Windsor, who beat a bunch of pale sailors into red pulp and got to be
the Middleweight Champion of The Dominion. He'd always had his
two leather-puffed mitts in some patsy's suddenly bleeding face. Then,
Jones loco'd to Montreal to fight Murray Sparks for a payday, but got
slain by a demonic punch, one that even the referee could not describe
because it had come from Hell. At the funeral, Clyde Gray—no slouch
himself—laid two brand new, red boxing gloves on the casket.

• • •

Being a paper boy, delivering each day's narrow obits, doom-n-gloom
headlines, and sports scores, Carl learned the ways and means of Bluenoses
and Scotianers. Okay, he was merely passing the daily gossip, rolled tubular,
to subscribers or to passersby. But news reveals august truths.

On his rounds, Carl got to eye mothers, wives, gals, and also call girls. On Fridays, collection days, if he were lucky, a *belle* would open her door but forget to sash her housecoat. While a cigarette protruded from grimacing, garish lips, she'd count out coins to Carl's cupped palm. Her nipples, brushing against thin fabric, would harden, exciting the lad as he squinted surreptitiously at her chest. Once the lady-of-the-house'd paid him, she'd smile, or dismiss him coldly. He'd pocket his coins and savour the memory of her yawning, puffing, sipping a drink, or lounging so carelessly on a sofa that he'd glimpsed her sex.

(Carl's weekly reckoning amounted to a lion's share for *The Morning Herald*, but a tally for himself. Thus, he splurged on comics, pop, records, a baseball glove, a book, a movie ticket. But he volunteered a portion of his profit to his ma, to better the poverty of the barnyard-domiciled clan.)

Carl viewed his route as a straggly mission among beer-perfumed dives and oil-scented alleys. He stopped at several taverns, seven rooming houses (three that doubled up as brothels), and three-storey houses that were virtual hospitals due to all the blood shed on their beds and floors and walls, thanks to razor blades used as scalpels and broken bottles used as saws.

• • •

Childhood is clean, yes, but no one gets out of childhood cleanly. It's even tougher to do so in Halifax, where sailors' *Poesy*—smut—passes for literature, impossible to avoid. In fact, in Halifax, Adult Education teachers swear that it is profitable to use sex positions to help illiterates learn to draw Roman letters and add and subtract Arabic numerals.

Corruption's inevitable here. "Cocksucker" is to Halifax what "motherfucker" is to Harlem. So, Carl eyed cock-and-cunt graffiti, riffled Tijuana bibles. He digested sweaty scripture—*Porn*.

It is disreputable *Art*, yes, but it depicts a *desired* life—as lurid as a corpse and as honest as a babe. (*Truth* be told.)

Carl saw its radical, dizzying beauty—how it joins unlikely persons. In smut, *any* pairing be a couple—black/white, young/old, hockey player/ballerina, blacksmith/nurse, chimney sweep/bathing beauty. There's no respect for person; *every body* can ply *Pleasure*, if comfort—or commerce—can be arranged.

On his newspaper circuit then, finding crumpled pages near a church, Carl chanced upon sordid, glaring photos: a mechanic and a nun; a cowboy and a figure skater; a lumberjack and a society lady. (Off and on, Carl repented for ogling such scenes, but he never felt guilty enough to quit this wicked delight.)

His favourite reverie recalls that crime at Italy Cross: In one scrofulous volume of snaps, a charcoal Negro pounds a sunshine blonde. He screws her so hard that any baby born will have a dent in its head.

Carl finds these sagas irresistible. No way to launder these besmirching images from his head and heart.

At twenty-three, Carl leagues with guys in shuttered garages down gravel driveways, or he descends into off-limit basements. To cheer on Hollywood–Las Vegas striptease strips—those looping, grainy, unreeling films of fat girls, garishly made up, being fucked—or flogged—by white men in black masks. More rarely, Carl glimpses close-ups of dark phalloi filling ivory-face, pallid mouths, and black-bushed scallop-pale sexes. A grave *Joy*.

In some flicks, circulated underground (for they're notoriously liable to confiscation or censorship), the camera cuts from a biker to a bedroom, from a man aboard a bike to a man aboard a broad. The man always arrives as an avenging angel, and never a pacifist. The hero is either gunning his bike or "shooting his wad." A model is either so skinny that she always seems to be in profile, or so fat that ordinary mirrors bulge just like funhouse mirrors.

Wisdom: the only public history that matters is military; the only private history that counts is sexual.

• • •

Though a minister's daughter, Victoria—never Vicky—Black had her five sons by five different Negroes, whose tints range the spectrum: a multi-hued brood. The first-born is Granville, whose father had been an army bugler with a cracked horn and a crooked jaw, and who perished due to a doxy who cut his throat because she couldn't stand his squawking. Next came the twins, Premiere and Encore. Their father earned a medal in Great War France because, being stone-deaf, he couldn't hear the machine-gun firing as he charged and bayonetted the Kraut gunner. Following Carl, the youngest boy is Huckabuck, whose father is, sayeth *Gossip*, Buddy Sun, the Negro milkman. Unlike his brethren, Carl looks coppery, mahogany-like, not jet-black or ivory-yellow.

Née Victoria Waters, Carl's mom had slid from well-bred Negress to common laundress, a genealogical disappointment who scoured the dank drawers and scrubbed the stained shirts of the Tars and Tommys who trooped to her home (and, if they had a spare drop to drink, could stay the night—and not spare her bed). Cleanliness—*fake purity*—was now her vocation. Despite her austere *hauteur*, despite her flawless German, Latin, Greek, and French, and perfect English, a *lingua franca* that she flaunted with the elocution and enunciation of a natural-born Royal, this ebony woman was always elbow-deep in bleach-stinging water and caustic soapsuds. To erase—from linens, lingerie, and livery—the remnants of semen, shit, piss, vomit, wine, coffee, beer, nicotine, snot, and blood required such scrubbing, such personal degradation, that Victoria's tears surged and merged—not infrequently—with her sweat and soapsuds.

Unfortunately, Victoria's expert governance of lingo was no match for her unruly heart. She had a yen for Coloured veterans who'd seen too many horrors in the Great War, and hardly any love. She herself had felt unloved; she wasn't pretty; she couldn't sing; she couldn't aspire to be a man's darling or a showbiz queen. There was no room in 1920s Nova Scotia for a black woman who could backtalk in five languages and rewrite musical notation upside down and backward. So, unable to bow her head to Dalhousie University or, say, Wellesley College, she took betwixt her legs, instead, local Negro grandees, much to the pitiless chagrin of her most distinguished and decorated sire, Rev. Dr. Capt. Victor Oliver Waters, O.B.E., B.Div., D.Div.

Impossible was it, then, for Victoria's 90 per cent high school grades to cancel out her dad's dismay at her fetching home one pregnancy, and then another, and then another. Although innocent of Freud, the Rev. Dr. Capt. Waters did suspect that his daughter's generosity to the soldiers he'd once chaplained and chaperoned enacted her rebellion to his strictures as well as her revenge for having been spurned as being too dark in colour and indelicate in feature. Victoria Waters had thus determined to be a better flapper than she was a Baptist. Shortly, her pressed hair was bobbed; she took up cigarettes and rum; if she couldn't have a groom, she could at least have "pets."

Discomfited by his backslid daughter's embarrassment of his sermons, the African Baptist pastor hit upon a save-face (if not save-soul) solution. Knowing that few selfish men would want to marry a woman with three boys already by three strangers, the Rev. Dr. Capt. Waters plotted to affiance his daughter's lust to a poor man's money-greed. His scheme: Fix a *concordat* between Victoria and a B.W.I. sailor surnamed Black, who hailed from either Barbados or Barbuda. The sailor seemed as dodgy as Don Giovanni. *But* if Mr. Black would take Miss Waters as his (temporary) Mrs. Black, in exchange for two hundred dollars, he could weigh anchor and steam off to seduce veritable virgins and swear new betrothals elsewhere, his in-good-time exit never to be questioned.

Thus, Mr. Able Seaman Black gifted Miss Waters with the respectable title of Mrs. Black and a new son—Carl, born in 1935, the Year of the Pig, and in May, thus rendering him a *Taurus*, bullish. Papa Black then disappeared. Either he decamped chilly Halifax for the sunny Caribbean to start a new family; or, he became an unsung martyr of the Battle of the Atlantic, dying, as it were, for the ex–Edward VIII's sick-to-death brother.

After the nuptials, Grampy installed Victoria and four sons in a barn behind a house of his on Belle Aire Terrace. (He resided in a manse; his daughter and grandsons stabled in a manger—a disreputable Mary, a long-gone Joseph, and a brood of downscale Christs.) There, Carl grew up, with a floor of straw and newspapers, bedding of rags and cardboard, rats for games of hide-and-seek, soap bubbles for early toys, and gruel, porridge, soup, and tripe for feasts, and eventually four illegitimate scions for siblings.

Despite his youthful ignorance, Carl sensed that his mom's apparent *Lechery* scandalized even Edward VIII–Fan-Club Nova Scotia. Too, Grandpa Waters was *somebody*, being the most distinguished black minister that Coloured Scotianers had had since Father Richard Preston—also Virginian—had died in 1861. So, *Shame* shadowed Carl's childhood. Being Victoria's only legitimate son, Carl blamed his mother—he blamed *women*—for blighting the family's pseudo-heraldic *Honour*.

Yet, Victoria had desired, merely, to be able to be—and love—as she wished, rather than kowtow to the bleating of a white world that wanted black women to suckle white children at the expense of their own (who could—and did—bloody well die), and buckle under the tantrums of black men who wanted them to be their slaves, so these guys could posture and pose as real—metaphysically white—men. From her standpoint, her decorated dad was as much a tyrant to her mom as the tavern brawlers were to their molls. She'd rather be poor but proud, and independent. However, as progressive as Victoria's individualism was, it looked *backward*—sinful—to others and merited censure: after all, she was raising her family in a barn.

Carl did see his mother as a trim, tall, molasses-tinted bluestocking, who had to play dumb and grin way too much to garner trade and tips from the scruffy troops whose dirt-slathered uniforms were her gold mine. Carl knew there was more to Victoria than soft soap, hard water, and lye. She wafted chalk dust. Her son could choke on his oatmeal, yeah, but Victoria forbade him to choke on his syllables. It was *Verboten*, in her barn, to deploy vulgar vocabulary *or* slipshod grammar. *No horse French, no pig Latin.*

Victoria laboured as a laundress through the Great Depression, World War II, and the dawn of the Cold War. A dreadful living, was it; grimy by definition. (Servicemen seldom come spic and span.) If a sailor pressed himself upon her, or bent her over her laundry tub, she could prove flexible. She was the Ophelia of suds, the Cleopatra of ironing, the Juliet of any desirous Jack Tar.

Yes, Victoria tolerated the sex stains and smoke-reek of the dregs of the ships, the docks, the pubs, the wharves. Whores—the underclass of the underworld—brought her their underthings too. Mondays, the barn looked like a Barnum & Bailey big top, with wet glitz, dripping stockings, gossamer panties, and clothespins dangling show-stopping bras amid the drab, damp darkness where horses once shat and cows once mooed. But Carl and his brothers enjoyed the sight and sound of the gum-cracking, loud-talking, lollipop-sucking sorority of the streets, who always paid well and on time, and who never cursed or drank in front of the boys. They were brownskin or black-to-the-bone, sporting crimson lipstick and blue mascara, so that when they flitted in and flirted with a shy-shy Carl, he felt that tropical birds were caressing him with their feathers. Victoria never hinted that she thought any less of these women than she did of the pale, upper-class ladies who, if they turned onto Belle Aire Terrace, would streak through the dire-straits street, ordering their chauffeurs to brake for no stray dog and no stray pickaninny. As for Carl, the vision of these barnyard lovelies reinforced the idea that women were fanciful creatures, half feathers and half fangs, and had to be tamed if they were to be trusted, let alone loved. A difficult prospect, really.

• • •

The streetwalker seared into Carl's memory is splendidly sultry, with straight copper hair, freckles, blue-green eyes, and a tan, sullen infant. This "Onondaga Madonna" would sit, smoking and gabbing with Victoria, while waiting for her shimmering undies to dry, and she'd breastfeed her golden urchin with dusty curls and sombre, coal-black eyes. This real-life Nativity—*Madonna and Child*—erased the picture book tales about farmer-dads and baker-moms, and storks bearing babes to cradles. One day, Victoria had to run errands, and so left the lady, Laxxy, with her own babe, Carl, and his younger brother, Huckabuck. In Victoria's absence, Carl had got up the gumption to ask, "Laxxy, give me your titty to suck." To his delight, she'd switched her snoozing bundle from one arm to the other and reached inside her cleavage to give Carl her plump left breast and instantly stiff nipple to tongue. He was ten then and didn't need the teat but had wanted to test his powers of rhetoric with a woman who was easily twenty. That Laxxy had yielded to his pleading was an object lesson. He had enjoyed her milk and the perfume soap of her skin, while both he and she kept a nervous watch, out of peripheral vision, for the return of Victoria. Disappointingly, after that encounter, Laxxy, who had purred and sighed as Carl had suckled on her teat, never showed again. She found a different *and* childless laundress to refresh her tawdry glitter.

• • •

Victoria's slide from high heels to round heels can be traced—in part—
to her rivalry with her sister, Pretty, Carl's aunt—sepia in tint, plump in
waist, and posh in bust; with slick, raven hair and a smile of bright, tantalizing incisors. Their preacher-papa, Rev. Waters, had cursed Victoria,
but he'd doted on Pretty, whose singing genius had hooked his adoration
along with *hoi polloi* adulation. Too, Pretty wore her name well, while
Victoria was book-smart but homely. The sisters traced opposite trajec-
tories: Victoria became a laundress; Pretty a songstress. Victoria was a
good-time girl gone wrong; Pretty was a never-a-false-note gospel singer.

Even as a disembodied voice pulled from ether, Pretty delivers
a spine-tingling contralto whose acid dissolves the pap of radio tunes.
She exhibits the pitch of classical perfection—thanks to her training by Dr. Ennio Piccioni, Halifax's star-turn Jewish intellectual exile
from Mussolini (and Hitler), who heard in Pretty a voice to rival that
of America's Negro art-song *chanteuse*, Marian Anderson (nicely *not*
an irritating Commie—unlike Paul Robeson—but comfortably liberal).
Dr. Piccioni took Pretty Waters to his bosom, pulled strings, plucked
heartstrings, and the scholarships and fellowships came a-tumblin
down: soon, pupil and tutor rose mutually from their depressed circumstances, hers suppressed by Negrophobia, his by anti-Semitism.

Though glamorous globally, with an RCA Victor recording contract, trophies and medals, fur coats and fan letters, superlative reviews
in *The New York Times* and *The Times* (of London), and, even, in 1958,
a *third* Royal Command Performance—this time before the Queen,
Pretty-as-a-picture wasn't picture-perfect: like Victoria, Pretty also had
borne a babe out of wedlock. But, in instructive contrast to Victoria,
Pretty left her newborn boy with a childless couple who'd sworn her
maternity to secrecy.

Also, Pretty damn well denies the jealous gossip that says she went from operatic song-sheets to Doc Piccioni's baroque bedsheets. But her shut-away son was shades lighter in colour than other Waters offspring, and, by age seven, he exhibited a remarkable aptitude for languages and a special affinity for Italian. Pretty's disavowal of her boy excised him as an impediment to her lauded belting of arias. She could steadily burnish her star *and* offer her teacher relief from the monotony of *Monogamy* and the sterility of exile.

Thus, Pretty's fame flourished, unmolested by motherhood, while her sister got affianced to a soon-vanished sailor—Mr. Locksley Black— and then consigned to a barn. Victoria had to lave and lave (swish sweat and soap), while Pretty, inclined to propeller in from Carnegie Hall or Royal Albert Hall or Rideau Hall, would bestow upon her sister a discard mink, a throw-away throw, but grant Carl and brethren a Christmas trove of toys and Meccano sets from Liverpool and ukuleles from New York City.

Carl lamented his mother's struggle to satisfy her family's needs. He couldn't help but eye Pretty's smooth success, her sunshine gleam, her lolling in glitz. Whenever she appeared in their doorway, she shed an afterglow, a radiation that transformed newspapers into silk and pine planks into gold. Her mere presence nudged Belle Aire Terrace, Halifax, nearer Bel Air, Los Angeles. Carl found it incredible, but ultra educational, that his mom and aunt were so different in material accoutrements, given their not dissimilar morals. (Aunt Pretty is and was as *pretty* did and does.)

Despite the grungy drudgery that was her employ, and the sooty dungeon that was her home, Victoria exercised thrift enough to install a phonograph. The instrument of instruments was a godsend (even if classical music was incongruous—surreal—with the sounds of suds foaming or water gurgling as Victoria sluiced away the filth of others). Yet, if chain-gang Negroes had to swing their sledgehammers and pickaxes in time to some antique spiritual or newfangled blues or heartfelt hollers, so did Victoria need to churn through hampers of ordure, buckets of soap shavings or bleach, and mountains of froth while spinning platters of Verdi, Chopin, Puccini, Beethoven, and Bizet. Salvation was hers if she could match her labours to trilling arias. Soiled clothes emerged extra bright if *Madama Butterfly* was warbling through the barn. If there were bloodstains on a uniform, *Carmen* was a prerequisite. Later on, even Pretty Waters's voice, scatting through Goldschmidt's *Beatrice Cenci* (1951), seemed to make smears and dirt-streaks scat.

• • •

Grampy Waters never lived to see bad-girl Victoria attain *Redemption*, for he perished of a heart attack when Carl was five. Still, the pontiff Waters's majesty attracted the premier of Nova Scotia to his sob-orgy funeral. Here the leader of the white New Scots seemed suitably downcast that the leader of the black Bluenoses was unanswerably deceased. Here, too, the humiliation of Victoria and sons was publicly accented, for they were banished from the first pew of the church, near the saintly grandfather's lavender, satin-lined casket. They had to look on, from a side pew, a distant pew, as the *Paterfamilias* got carried out from the church to his sacred slot in spade-opened earth.

Still, Rev. Waters would've been unhappy to know that Victoria's later uplift was due to her abandonment of one-afternoon or one-eve stands to accept, instead, to be mistress to the black boss of the Halifax Coloured railway workers. Thus, she experienced the identical ascension as did Wallis Simpson, more notoriously: to move from the arm of one man to the superior arm—and bed—of another.

Thanks to these determinations, Victoria was able to cease being a laundress at about the same time that Carl ceased to be a boy; she became, in a post that flattered her elocution, a telephone operator for

Maritime Telegraph and Telephone. Quickly, she moved her boys and her record player into a house that her lover, Mr. Grantley Beardsley, that "black bear," assisted her in leveraging.

To Carl, Beardsley was—and is—a fat but vicious cat, looking pampered but with ever-sharp claws and teeth, ready to dissect and digest any wayward mouse. Stout, portly, and the colour of stout or port, Beardsley needs only a derby hat to effect the darker likeness of canny, cagey Winnie Churchill, but one whose *V* stands for *Vice*, not *Victory*.

As the highest-ranking secular Coloured in Nova Scotia, who had come from the British West Indies, Beardsley needed the legitimacy that a daughter of the highest-ranking (though deceased) divine Coloured in Nova Scotia could provide, even if she was considered, by some, a "fallen" woman. Like many kings before, if he could not be happy with his queen (a sour-faced dame whose mouth spat piss and vinegar), he could choose to elevate his comfort woman.

For her part, Ma Black was nicely accommodating of "Pa" Beardsley. Her own father had put her in a barn, but her lover had put her in a house—impossible not to notice the bottom-line, top-dollar difference. To get out of the barn was like going directly to Heaven: to go from sniffing definite rat shit to being able to chow down on savoury venison, its spicy flavour not spoiled or turned by underwear stink or vermin-defecate stench.

In spite of their improved status wrought by the appearance of the benefactor Beardsley in their lives, the continued derogation of the Black family was clarified excruciatingly when a delegation of African Baptist Church women—a gaggle of dour, monocled *Gestapo*—dared to ring Victoria's doorbell to tell her that her profitable adultery with Mr. Beardsley, a husband and father, made her unfit to remain a member of the Ladies' Auxiliary. Victoria kept a steely face; she asked if anyone had thought to ask Mr. Beardsley to address these allegations. (She might have asked how many of her inquisitors had been virgins at marriage or how many had had babes by men other than their husbands.) But the damage—so to speak—had been done: Carlyle Black was now convinced of the unutterable hypocrisy of *all* African Baptists. Carl realized that he'd been born to a ma who'd just sinned and sinned and sinned— only outside a sorority of sanctimonious bitches. (Hard not to remember all this when he became Baptist Youth prez.)

So, as soon as he was able to work to help finance Victoria and his brothers, Carl set to institute a stern morality—as if reviving the right dead Rev. Waters. At age seventeen, he changed the locks to Victoria's house. He hoped to bar patron Beardsley from rendering the new home his extramarital love nest. He kept one key for himself and hid the other. Victoria protested, loudly, her son's imposing upon her *his* notions of *Chastity*. She complained most bitterly: "Bible lessons are Mother Goose tales for adults!" But Carl was unmoved by her upset (induced by her fear of losing Beardsley's benevolence). Carl thought he could govern now like a *Harem* eunuch, guarding any entrée to Victoria's boudoir. He'd decided that five fatherless sons were enough. He would discipline the loose womb that had borne him. So, come ten p.m. each night, Carl locked the door to bar Beardsley's intended, amorous liaison.

This regime lasted one week. Carl revelled in his power to lock out Ma Black's gentleman caller, who dared to rattle, drunkenly, the doors. The son was pushing Beardsley to seek his scabrous pleasure far from Belle Aire Terrace, this shantytown street with a Tinseltown name, this street of crooked, wooden houses, most no better than splinters pinned together with tacks and papered over with *Crime* reports, painted in riotous colours.

But Carl's prudish experiment ended when Victoria offered him the dignity of his own room. He'd guard *his* space and leave hers to herself and whomever she chose to invite upon her premises. She was damned sure this compromise would hold. Her voice had hissed as her eyes had flamed. Carl scowled, but relented, and he and Victoria were able to access house, home, and rooms as freely as they wished. Yet, Victoria did choose to be more circumspect, arranging to meet Beardsley in sleeping cars stalled overnight at the train station.

• • •

Carl's teens were improved by the largesse that Beardsley visited upon Mrs. Black & Sons, and his twenties have unfurled as fairly prosperous because Beardsley got him hired at the CNR train station—a plum post, sure. Though his mother has long ceased to favour G.B. with coitus in her home, due to Carl's puritanical gestures, Ma Black still has the last word, the last laugh: now she trysts, supine for big-boned Beardsley, in their train-station, sleeping-car beds; and Carl launders the sheets that mom and lover besmirch—or, rather, baptize. Too, his paycheque shackles Carl to Beardsley, which is his boss's sweet policy.

Carl is conscious, daily, nigh the point of anxiety, that his way-of-life depends on Grantley Beardsley—G.B. "Great Britain"—because he's merely slotted in, at Beardsley's discretion, to cover for Burl Bundy, who's tenuously away to suffer cancer treatment. When—if—Burl returns, Carl will hit the unemployment insurance claimant lines, *unless* Beardsley wroughts his usual financial-politic magic.

Carl's plight is definitely a raw hurt. Beardsley, the B.W.I. ex-officer who loveth Victoria whenever he wants, is Carl's boss because the man scored the Order of the British Empire medal by recruiting a couple thousand Coloured chaps to serve in the Battle of the Atlantic and get torpedoed, blown up, and drowned, after first being called "niggers"— incessantly—by their strutting, spitting Anglo-Saxon commanders. Likely more than one Caribbean sailor had perished while cursing his bad luck in choosing to defend the Empire rather than back Marcus Garvey's fascistic Back-to-Africa dream.

Bad enough that Beardsley's chief; worse is how he won this fief-dom. Unlike most Coloured railwaymen, Beardsley don't ride the rails, not now. Still, the railway has been and is—even for this prime "Uncle Thomas"—a locomotive of *Liberty*; or locomotion for class upgrade.

Beardsley started off on the CPR—the "Coloured People's Railway" (employer of East Indians and West Indians)—working its ships, and then he migrated over to the CNR—the "Canadian Negro Railway"—as a sleeping-car porter. He had to launder white folks' sheets, shine their shoes, get called "George," or "boy," or "Tom," or, yes, "nigger."

Some get rich by distilling; others get rich by stealing. Beardsley got rich by smiling. To wit, whenever a white passenger branded him a "nigger," he'd answer, "Nigger's ginger-coloured, and so's a cent, / Tip me a copper or your nigger's spent!" This wit won him grins—and coins. Beardsley even told white passengers, "Call me 'Bojangles'—cause I's a 'beau' and I sure do 'jangles.'" His jovial jive hit jackpots. Acting the wily vassal, he was soon as successful at shining shoes as Al Capone was in merchandising bootleg. To whites, *porter* denoted "Negro fool." To Beardsley, *porter* denoted "self-employed accountant." No bones about it. By cagey *playing to* white stereotypes, Beardsley won black power, royal-purple influence, and pure gold—his own paid-off house plus other real estate.

Greasy fat, if a skinflint, Beardsley believes in his Negro-go-slow gradualism and his rapid, capital accumulation. After all, he's wit-nessed horror: in the 1930s, he found the castrated body of a fellow porter, the erudite Mr. Booker, hanged—lynched—in his porter uni-form from a Dixie pine. Weirdly, Booker had somehow maintained his funereal dignity as he floated, crotch still dripping blood, suspended from a rope between the white man's Heaven and the white man's Hell-on-Earth-for-Negroes.

Beardsley swore to never be a victim. He be cut of rougher stuff than most Coloured men. He's been propelled upward in the world by shitting downward scrupulously.

Indeed, Beardsley used to sell call girls' phone numbers to select sleeping-car passengers, on runs where the train would overnight in Montreal, Chicago, New York, or Toronto. For anyone detraining in one of these cities, if only for a night, and needin companionship, Beardsley could furnish a sure-thing phone number for an extra-something tip. Later, after a gent had been entertained, and had paid, the benefactress would wire Beardsley a retainer. Smartly, Beardsley kept a discreet notebook of clients and calls, so that, if he needed assistance with a problem or just extra collateral, he could call quietly to a gent, mention his past help in fixing up a righteous rendezvous, and then make his pitch for aid. Usually, the request was granted promptly by a "Yes, sir" telegram or a wired money order.

On a 1950 foray to "Naw Leens," Beardsley ogled Bourbon Street belles wearing baby dolls, the dresses that bare panties deliberately. It so excited him, he brought a consignment to Halifax, for use in the cat-houses, where he advised the lady inmates to wear high heels and string pacifiers about their necks. They did, and soon found that jerks adore lavishly the *Pedophilia*-provoking getup.

White guys mistake Beardsley for a buffoon; but he's a czar. He has served every prime minister, from Borden to Diefenbaker. He's pure starch in his trousers, iron in his backbone, spit on his shoes, and silver in his tongue.

Not only does Beardsley direct Coloured railway workers, his prominence makes him the natural Maximum Leader of the Halifax Coloured Imperialist League (HCIL), a shadowy, *Race*-uplift enterprise. Running the HCIL also lets him run Victoria. As a daughter of the now-deceased Rev. Waters, by lending her prestige heritage subtly— nominally—to Beardsley's board of directors, Victoria ups his status as well as her own. He acquires mo' legitimacy; she's acquired a house.

Being head honcho of the HCIL, a group that views *Race Relations* through rose-coloured glasses, Beardsley salivates to pose with patricians for photo ops and plead for minor jobs for Scotianers, so long as Coloureds don't protest their treatment as third-class citizens, subject to cop beatings and store clerks' snubs. Better to hobnob with paid-off police than berate their shooting down of hard-up Coloureds.

Being, too, an intent student of *The Race*, Beardsley knows every Negro prefers *Carnival* to suck-teeth *Survival*. Any weekend, Scotianers transform from Saturday-night flash to Sunday-morning best; to go from canvas sneakers to patent-leather heels. The function of the HCIL is not, then, to combat *Segregation*, but to toast the Queen and pass the marmalade (morning) or caviar (evening). To put on revels, not elevate or equalize.

Gossip posits that the HCIL is just a prostitution ring, acting to procure brown gals to service sailors of all nationalities once their vessels put into port. If true, then, Victoria shares in the moneys that Beardsley extracts for being a shady pimp for lovelorn Tars.

Yep, the HCIL is a fusion of opium den, blind pig, and house of ill repute. But Beardsley thrives because times are usually hard, women always soft, and currency best held cold. This combination, fit to docking schedules for ships and the shunting of trains, hither and yon, produces a steady drift—tide—of income into Beardsley's pinstriped pockets. He is less corporate than Kennedy and less conspicuous than Capone, but still an A1 capitalist *Success*.

• • •

Seduced by Aunt Pretty's graces and her luxuries, and cashing in his paper boy—and later sign-painter—coins, and still later his CNR pay, Carl began to make a fetish of purchasing classical music records. Despite a local, scandalous link to jazz—namely Duke Ellington's ducal-style adultery with the daughter of an Africville man (who'd traded Halifax's granite curbs for those of Boston)—Carl can't take black classical music seriously, though he does admire the sartorial panache of the Negro players. No, Carl prefers egghead pianists, those shades of Dr. Piccioni, who tune up the old-time repertoire, rendering it—*via* Leonard Bernstein and Arthur Fiedler—a cabaret (Fascist critics say "degenerate") grace.

Finally splitting from his mother's Beardsley-financed abode, and moving, to rent, at eighteen, his own Belle Aire Terrace apartment (where *Stag* mag shares shelf space with *The Watchtower* Witness screed), Carl devoted a buck or two each week from his CNR cheque to canvassing classical music aisles in record shops. His LP collection thus came to boast Fiedler's Boston Pops Orchestra recording *Classical Music for People Who Hate Classical Music*; pianist Amparo Iturbi's *Spanish Music*; and Ernest Ansermet conducting L'Orchestre de la Suisse Romande in *Stravinsky: The Fire Bird (Complete Ballet)*. Other albums spin to round off seductions: platters by The Platters, Nat King Cole, Johnny Mathis, and Yma Sumac. Carl is set erect by Sumac's poignant clarity, her piercingly guttural trill, her ability to reverse from crystalline soprano to smoky contralto, to blend Maria Callas and Billie Holiday. Startlingly black-haired, ivory-skinned, and busty, she's Peru's Sophia Loren.

Carl's classical predilection means he *outclasses* most folks (or so he thinks). By playing Beethoven, Bizet, Brahms, and Bach, he announces he's no layabout beatnik, slapping bongos. Thus, lugging suitcases at the Halifax train station, he whistles snatches of Debussy or fragments of Gershwin. Anything to lift him above the unlettered—and unwashed— herd. Carl loves Copland's "Fanfare for the Common Man," but he sure don't wanna be mistaken for one.

To subscribe to Tchaikovsky, not Chuck Berry, means that Carl must want a woman who can gussy up, who can wear the black gown, black pumps, and black gloves of the pale brunette gracing the cover of *Oscar Levant Plays Gershwin*. He desires just such a debonair dame. Yes, he ogles the college gals of *Playboy* centrefolds, who disrobe their tits to achieve a month's sum of immortality, but still dwell at home with mom and pop. These suburban sophomores suit Carl's Licia Albanese (Cio-Cio-san) devotion, his pretension to *Wholesomeness*.

Gleaned in part from trashy, yellowed paperbacks featuring hard-boiled dicks and mushy dames, his polysyllabic vocabulary also backs his *Elegance*. (Better a hardcore paperback commanding, "Let's do it," than a hardcover novel asking, "Whodunit?") Carl relishes his ability to dizzy unsuspecting folks with a flurry of vocables. By speaking before a mirror, he learns to enunciate.

Later in life, Carl's friends will be lawyers—men who'd savour his puns, his insinuations, and his enlightened dirty jokes. He don't say to a *she*, "Let's make love"—nothin so vulgar. He say, "Allow me to introduce you to the divine raptures of earthy levitation, the commingling of senses ordained by Eden and sanctified by Heaven." Sumpin like dat.

• • •

A classical music aficionado because of Aunt Pretty (and Mrs. V.B.), Carl's become an amateur painter because he wants a trade to transport him beyond his railway luggage and linen-laundry service. Nicely, *Art* aids seduction as much as does a motorcycle engine throbbing and pulsing neath a lady's stimulated *pudenda*. If Carl can't woo a woman by offering a jaunt, he tenders his rendering her a pastel portrait, a charcoal likeness, or (if she's willing) a watercolour nude.

Painting's become Carl's forte due to hard-faced Leo Fennel's eschewal of soft drink. The sign painter—a two-fisted alcoholic always adrift from job to job, flophouse to flophouse—had no pocket money to pay his laundry bills, including those racked up with Victoria. (Whenever

Leo acted a "recovering alcoholic," all it meant was, he'd recover empty bottles—wine, beer, liquor—to exchange for drinkable coins.) Resourceful, Victoria held that, in lieu of paying for his fresh-suds duds, Leo should teach Carl, then fifteen, to illuminate letters. The drunkard'd said, "Aye."

Thus, fresh from newspapering his hood with news of the latest killings in North End taverns and in North Korean trenches, Carl apprenticed to craggy-nosed, thin-haired, flush-cheeked Fennel, a stick-skinny man (who drank strength from liquor but also pissed it away). Being a devout drinker, Fennel was a conscientious teacher. Promptly, at five p.m., he'd set down his brushes and paints, his level and his yard-stick, and get he either to a tavern or to his rooming house—wherever there was drink stashed or on tap. Usually, he'd already be shaky and staggering in anticipation of the first steadying drink. Though his alcoholism was a hiccough, Fennel's fine sign lettering merited emulation, even worship. Trained in a dying branch of deathless advertising, Carl absorbed the tricks of carpentry (crux of *Architecture*) and illumination (*Art*). He learned to depict vivid, dreamy life. Too, given Fennel's stupors, Carl pocketed plenty scratch for helping to finish firm-hand-needed jobs that the grizzled Ol Massa's drinking threatened to scotch.

After he got comfy with inking the alphabet's twenty-six tricky figures, Carl began to experiment with depicting magazine starlets, cutie-pie classmates, or dudes goofing about diamonds or sporting in gyms, dropping barbells on each other's throats or braining each other with hardballs. He imitated Disney cartoons and the look of comic-strip cowboys and detectives. *Pleasure* there was in blacking in an image, applying oils or pastels to limn a tree or flower, or simply pencilling the delicacy of a woman.

For two years out-of-school, aged fifteen to seventeen, Carl lettered signs alongside Fennel, playing his prop and often his crutch. Fennel swayed; he had a cranky list. (He termed it "a limp" so that it would look more like a war injury and less like brain damage.) Still, his eye and hand were gifted enough to guide Carl and keep his throat lubricated. Thus, Carl got expertise in inventing eye-catching signs or luminous drawings or radiant anatomies. A charcoal-ink pen, a maple-clad lead pencil; a pine-colour or cedar-colour crayon. Carl liked most media—watercolours derived from rain (residue washed up from Paris or Venice), or sun-brilliant oils, or the weather-beaten, sun-faded look of pastels.

With the income got from "signing," Carl bought model kits and their specialty paints, and learned to wield tiny, pointed, finicky brushes and dab pointillist daubs as he fine-tuned the assembly of a bike, or a buggy, or a bomber, to be sold to a collector for pocket change. Thanks to Fennel's penchant for painting palm trees and Hawaiian gals on rum bottles, Carl started to apply the cool gleam of model-kit paints to glass. Framed, with tinfoil stuccoed between the glass surface and cardboard backing, the painted scenes could be set shimmering—sights irresistible to many billfolds. Carl owned a good eye, an ogling eye, a for-sale-sign eye.

When Fennel drank himself to death in 1958 (he stumbled, zombie-like, in front of a freight train), Carl had purchase on a near-monopoly as a sign painter in Halifax. Problem was, the railway pay was too addictive. Because neon and fluorescent tubes were the new fixtures in many store windows, sign-painting assignments had dwindled, but there was still enough for a man to prosper, had he gumption. Maybe Carl did. But he'd have to dicker for painting gigs, whereas the railway cash was weekly and arrived with unemployment insurance, a prized perquisite for Haligonian Coloureds, always cash-poor twixt jobs. (Too poor to even pay on time their pennies-worth burial policies, thus renderin em "non-cents." Get it?)

Carl went to Queen Elizabeth High School in 1952–53, for one year, Grade Ten. Gifted with Victoria's brains, Carl breezed through the curricula but concentrated on *Art*. He wanted to supplement Fennel's hand-and-eye instruction with *Theory* got from classroom praxis and watching pliant teen models: a blue-jean-jacket blonde with a cigarette always pursing her lips; a brown Negro dude with cherry-red lips, gazing off into a blue-sky, skyscraper distance; a sable Negro with a square head, no lips, and frenetic limbs; a cream-faced brunette with curly hair, bright blue eyes, and smiling red lips.

Although two years older than most of his classmates, Carl did not let his seniority split him from his peers. He won praise by painting animalistic dudes and drawing animated women. He aced the class. *Cool* it was to spread-eagle an easel; to splay paint, charcoal, ink, or pastels; to master whiteness; to use colour to colonize blank paper or canvas. To make a woman look super and a man look souped-up.

At eighteen, in 1953, after Grade Ten, Carl quit schoolin. Now, he leafed through art books, but riffled through Rembrandt, whose brooding scenes admit that light is everywhere, but sordid, stewing in shadows. Carl saw, in Rembrandt, the same demented faces that haunt Halifax alleys and hovels. In Halifax, as in Rembrandt's *The Night Watch*, one turns a corner and sees a shimmering, half-savage visage looming out of a doorway, a window, or fog, looking ready to kiss, or kill, to be either the Ripper's victim or the Ripper his hellish self. But Rembrandt's nudes glow pink, plush like shameless roses. Carl treasures the painter's zest for light amid all Amsterdam's sodden, black velvet.

Carl saw that *Art* has three stops: *Religion, Nature, Woman*. Period. Out of chiaroscuro, out of pastels, out of oils, out of watercolour, every feminine form emerges, like a Botticelli Venus, a gorgeous Medusa, to transfix and trouble a dude. Yet, his gaze cannot be sated. A woman's beauty—her exquisite look and liquid sculpture—is light, brilliant and ephemeral, never to be captured.

Naturally, Carl's always idolized the sultry temptresses who beckon paperback readers. Even a high-class author like Billy Faulkner looks more appealing when his novel cover shows a blond, barefoot belle in a skin-tight, crimson dress, leaning against a wooden porch column and eyeing, brazenly, a bare-chested Negro labourer as he passes by, a boy from Ipanema. The book cover is a mini movie-poster, suggesting that black words on white paper can yield as many thrills as silvery light in a darkened cinema.

So Carl has gravitated toward Alberto Vargas's pin-ups. The Peruvian's women model Leda-as-swan, svelte, feather-light, and feather-white. Too, Vargas gals are never girl-next-door average, but shiny and statuesque. His palette is blond—gold, ivory, peach—and his palate favours blondes. Vargas pin-ups look pinned down, arrested in their nudity. It's difficult to imagine them as physical women, as *avoirdupois* women; they seem more like soft, thin clouds, pinkish-beige, creamy, but still so incandescently white as to vanish against whatever sheet they could ever be set down upon.

Carl's other major model is local—namely, W.R. MacAskill, the Nova Scotian marine photographer, whose scenes of fishermen battling gales are an East Coast version of Walker Evans's social-realist pictorials in *Let Us Now Praise Famous Men*. In lieu of a dust bowl, MacAskill shows a florid ocean, all ivory spray and charcoal depths. His apple blossoms and clouds are explosively white, but seem as posh and glowing as the innards of potatoes; his seas are lustrously dark— like India ink come fresh from a German pen. Because MacAskill is so unrepentantly *Romantic*, he is out of fashion in the era of *Time-Life*. But MacAskill depicts a Nova Scotia of gleaming leaves and of electrified sea-spray. His photos are moody, yes, but supernaturally voluptuous. His cloud banks are so lush as to seem roseate; his waves, violent in pitch, exude a bruising purple; his suns, ostensibly ivory, seem to pulse and throb with gold, vanquishing or dissipating some gathering storm. MacAskill photographs need no obscuring tints: he wrings entire rainbows out of collisions between natural blacks and native whites, orchestrated by sun or moon or rain squalls, and that vast horror that is the Atlantic, seething with sharks and shipwrecks. MacAskill's photos brood like Hitchcock stills. (Cf. the opening shot in Hitchcock's *I Confess*.)

Carl critiques MacAskill for wasting his talents on sailboats. He should've gone to Cannes, shooting starlets whose skin glows like cream. (MacAskill should've been a bit more like Vargas: posed a bikini'd babe on a heaving North Atlantic fishing trawler.)

Carl also copies Alex Colville, the official Dominion World War II artist, now finding acclaim with simple oils such as *Milk Truck* (1959). The painting could be low-key realism: a small-town truck is out delivering milk, but the black dog gazing gloomily from its rear seems symbolic of dread. Milk is white, but men's souls remain damned, or so impish Colville implies.

Carl's charcoal pencil pays homage to cartoonists, such as Bob Chambers at *The Morning Herald*, whose *métier* is hokey caricature. Chambers images the taxpayer as the archetypal little man, nude except for a fig-leaf-barrel suspended from his shoulders and a few sprigs of sweat leaping from his forehead and a few sprigs of hair sprouting from his legs. So, Carl doesn't mind aping Francisque Poulbot of the "Republic of Montmartre." His pictures of *les gosses*—Parisian urchins—are dowdy beauty, romanticizing rags and hovels. Carl spies his own childhood poverty in Poulbot's edgy sketches of naughty waifs and dreaming ragamuffins (the Parisian version of Dixie pickaninnies). If Poulbot's art remodels slum kids as Hansel and Gretel, so that *Deprivation* seems endearing, still he's no Norman Rockwell, flattering middle-class notions of pre-Depression, pre–World War II *Normalcy*.

All things considered, Fennel was a good introductory painting instructor, of sorts. And Grade Ten *Art* taught Carl much. But Carl considers taking a mail-order course.

The *Male* ad reads, "Art—Learn at Home," *and* showcases a painted robust nude. The come-on commands:

Enjoy glamorous high-pay career or profitable hobby. Learn Painting, Commercial Art, Cartooning, Fashion, Art, Lettering, TV, etc. We train you at home, in spare time. TWO 22-pc art outfits (worth $25) included, without charge. LOW COST—only 20¢ a day. Write for FREE BOOK describing EASY course. No salesman will call. Lincoln School of Art. Studio 69, Lincoln, N.B. (Estab. 1918). Tear This Out.

The course is "Easier than You Think!" The ad swears, "You don't have to be a 'genius' to break into art" and "No previous art training is needed." *Promising*. But this ad flanks others exhorting readers to "Be a LOCKSMITH" or "Study Law at Home," or "Be a Fingerprint Expert [There's a thrill in bringing a crook to justice through Scientific Crime Detection]" or to learn to "Hypnotize Easily," or, the top choice, to learn "Meat Cutting—The Best Established Business in the World: PEOPLE MUST EAT."

These ads suit carnivores, or patriots, or men who know that more education is like taking an endless vacation from *Poverty*. Carl dismisses the pulp mag tales of men "kicked to Kingdom Come by mad horses," or tell-alls about "What You Don't Know about Nymphomaniacs." Still, he surely is "TIRED OF WORKING for someone else."

He chances Lincoln. Maybe *Art* can emancipate him from shackles of "class oppression," just as Abe Lincoln emancipated slaves, well, *sorta*.

When the Lincoln *Art* kit lands at his door, it is full of standard, paintable images—lighthouses, churches, horses, nudes. There are also paints—oils—and brushes, and a how-to booklet. Also included is a pamphlet, "How to Make Money with Simple Cartoons." Carl dreams now of drafting—i.e., courting—models, choosing from among the waitresses, maids, secretaries, teachers, and Sunday school madams, all within his lower-middle-class, Negro orbit. Such are his available mannequins, who might very well strip down—not for cash, but for relative *Immortality*, the satisfying monument of a portrait.

• • •

The Halifax train station, with its sculpted image of Britannia ruling the waves, executed in white marble, set above the main portals, graced also by thick, concrete Greek columns, is a salt-spray White House, a Maritime slave mansion, where dark-black men still shine shoes, porter, lug baggage, and tote linen. From the station's entryway frieze, the profiled, helmeted Britannia, her triple-penile trident held erect, peers dismissively down at the Coloured porters and shoeshine boys, the Negro Scotian flotsam and jetsam of British slavery and royal wars. In enticing revenge, however, they are far more real than is the Empire, having "lost" India and Pakistan, and now slowly "losing" Africa and the Caribbean possessions (confiscations). White Britannia overlooks a station that is a quaint, outpost relic of the Raj.

Carl respects the sleeping-car porters. Their service is never insolent; their courtesies are those of chevaliers. They are the dark knights of the steel roads. Each talks like a professor and struts like a potentate. Bold, they possess the vocabulary to make their arguments register as lucidly in taverns as they could easily do in legislatures. These guys personify *Dignity*.

Too, by picking up discarded newspapers, thrown-out magazines, and refuse books, and by accepting gifts of Bibles and poetry, a porter can become an expert—with the lingo to accompany it—on any subject. The King James version is fine for morals, but Jesse James is better for finance. (Carl trusts that bankers are the best bank robbers about, preachin, "A dollar stolen is a dollar saved.")

The railway *is* frustrating, even for aristocratic, richly tipped porters. Yet, Carl likes the grit of the work, the gravel that chuckles under his feet, the steam and oil smell of the old locomotives. Whenever Carl hears a train whistle, he hears a cry for *Freedom*, if also the moans of *Lust*—his two imperatives. He suspects the very phrase *rock 'n' roll* got bo'n due to Negroes copulatin in sleeping cars (Victoria and Beardsley being a case in point). Trains *are* romantic vehicles: Carl prays to pull out of Halifax, to exchange Africville and the Halifax garbage dump for Chicago, home of Black Muslim toughs *and* bandy-legged Playboy Club heifers.

He be only a linen-and-equipment checker, but Carl sees himself as a subversive menial. Surely, the world of the Negro custodian—as railroader—in Halifax, as in Harlem, is never pure black and white, but full of greys. Carl understands himself as a struggler, as Trotsky with mahogany skin and Brylcreemed hair, as revolutionary even when he is saying, "Yes, sir," vivaciously—as if he means it. The railway is just a way station until he can make his own way forward as an artist. To be a man not reading *Male*, but profiled therein.

That's his dream, but Carl fears the CNR has him penned up and pinned down—like a stallion, a Black Beauty, corralled by railway tracks and outpaced by those steel wheels. No wonder he's got to jump on Liz II and have his *Freedom* the way the Queen has hers, happy aboard her horses.

Certainly, his immediate bosses treat Carl like crap. "Sparky" Jollimore—razor-pitted and red-dotted scabrous—and "Studs" Sponagle—nerdy with Scotch-taped eyeglasses—are, by rank, subservient to Beardsley. In practice, they run roughshod over him and run herd on Carl. Neither Jollimore—skinny and hatchet-faced—nor Sponagle—fat and Mussolini-bald—can cipher or letter worth a damn. But they've been at the CNR almost as long as *Rex Georgius* VI had his smoking problem. However, they resent Carl because he looks "pretty" (as Cassius Clay would word it), speaks way too intelligently (grammatically), and is only tangentially deferential. Because Carl reminds em they work for Beardsley, Sparky and Studs slag him as flippant. They also loathe Carl for chatting up so breezily the station's white, black-coffee waitresses. So, the two louts serve Carl grief. If he drops a suitcase, or finishes loading or unloading a train too slowly, or fails to fold a pillow-case or sheet "just so," they dock him precious-precious coins.

The Abbott and Costello of the Halifax station also loathe Carl's lit-eracy. ("*N-i-g-g-e-r* is how ya spell *stupid*.") Two years back, in '57, Carl committed the crime of leafing conspicuously—in the lunchroom—Trotsky's *The Negro Question in America* (1933). His act agitated Studs and Sparky. The boss-men buds tried to get Carl fired for bringin "pinko shit" to work. They got up so close into his face that Carl could smell the urine in their underwear. Carl had to satisfy the inquisition; he intoned, "Yes, sir; no, sir." He did want to slug his overseers, but decided to drop ice-picked-on Trotsky for Ian Fleming's nasty but hip-hip-hooray Bond capers. Didn't help: Jollimore and Sponagle still dub Carl uppity.

Matters worsened when that innocently lurid photo of Carl, as Baptist Youth prez, surfaced in *The Morning Herald* in January 1959: he was positioned directly behind two young white women, bent over a table, with their crossed arms before them and their sheepish rears prof-fered invisibly to their black male ram. Sparky and Studs espied inter-racial hanky-panky in this provocative posing, and summoned Carl to their desks to complain. He could only grin inwardly at the discomfiture of his superiors. Spittle seethed at the corners of their yellowed teeth; red veins X'd the whites of their eyes.

No wonder Carl is so circumspect in his parley with white female train passengers. Especially if they are single and travelling solo, his ser-vice requires a kid-gloves aesthetic. A too-familiar glance, an accidental touch, and he could be tossed from the railway and tarred for life. In his daily rituals of lugging baggage and laundering bedding, he must be as ascetic as a Shaker and as asexual as a eunuch.

Recently, one grey-haired, skinny schoolmarm, with glasses, asked

Carl, "Do you credit Mr. Will Faulkner with being correct in describing an oddity of the Negro male anatomy?" Carl looked at the attractive, perhaps lonely, lady, and could not help but smile, sincerely, and whisper, "Ma'am, it's no oddity, I assure you. It really is a dilly." A twitch ran through his manhood when he saw her eyes glaze over, fantasizing. But he's had to keep the episode so private that it's come to seem more dream than memory.

• • •

Relations between Victoria and son were—in his teens—frosty, given Carl's blinkered attempt to police *her* genitals. Their relationship warmed only when Carl admitted being sweet on a white classmate, one Liz Publicover. Both named Head Boy and Head Girl for their school, their proper photos had appeared, cheek-by-jowl, in *The Morning Herald*. Thus, her apple-blushed face highlighted his almond-dark complexion, while both gripped the trophies demarcating their triumphs. Carl's smile was tentative, while Liz's teeth shone fulsome. This contrast prompted Victoria to ferret out the truth that Carl fancied the filly. Having been herself, severally, the *not*-quite unwilling recipient of Caucasian male lust *and* largesse, Victoria had no illusions about *Respectability*, and believed white folks were no way more virtuous than Coloured—just better able to parade a torch-lit wholesomeness (shades of Nuremberg). She'd toast happily the knowledge that Carl—and her other sons—were regularly ploughing any number of Caucasiannesses to reveal them all as consummately *Concupiscent*, despite all their soap, silks, and sermons. Thus, Victoria badgered Carl to pester Liz for a date. She smiled and winked at her son whenever he mentioned Liz—he thought *nonchalantly*. She'd vindicate her self-taught morality if a white girl from a proper home were to be caught, *in flagrante delicto*, with an amorous Negro. When Carl courted Negresses, Victoria was less interested, for a Coloured woman's hymen wasn't worth shit (as, slurred white and black dudes, *hers wasn't*).

Victoria's sentiments were acrid but accurate, for they were derived from experience. Convinced that humanity *is* depravity (a notion every laundress affirms), and that *Purity* belongs only to *Nature*, Victoria lusted to read accounts—or eye photos—of brown babes at white breasts. To her, the British Empire itself was royal rapine and crowned *Criminality*. Encouraging her sons to screw white daughters was her vicarious way to rub upturned Anglo-Saxon noses in African and very earthy soil. To use *her* black sons to hit *their* white daughters executed a Garveyite vengeance in the style of Euripides.

Thus, Carl credits that, yep, the most desirable women are white and are the most satisfying once subjugated. It's an imperious attitude, imbibed from *History* and from his home, and he spied its workaday reality in the North End of Halifax. Coloured women are for work, white women are for "sleeping with," all women can be beaten, and none can be trusted. Thus did Carl chew up the boiled-down misogyny of hard-boiled crime comics and Tijuana bibles. His dark-complected (and complex) sexism became his answer to redneck racism and blueblood classism.

This Negro male *revanchisme*, the battering of women (principally wives) was prevalent in Carl's childhood. Right on Belle Aire Terrace. The brute idea that manhood was what was distilled—left over—from a smashed-down woman's blood and tears.

● ● ●

The woman splintered the pine door as she come through it, screamin as if bein born. The locked front door should've blocked her egress. Except the small, brown woman—pure five-foot-two and ninety pounds—come crackin right through, then roll down the steps and onto the sidewalk. She was hollerin and cryin and gaspin, her arms flailin, clutchin at air, as she was projected through the door and down the rough wood steps. She looked like she'd fainted, once she hit the bottom step and then sprawled—a disjointed mannequin.

The Blacks lived side the Downeys. Behind and above smashed-down Mrs. Downey loomed her gross husband—summide three hundred pounds of plus-six-foot-tall muscle. A railway porter, often away from home, carrying suitcases, shining shoes, and making beds for people who called him the homely, gutter-language, trash-talk names. All of Belle Aire Terrace—white and black, Catholic and Protestant, sweatin class and petty *bourgeois*, stood and watched nice, neighbourly Mr. Downey "put a hurtin on" his missus.

Mr. Downey always strode ramrod straight, and he might say hi or he just might tip his hat and keep on goin, acknowledgin you even as you got dismissed. But he was a serious Negro, tannish, while his wife was caramel in tone. His face was as hard as algebra. His voice was quiet, but his hands—his fists—were huge. Carl was wary about those fists—that temper—just like everyone else.

When he'd heard the hubbub and come outside, Carl saw Mr. Downey, forty-ish, adult enough to get shot by a cop or railroaded to a jail, hulking in the splintered shadows behind the jagged hole that his wife had made. The man was too far away and he was too dim in those sharp shadows; still, something human had vanished from his guise.

The moment seemed still and silent. But it weren't. Folks'd come streamin out their own homes, wives especially, to pick Mrs. Downey up from where she lay, all akimbo, blubbering, her hot-comb-straightened hair awry, and to take her into their homes, their arms, to nurse her bruises, bandage wounds, dry her tears, fix her hair, and later let her return quietly home, once again walking—or *limping*—with *Dignity*. Simultaneously, her husband and one son went about repairing the breach in the door—the breach of the Sunday peace—with boards. Did one of em whistle?

But nothing could erase for Carl the image—fact—of Mrs. Downey breaking the door as she flew—or fell—through it, at the butt of her husband's fists. And no one phoned the police (for that could have been a death sentence for Mr. Downey). Carl did think the incident one on which all of Belle Aire Terrace agreed: a man's home is his boxing ring (if he so desires), and wife and kids are handy punching bags.

Carl couldn't dismiss the incident, though never did his respect for Mr. Downey cease. He still said "Mr." and "sir," though it was hard to ignore Mrs. Downey's bruised cheeks and her loss of a smidgen of *Vitality*, even as her carriage became ever more rarefied. Carl saw that the high-prestige job of sleeping-car porter had a downside. A man like Mr. Downey could be a travellin man with shiny shoes, status, and an address that lacked "Apt" as a suffix. Plus, he could carry home enough cash to keep a house and a wife who was *not* a white man's "help."

Had Carl mused on Mr. Downey's behind-closed-door *Violence* that had exploded, accidentally, into a spectacular, *alfresco* affair, he might have said, as if quoting *sociology* mavens, that Mr. Downey felt frustrated by his lot. Thus, he'd morphed into King Kong, caged inside a dinky kitchen, knowing impossible energy, translated into muscles— arms, legs, fists, feet—and, to his own surprise, perhaps, turned his wife into an ungainly football, or a soft-tissue battering ram, that, smashing saggingly through their door and out into the sunlight, had transformed their in-house squabble into outdoor entertainment.

But *Violence* was all about: Japs, Krauts, Commies were being atom-bombed or firebombed or hit with flame-throwers, *depending* on whether the foe was Red Scare or Yellow Peril or Blackshirts. Murderers might be hanged at Rockhead Prison (overlooking Africville in geography, but never overlooking Africville for prey) or face lynching at Italy Cross. Men took cleavers to rivals' necks. Women stomped on the babe-bloated bellies of rivals. Everyone learned the sign language of fists. Cops shot up everybody who was poor, as if lead was a charitable donation. Churches preached *Peace*, but it was a nebulous notion. Those who were pacified were either in coffins or in shackles. *Violation* was the norm. Even hockey was about thin steel blades slicing into ice—or about ice-borne slug-fests and hockey-stick bludgeonings.

How does a Coloured boy—man—get to feel safe and free enough to *Love*? That he can love fearlessly and be loved fearsomely? That his too-free kisses don't put a lynch noose about his neck (if he's caught neckin with the *wrong* shade of gal); or that his gentleness doesn't send his *uncorrected* sons to gaol or the gallows? Hard to give *Love* when you must police all that you do. Dilemmas to stump Plato, let alone Carl.

• • •

Sailor Black had vanished—perhaps into the anonymous mass graves of the eponymous Black Atlantic, where Africans had been unceremoniously dumped if they became hostile inmates or cumbersome cargo, en route to *Slavery*, but also now where black sailors could drown in defence of white Anglo-Saxon plutocrats *vis-à-vis* white Nazi goons. Whatever: Carl's father was gone from his life, almost as soon as Carl had it, but he didn't resent his father for vanishing, for that's what sailors do. They go down to the sea; they sail off into *Oblivion*.

Carl couldn't look to his mother's lovers—bed friends—as surrogate fathers, for they were mere glimpses of masculinity. Nor could he look up to Beardsley, even though he was a more permanent gent at his mother's side than the other guys had been. The problem was, G.B. was, in strict terms, a fink.

Nor could Carl idolize Grandpa Waters, who, after all, had stuck his daughter and grandchildren in a barn. Rev. Waters had immured his own flesh and blood in a castle of once–cow manure, once–horse manure, and a warren—still—of rat feces. Capt. Waters had—thanks to his high principles—placed his descendants in *Squalor*, hardly alleviated by laundry soap and turntable operatic arias.

So Carl's first hero was Jesse Owens, the star Negro of the '36 Berlin Olympics. Owens's fleet speed had scooped four gold medals and scuttled the *Race* theories of the Third Reich *and* the Southern-fried Dixie Nazis. Before his foot racing won him those Olympic gilded laurels, Owens had been a humble worker—like Carl—bagging groceries, shovelling coal, and rubbing in *dat* shoe polish. Even in university, he'd had to take part-time jobs, still reeking of shoe polish.

(Hard was it for Owens to wait tables, though: hard to take orders for steak and hamburger when he stank of blacked-up leather. His fragrance would remind diners that the beef they were set to consume could just as well be the leather shoeing their feet.)

After his Olympic triumphs, Owens found his gold medals inedible and so gobbled humble pie instead, turning his athletic prowess into small-town titillation, running against racehorses. He even pumped gas and dry-cleaned clothes to make a penny-ante buck. Carl liked this bio—of a Caesar of the track who struggled against the colour bar and anti-black codes by just sweatin and holdin high his head. Carl also liked Owens for refusing to raise his fist against *White Supremacy*. Owens had said, reportedly, the only time it's worthwhile to make a fist is when ya got dollar bills inside. So Owens was, to Carl's mind, a real Olympian, able to stroll with kings because he could outrun steeds—and not worry the seeming *Humiliation*. Owens fronts the *Equality* of folks of *Quality*, not the Negro mass cravin entry to the middle class.

But Paul Robeson is another matter. A superlative singer, actor, and athlete is he. But, as a declared Commie, he'd never warble for Edward VIII. So, though Aunt Pretty once shared a stage with the "Ol' Man River" singer, the man who exchanged the Hammerstein lyric "niggers" for the Comintern plug "workers," his anti-royal leanings make him an unsavoury character to Carl, who prefers lusting after Liz II to ever having to bunk down in the bunkum of a "Democratic (Peoples') (Socialist) Republic," the very moniker that translates as "no good martini available."

Joe Louis did the anti–*White Supremacy*–right thing by knockin out Hitler's champ, Max Schmeling, in the first round of their June 22, 1938, bout, when Carl was but three years old. The Brown Bomber had become such a hero that the Vachon pastry bakery outta Quebec had begun marketing its own Jos. Louis sponge cake, wafering vanilla cream between chocolate layers and under a chocolate coating. But, as a teen valuing classical music and elocution, Carlyle needed his heroes to project good grammar, not just throw redoubtable punches.

As a child, Carl's only other "Negro" hero was Batman. A white man by day, but a black avenger—leather-fisted brawler—at night. Carl viewed the comic book superhero as a modern type of Nat Turner, the swashbuckling swordsman and prophet who had campaigned bloodily for slave revolution in Virginia in 1831. A courageous and righteously Gothic dude.

But as a motorcyclist, Carl looks up to only one, if dead, man: T.E. Lawrence—writer, artist, war hero, camel jockey, and motorcyclist— the Batman, so to speak, of Arabia.

• • •

Astride the BMW, even when he's bent over the fuel tank, trying to duck the tonguing wind that washes under, over, around his helmet and his jacket, Carl feels erect, like a gunfighter in full gallop, stream-lining with his stallion, ready for the showdown, the high-noon or midnight fray. His legs are sturdy wishbones and his arms are Frankenstein-monster outstretched and steel-hard. His manhood too, even at rest, is cocked. Liz II, his "queen of *queans*," transforms Carl into a black-leather Priapus, a dark roustabout darting cupidic, or so he doth believe.

Aboard that machine, he imagines that he's Jesse Owens, streaking always to *Victory*, with style, with panache, with a kind word for all women and any and every tipper. *Liberation* is going, floating, flying; i.e., *feeling* actually free.

With polysyllables and a whistle at his lips, eight-millimetre sex loops in his head, the wind and Wagner in his ears, crisp bucks in his pockets, and a motorcycle as jockstrap, Carl is ready to sally forth, to seduce as many (milk-white) ladies as he may. He plans to introduce the motorcyclist Lawrence of Arabia to the plushest bedrooms of mainland Nova Scotia, wherever swagger and deft heft are welcomed. Carl will borrow the cap and garb of Rommel—The Desert Fox—to be a man of action, never *Alienation*. To lay down ladies, not lay down switchblade-rumble-in-dark-alleys *Nihilism*. *Vroom! Va-va-voom!*

TOUR II

Take from beauty ultimate beauty
and from truth ultimate truth . . .
and from femininity tenderest tenderness. . . .
— Juhan Liiv, "The Last Chance"

Wednesday, May 13

After his May 9th cruise with mercurial Muriel, Carl sets his heart a-ramblin—as is his wont. The women swirling past his dark sun-glasses seem delectable *bonbons* in rainbow-colourful sheathes. Even a repugnant face becomes acceptable if heading and fronting a curva-ceous physique. Loose morals make a tight butt way more enticing.

Carl's aesthetic is, luckily, portable—and instantly applicable—as in his on-and-off flirtation with Laura "Blue Roses" States. Carl spies her at the Chinese-operated Sunrise Café on Gottingen, south of Cornwallis, facing the Vogue Cinema. She's in from out of town (up Windsor way, where the States clan—of ex–U.S. slave descent—settled). He pulls Liz II over, letting the engine's rumble vibrate the restaurant windows: to broadcast his fanfare, as if he were Queen Liz, cross-dressed, exchangin royal-purple satin for *Lumpen* black leather.

Carl enters the door as if parting a theatre curtain. He's on stage now. Laura sits in a booth by the front window. She wears a flirty skirt; plaid pleats flatter her thighs and ivory legs. Carl grins into her face: she smiles into his mirror sunglasses. She seems invitingly guileless, and yet—as Carl knows—she hides her limp, just like Laura "Blue Roses" Wingfield in Tennessee Williams's play *The Glass Menagerie*. She is about to stand when Carl, the gentleman, tells her, "Relax," then slides into the booth, sitting opposite her. So the States girl perches: her hair, an exciting ponytail, flops up and down. Spiting her handicap, she moves as fluidly as water. Yes, she has a limp, but the extra rubber piece on one heel—the right—grants her posture an illusion of equilibrium. Carl studies an ever-radiant face, a Marilyn Monroe beauty spot off one Shirley Temple dimple. Her skin is pass-for-white cream, but Laura's dark sable eyes hint at her Negro *cum* Micmac mix. Carl is surprised to find her here, this Wednesday, for he knows that she's at the teachers' college in Truro, an hour away by train or by car. *Why she gracing Halifax t'day?*

"Spent a winter cooped up in Truro. It's big for a town, but still just the right size for small minds. Teachers' college is done. Time to kick up my heels in Halifax."

Carl flashes his teeth: *How can "Blue Roses" kick up her heels easily?*

"Finish your Coke float! I'll float you on my bike."

"Right away, alligator!" She wrongs the slang, but her error is endearing. Laura even flutters her eyelashes—as if she's taken *Gone with the Wind* as a tutorial in Southernly seduction.

But Laura's mistake is intentional. She likes the slick, eligible bachelor, and is very pleased he's noticed her. From the perspective of Bay Street, or Wall Street, or London's City, Carlyle Black is a nobody and worth nothing. As a teacher-trainee, however, Laura lauds all who complete Grades Ten to Twelve. Carl Black is a high school dropout—a plain fact. Having finished Grade Ten, though, Carl exceeds the average

Coloured Scotian and the Coloured Scotian average. Carl be, then, a good *local* catch—an iridescent, marine-sleek being.

The motorcyclist studies the light-complected, secret-Negress brunette: she mirrors the Columbia Pictures goddess, the icon holding aloft a torch—*La Liberté guidant le peuple.*

Politely jarring the Sunset Café door open for Laura, thus facilitating her egress to "Got-a-gun" Street, Carl is able to observe the extra perky swish of bottom and skirt that her uneven walk creates. Her seesaw step mimics a Hollywood sexpot's red-carpet strut.

Carl proposes a spin to Miss States's homestead, i.e., Windsor. Despite probable wet weather, Laura agrees.

She's a trouper, Carl wagers, to face such imminently inclement conditions: but Laura says she's a farm girl who can face the elements, the looming black clusters of clouds. The afternoon copies an English April: dismal, smoky, chilly. They board the bike and go, but sudden wet turns tires spongy. Wind raises clay-splintering cold. Slab upon slab of rain makes for intense work, hard going. Still, the two wheel two wheels to Windsor. Then, rain ends. The highway looks a gold-brick beauty. After the jolting ride, arrival finds the pair groggy, feeling a perfect chill, and Laura's garments—sweater, blouse, and skirt—are see-through wet. Still, her skin looks a milk bath. Her black hair flares over her shoulders and bosom. Her beguiling scent washes over Carl lightly, loosely, almost erasing the clinging saltiness of fog, the silvery damp they passed through miles back, round St. Croix and then Three Mile Plains.

Sure: the trip means silly driving. Windsor is just a bush-league, rained-out Windsor, England. Unwelcoming. The Avon—Shakespearean—River mud flats, usually ochre, look gory, now engorged with rain and pitted by the splattering gouts. The Windsor Wear factory workers, released from spinning cotton into delicates and denim, mill about the riverfront, dreaming of rainbow panties or drab underpants in which to outfit the uncaring cadavers in the Windsor Funeral Home. A Victorian, red-brick hotel bleeds red rain, while ivy vaults across its back, shielding the Nova Scotia Liquor Commission outlet from tee-totallers and the casual bordello above it from wives. (Entertaining it is to stand in line to buy a beer here while listening for the tart squeals and bedspring squeaks that penetrate the ceiling as bottles clank into boxes and coins clink into hands.)

The motorcycling pair takes tea and sandwiches at a café on Avon Street, bordering the Avon River. Gee, they feel just fine. Conversation is quips, puns, jokes, and gossip. But it's rainy, foggy, again, all this evening. The sky's dreary velvet. Mists of cloud swamp early stars.

The journey back to Halifax—to lights and shadows wobbling upon the harbour—sees Carl and Laura tunnel through fog. Carl's headlight shines a queer, pinpoint brilliance that's almost futile.

Back in Halifax, they feel frozen. A cold, miserable night. The fog drops like snow; rain drills down pointedly like icicles.

Laura jests, "There was so much rain today, I don't need to get a tan. I can just stand around and rust."

Carl laughs heartily: he wonders if Laura intends the pun on *stand*. Even with the half-inch extension cobbled on the right shoe heel, there's something courageous about her limp. Now, they're kissing hotly. But curtly.

Laura shivers. "Shouldn't we be getting someplace warm?"

Carl jets Laura to the Poesis Restaurant. They're starved after their trip—and then those kisses. They have fish and chips, with green-tomato chow-chow garnish, then lyrical custard and melancholy wine. Next: time to eat tea. Carl scrutinizes her physique, but Laura is as elusive as Confucius. She seems to like him, but Carl can't coax more from her than smiles and lively laughs. He's met now a Coloured woman who welcomes his humour. His dark face grins back pallidly from a china plate.

Afterward, agreeably, Laura rides with Carl into the glassy smoke of night. He swerves the thoughtful beauty through cloudy indigo to her temporary quarters at Princess Place. All about them, fragrant apple blossoms flounce.

Nervous, Carl swallows hard. He asks "Blue Roses" back to his place, finally. No more dodging. But she says she's bushed. He tries to hug her, and he can, but still she feels ungraspable—like a dream evaporating in cigarette smoke. She turns and leaves.

Dejected, Carl zooms uptown but runs out of gas on Robie Street. He gotta jog to a service station to pick up more. His feet squish through minor puddles at every step.

Back at his place, *Despair* daunts Carl. Loveless, wifeless, childless, shiftless, and worthless (though not penniless): that's him summed up. By his own account. Uninviting is his cold bed after Laura, hugging, was so warm. Warm as red wine and buttered toast.

Too damn lonely, he tunes in CJCH, *The Hit Parade*, and audits the whine and gasp of crooners, some songs as clear and as mysterious as lingerie. Then, even though jazz does not please him, unlike classical music, Charlie Parker's tune "Laura" slips him into a dream.

It bests anything imagined in the adventures of author Lawrence's "Shady Slatternly": Laura begs Carl to stick his paintbrush in her inkpot. He does. Soon she's an eel wriggling at the point of his spear. Her wide mouth, those pomegranate-red lips agape, cry such sweet love, his blues turn to *Bliss*. She's a pretty queen: gleaming brown eyes; the smell of a mint-scented lynx; fine, vanilla ice-cream skin; crystalline speech.

Carl awakes; a milky scent saturates the room. But now he hears Herbert W. Armstrong trumpeting *Damnation* all the way from "beautiful, downtown Pasadena, California." Carl doesn't crave *Penance*; no, he feels like taking nurse Marina and having maid Muriel and giving a nice slice of himself to teacher Laura.

Restless, Carl opens up Henry Miller's *Tropic of Cancer*. The U.S.-banned but sailor-circulated (contraband) novel is like a study of his dream life: *Lust*, ladies, liquor. And *Love*, but only if it entails *Liberation*, *s'il vous plait*!

• • •

Laura is sad to spurn Carl's company after the damp but truly transporting evening. But a man must not know a woman, or know all about her, too soon. Nor does she feel obligated to bat her eyelids for just one beau.

As a teen, not too many birthdays behind her, Laura'd been bewitched by the Negro chaps off the gypsum boats plying the Caribbean, the Bay of Fundy, and the Minas Basin, ricocheting (lazily, very lazily) among the British West Indies and the Dominion of Canada, all ports of enlightened, easygoin Buckingham-Palace rule, plus hard drinking. Sweet it was for Laura to escape the gruff, untutored embraces of country bumpkins. Instead of suffering those clod-hopper, two-left-hayseed feet, she could waltz with a walnut-handsome foreigner, in town to exchange sugar for gypsum and a *Cuba libre* for a kiss. Nor did such ocean cruisers "tsk-tsk" at the sight of her slight deformity. Rather, they eyed a petite, buxom lady, whose mixed-blood might have dismayed segregationists, but whose complexion was translucent, whose rump was *pointue* in the patented African fashion, and whose hair compiled scalloped curls.

For her part, Laura likes to press her ivory face against a cocoa-coloured or iron-coloured man's face. But she also wants to help uplift Scotianer Baptists by securing a teaching post, now that, as with nursing, the opportunity is open to provincial Coloured ladies. Took a lot of fuss and fight to open outward those white-collar, once pink-face-only professions.

Yet, unlike Marina White, who also hails from Windsor, N.S., and is a co-religionist with "Blue Roses," Laura welcomes the courtesies of illiterates, so long as they're not also dolts. Okay: she'd reject the hand of any uncouth, ill-mannered, badly dressed, ill-coiffed, or poor-mouthed

Negro. Yet, her dances with lonesome but black, handsome sailors docked in the anti-Negro, crucifix-burning town of Windsor has taught her not all personable and enchanting Island lads are sons of lawyers, engineers, or doctors, that triumvirate of *bourgeois* nobility. Thus, she is as willing to date a Jamaican deck-swabber as she is to date, say, a fellow like Leicester Jenkins, M.D.-to-be, who's scheming to fit in some Bluenose gynecological "cramming," before steaming home to doctor Grenadian vaginas.

Not to say that Laura considers maid Muriel her equal. *Au contraire*: she knows *she* has options—choices—that Grade Three–schooled Muriel can only lip-read about while fingering borrowed Harlequin romances. Laura won't lord it over most guys, even if she *is* their superior in terms of education and (eventual) salary, but she asserts her superiority to most Coloured women, due to her cream complexion, her college reading (John Milton, y'all, not just Mickey Spillane), her poise and elocution, and her fashion sense to garb herself so that her limp becomes a prop. A man sees, eyeing her, a Calder mobile, a Picasso-cubist-clothed nude, whose curves play one riveting jiggle upon another.

Laura need not compete with Marina or Muriel for male Negro courtship. Her only rivals can only be *real* white girls—schooled in chat and talcum-powdered of skin, and whose chewing gum is really Goldschläger's gold flakes, the additive that makes that schnapps a veritable, tax-deductible *Pleasure*.

Saturday, May 16

U p north from Mar's place, Carl spies "Blue Roses": so lovely—all-day and all-night lovely. She stands outside Halifax Motorcycle Shoppe, chattin with Corkum. This good-lookin cookie's been lookin for Carl. She's in town just for the day (now night) and wonders if he might take her for a treat before she vacates to Truro tomorrow.

Carl says, "Hop on." Goodbye, Corkum. (He hopes that the married man envies him for transporting—sporting about with—yet *another* lady today.)

Again Carl asks Laura if she'd just like to come back to 1½ Belle Aire Terrace since it is late—already eight p.m.

"Yes!"

A delectable answer.

(He's planned—promised—to call Mar. Instead, Carl has Laura. And he'll have Laura now, and he'll try Muriel tomorrow.)

After a "beauty" run, a spin, just for looks, for kicks, through the night-darkened city, the harbour waves rushing up inky and ivory, the houses blinking blinds and curtains and yellow light upon the streets, the maples and chestnuts waving in their boulevard formations, the pair scoot finally to Belle Aire Terrace—B.A.T. (*Bountiful Action Tonight*), the lair of a truly black Batman. Here, Carl unfurls the art of the proletarian gourmet, serving smoked oysters on crackers, olives with cheese, olive loaf (with pimento), and red wine in two glasses, and sets Yma Sumac on the turntable and candles on the coffee table. It's all good. They're all in. Bongos and maracas await.

They talk. They kiss. Nothin ain't arousin.

Then, they hie to bed. He is fire; she is cream. He is Mozart; she is Motown. When full-bore climax hits, and Carl cries out, "Cripes! Laura! Cripes!" he understands why she has the same name as Petrarch's Laura. He sees her face behind his shut eyes as he sinks between this Laura's thighs. It's all "ooh-la-la" and "oh-oh-oh"! Can't sleep. So they do it again.

Not ambivalent, but ambidextrous is their coupling. Finally, it is ambiguous, so neither is sure who is giving, who is receiving. Carl wonders whether Marina could ever feel this good. He don't bother to compare Laura to Muriel. "Blue Roses" is—*joint*—ecstasy, and she seems as oblivious to any misgivings as he is now to her right leg that's a tad shorter than the left.

Laura deems *Sex* as healthy and healing. A student teacher, she's savvy, but her only contraceptive is rhythm method. Carl didn't find a rubber to don, but Laura holds she's safe from conceiving. Yet, were she to carry a child for Carl—a Negro with Grade Ten, a lustrous pedigree (Aunt Pretty and Grandpa Waters), his own apartment, and a steady job—she wouldn't rue this fate, for he's a match, compared to the freckled, feckless hicks of Windsor and the unlettered lechers of Africville-Beechville-Cobequid-Lucasville-Preston and the gypsum boats. Carl's cedar-and-ebony complexion dazzles; his speech and smile are snazzy. *What's not to like?*

Carl trusts that Miss States is in no rush to become Mrs. Black. He likes Laura, sure, but he wants Marina, to prove he merits the student nurse's committed *Passion*.

• • •

Despite romancing moist, pliable Muriel, plus difficult, if teasing Marina, plus *comme-ci-comme-ça*, seldom-about Laura, Carl begins to court a vanilla-ice-cream-complexion woman, Avril Phaedra Beauchamps, an American student. As a Mississippian, studying *Nursing* at Dalhousie, Avril enjoys her present liberty to ogle Coloured guys. Though Negro women revile her for her *Presumption*, none speak any word directly to—or against—her. After all, they could end up having to work for her, should she form a household with a Halifax (white) man and produce a crop of pinkish cherubs.

Like Marina, she's a student nurse. But Avril is also starkly *not* like Marina, for she need not bear the burden of symbolizing *Venus as Virgin*. Hailing from magnolia-hypnotic, if homicidal, Mississippi, her yen for Coloured gents would be a death wish in the South. She is twenty-one, flashes gold hair, green eyes, scarlet lips, and is plush enough to dispatch a thousand brothers of Emmett Till (the bashed-up Negro version of the carved-up "Black Dahlia") to lynching trees, just for glancing her way. She's a plump ringer for Disney's Sleeping Beauty, but she's no devotee of Disney *Morality*, which would outfit Sleeping Beauty in a chastity belt *and* a straitjacket.

Avril is friendly to Marina but thinks her snooty, due to the young lady's self-crucifying status of being "The First Negress to . . . [Fill in Blank Here]." Yet, Avril also guesses that, given her own Deep South roots, plus the reputation of her state, Marina could presume that her sister nurse-to-be is merely superficially courteous (like too many Canadian Cauca-sians), and so may wish to avoid any potentially strife-fostering parley.

Marina has only one asset Avril covets: the chic, black buck who zooms up on his bike, then spirits Marina off to some wind-blown-hair adventure. Avril has never before seen a dark-copper, dapper man, so fastidious in his black leather kit, helming a darling, dazzling cycle. She envies the gazelle-gold of Marina's legs as they gleam against the flanks of the motorcycle and she presses frankly against the dude's back; and he dons that black helmet tricked out by rainbow flames.

Thus, in mid-April 1959, after exams, when most female students had gone to distant homes, or summer jobs, or marriage (at last), Avril had asked Marina—with deliberate vagueness—about her beau. She'd focused her curiosity on the bike, for, truly, she'd not yet ridden on one. She also hadn't wanted to alarm Marina, who could have had a proprietary interest in a man who, nevertheless, she seemed only will-ing to kiss. Avril's gambit carried, and Marina did introduce her to Carl, who was the quintessence of circumspection, while also being avid to give her a test ride. However, Carl pointed out, the jaunt would have to occur in May, once his motorcycle was "born again." An Easter resurrection jest.

Now, to Avril, Carl projects ascetic cordiality. Privately, though, he's very intent on fathoming for himself her sweetest depths, for women like her have been blamed for thousands of Dixie Negroes' murders.

(On April 24, 1959, Mack Parker, accused of raping a pregnant white woman, was dragged from his jail cell in the dead of night, in Pearl River County, Mississippi, to be castrated, then hanged. Instead, he was shot to death and his body dumped in the Pearl River.)

One look at Avril, and Carl recalls again the fierce *frissons* that the 1950 Italy Cross incident had aroused. He now wants to ascertain, fun-damentally, just how deliriously evil a Caucasianess can be—in bed—as the Nation of Islam preaches and the Ku Klux Klan fears.

Yep, his black *Lust* be compounded—no, saturated—with Negro *Vengeance.* By having Avril and having her in ways squealing and squalid, Carl can sound the white woman soulfully. He'll act dervish-unstoppable. Yep, Carl recognizes that Avril seems gracious, exuding no airs. Nor is she the collegiate *belle du jour*—a Civil Rights Movement do-gooder. No: she wants to straddle the motorcycle, let the wind ribbon her hair, and feel the throb and pulse of the engine, exhausting itself, hotly, under her ass, and, next, she wants to grip and straddle the black man's waist, as he drives *Pleasure* into her coral-pink, coral-white core. *Humming.*

To start, though, phone numbers are exchanged—with extreme nonchalance. Neither Carl nor Avril wants to appear to be dating—nor to tip off Marina that her *Special Relationship* with Carl is about to face a stress test. The two—not couple—are just motorcycle enthusiasts who will put Liz II through her paces, objectively.

They agree to meet on Tuesday, May 19. (Round this time, Ezra Pound drafts Canto CXIII: "17 Maggio" and "May 19, '59." Back in Italy, the Italy of Petrarch's Laura, Sade's ancestral cousin.)

Tuesday, May 19

C ome the day, Carl rolls eagerly from faux-Harlem North End to faux-London downtown and on to faux-Baltimore South End. Speeding south on Creighton, then east—downhill—on Gerrish (aiming for Barrington), Carl brakes too hard and flips the bike over. He shoots skyward: Reverse Icarus.

At the instant of ejection, Carl is conscious of being airborne, a solid fluid, sensing the flutter and wash of air about his body, the stunning brilliance of sun shadowed by a pressing blackness, plus his actual tumbling, or slo-mo tussling with gravity. Then, instantly, he's heavy, gaining quick weight, until—like a show-off acrobat—he lands, thud-thud, on his feet, amazingly upright, whole, and conscious. An extra, money-saving miracle: Liz II is undamaged.

Carl believes *Divine Intervention* has just occurred—but no fuss. A positive, astrological alignment with his cheery, psychological state? Off he goes, on his way. Whistling.

Carl and Avril rendezvous at *rue* Trollope (named for the novelist, not a trollop). She's plush in her leopard-spot ensemble of capri pants, blouse, and white scarf; and dreamy, such awesome yellow hair, wintry skin, green eyes, red lips. Man and woman kiss lightly, politely. A start. He thinks, *Avril Phaedra Beauchamps: A.P.B. (All Points Bulletin on an Alarmingly Pleasing Beauty.)*

Carl's route will take them off the municipal peninsula and onto the provincial peninsula, then back to Halifax: seventy-five miles!

The spoils are not in speeding: the *spend* is in feeling Avril huddling against him, or hearing her squeal as they take a crest, flying, or a tight corner, dipping. He loves that her hair streams back; he loves that her full breasts mash his back.

Hear the poised thunder of the engine. On the road, Carl sees a Ducati, a Manx, a Harley, a BSA: priceless iron a-gleam.

The pair edge along the sapphire Atlantic, that lovely, heavy sea, where every drowned fisherman and sailor proves a failed Noah and a failed Christ. The water lazes like a sun-basking lion.

At Purcell's Cove, the surf hisses like a bat. At Peggy's Cove, operatic waves play soprano and bass tones against a beach of boulders and slabs.

Carl feels *Joy* ferrying Avril. She is flesh for speed and speed for wind and wind for flesh. Her complexion looks best when she profiles her face against his black leather. And her long hair suits a motorcycle mama. The blond-tressed, Cajun-descent beauty, with her ivory smile, her green-apple eyes, *man-oh-man*, must bless his bed, eh?

Returning to Halifax, Carl races spontaneously a 1959 BMW—brand new, manned by a fellow with a scar-blistered face. His rouge machine sounds as healthy as a wasp's nest, buzzing and humming. Carl produces a *brio* of noise, a bullet of speed. Slick devilry. But the memory of Mack's death, in Mactaquac, N.B., April '58, propels Carl to exercise safe propulsion.

. . .

Sky was as turquoise as Bermuda's waters. They'd fixed on a race, Carl and Mack, to enjoy a *lagniappe*—"a little something extra"—as New Orleans folks call added *Pleasure*. A brisk breeze propelled the brusque—not risky—decision: to have extra speed, a fillip of jet-feel.

Carl did experience exhilarating acceleration, passing a cream-pink Chevy Bel Air—a car named after his own street. In the rear-view mirror, the car colour began to resemble the "Flesh" tint marketed by Testors model-kit paints.

Two machines were purring away, this April '58 Saturday, horsing around in the intoxicating breeze, sweet with apple blossoms, ripe with cow-and-bull-and-horse-and-pig manures, and a mental whiff of the rum to be enjoyed after the racy ride. *Stimulating.*

A devil-may-care stunt, really, to occupy both highway lanes, to doubly skim their physical shadows, twinned with the mechanical conveyances, over asphalt, typically New Brunswick–faulty with pot-holes and pits dug out by the lumber and timber trucks servicing the logging and pulp-and-paper economy by making roads impassable for non-commercial traffic. But Carl and Mack had chosen the best of the rotten roads, hard by Mactaquac.

Carl zipped past a pink Impala outta Quebec (*La Belle Province*), and the driver yelled, "*Va te faire foutre!*" His railway French told Carl that he'd just been told to go fuck himself, and so he dropped his machine in front of the car and slowed down irritatingly, to enjoy, in his rear-view, the sight of the hyperventilating fedora'd driver, a blond woman beside him in an unseasonal summer dress, sunglasses, binoc-ulars about her neck, and the top of her tits jouncing every time the car struck a miniature Grand Canyon. Mack saw what Carl was up to. Grinning, he moved beside the Impala to trap it in its lane, boxing the car in and forcing the driver to move as slowly as Carl might wish. From the driver's side window, a host of expletives could be heard: "*Merde*" this and "*Calice*" that. It changed nothing: Mack and Carl continued to pace the Impala just above a crawl.

Soon, however, a speeding green car, with white roof and white-wall tires, approached from behind. Mack and Carl decided to release the Impala and race onward themselves, letting the green and pink autos play horizontal leapfrog with each other.

The bikers zoomed ahead, still doubling their lanes, approaching a mausoleum hill, perhaps too blithe, too blissful, to proceed with due caution. *Speed* held them in its deeps.

So, they shot over the hill, only to see one car bearing down on em in the opposite lane and a farmer and horse-and-buggy plodding head of em in their designated, legal lane. No time to react, to brake, to slow and dip behind the buggy. Worse, the oncoming car was moving like silk on wheels—dynamic, direct—floating right over the omnipresent potholes.

A mortal chunk of time disintegrated in a glass, steel, wood, horse-hide *Tragedy*. Unfolding sloshes of blood. Carl's bike went drifting and he was flying and then his ass was plunking softly down under an apple tree.

The scene erupting about him recalled Elizabeth Bishop's poem "First Death in Nova Scotia." Now, Carl saw "First Deaths" in—pitiless—New Brunswick. The black horse, its head out of whack, looked a bit like Bishop's "stuffed loon," so torn to pieces was it, as if a machine gun had blizzarded it with bullets, shrinking it down to bird size. The equine cadaver was tactical putty—a big black chocolate "cake coffin." As for Mack, no measure of medicalese—M.D. Latin or pharmacist Greek—could repair the horror that Carl could see in its unglued guise. Debris *impossible* to assimilate. "Debris" translated as *déchets*.

Mack was mishmash—like a black-ink typewriter page that explodes into red-ink handwriting because a ribbon has petered out. His face was porcelain grammar given a jagged, cursive erasure. Mack's body implanted an honest nest on the roof of a minister's car, the preacher's spouse dead within. Mack's poundage (e = mc2'd into tonnage) had smacked hard onto the roof, buckling it, so the underlying steel had hammered the Mrs. Minister's skull, bashing her dead. Beside the torn horse, Mack's bike looked like a tender mechanism, too easily mutilated.

Only an engineer could repair the grisly mix of glass, metal, horse, wood, rubber. The waste of animal and wreckage of human beings and the mutual destruction of Jet Age and Stone Age machinery. Only God could survey the scarlet-washed accident and identify the resurrection. *Killud*—the Estonian word for "collected fragments"—suited the jumble and carnage. Shards of glass, a motorcycle wheel protruding from the horse's rump, so much furious bleeding, slipshod, the ache of smoke, tears throbbing amid car and motorcycle pieces, the chrome mixed in with the steed's deep, black breast.

Then the Quebec car was stopping. The driver and lady could see terrible *biffures* all about. A man had buried himself in a car roof, and a woman below it would need burial herself. Everyone seemed to be in a deep, morphine sleep. A farmer and *un nègre* (Carl) were both emitting electroshock hollers. Metal parts, raw junk, goggles of glass for horse eyes, shackles of chrome on the felled biker: only a balm of fog could pacify. Everywhere was detached pissing: tears, blood. The minister, garbed for church, was, instead, attending suddenly his wife's funeral. Oil and gas and horse urine seemed perfumes as heavy as lead. The air was strident with stink. Unnerving. The animal showed the convoluted guts of a snake.

Carl felt drastic numbness. He went to Mack. No breath in the bones, no fever in the flesh: just breaks in the bones and wounds on the flesh.

Slowly, too slowly, a curious, mauve light bled into view: the ambulance. From the broken-roofed car, a matron and attendants withdrew the arthritic vertebrate—the corpse of a wife and mother. The blood from Mack and the woman made the ambulance nurse—Mrs. Bolton, in her Jack Frost–painted uniform—appear to be bleeding too. She had to shoo flies away from herself and from Mack's posterior, groin, and chest, not to mention the horse's punctilious wounds.

The once fully articulated horse was as dead as a royal portrait of George VI. But Mack showed the pallor of a "cold parlour," a room of unfathomable snow, and his body seemed a stunted lily. He looked the embodiment of disembodiment. Carl wept. For his dead friend. For *Joy*, too, truly, for he had staved off the cancellation of his own breathing.

• • •

Excited, Avril grips Carl extra hard, thrusts her Dixie Cup breasts ever harder into his back. She thinks, *The man is fast; his blood is hot; his muscles are hard.* Carl streaks past horizontal rockets of cars—until snarled traffic forces an *Armistice* upon he and the comrade "Beamer." They wave *goodbye* as they veer off in opposing directions.

At Cornwallis and Gottingen, a grey-haired, potting-soil-coloured elder—Deacon Dex Slaughter—looks Carl and Avril up and down, then winks secretly at Carl. He foresees a black arrowhead sliding into a white pelt.

Once back to Avril's sunny—South—side of Halifax (locale of doctored and lawyered *Vice*), Carl leaves her at the Miramar. Should he care that he'll see Marina in the morrow?

Exquisitely, Avril requests another ride. She feels hot, in her very fundament: her blood is leaping, surging, not just pulsing. Avril extends her hand like a Southern belle: "Why dontcha come see me at the Lord Nelson Hotel? I'm a-stayin there when the residence shuts for summer recess." (For Avril's plantation-floated purse, the hotel stay is chump change.)

Carl seconds this plan: "Just say when." He kisses her cheek—daringly in broad sunlight—while he holds her hand. Then, he jumps up and down, starts the machine, and roars off, his own heart tapping, in Avril's honour, a fervent tattoo. Echo of Civil War cannon.

Tomorrow, he's twenty-four. The New Age is a-lookin up.

Wednesday, May 20

Birthday day! Liz II is on the road and Carl is on the prowl. Maybe today—*his* day—he'll waylay Mar—lay her down. His way. *This time!*

He and Mar haven't dated, really, since the abortive sofa-seduction of last March. *Gossip* tells Mar that Carl's been satisfying his gross needs *via* assignations with Sluts 'n' Strumpets (the Haligonian definition of S.S.). But Mar's always liked Liz II—that queenly but stallion-size motorcycle—and so she asks Carl to take her, on his birthday, for a spin. They'll have a picnic. She plans a suitable surprise: she's curious now to observe a live man's sex, not inspect the dessicated, bent thing latched to a cadaver. She's nervous, yes, but has practised her planned sucking *act* and licking *art* while gobbling suitably dark and spicy pepperoni.

Carl motors to the Miramar. The day's succulent with light. Mar appears in saddle shoes, a white pleated skirt, and a yellow blouse. The picnic fits neatly in a saddlebag. She mounts the back of the dual seat, and her arms vise Carl's waist tightly. *Promising.*

Carl decides to ferry em to the Look Off, near Canning. The ride is smooth. The engine gallops up to thirty-five horsepower at 6,800 rpm, thus yielding exceptional glide. (Superfuels maintain *Perfection.*) Carl is thankful for the noiseless helical gear train for the camshaft, magneto, and oil-pump drive, mechanics that give him a machine quieter than other bikes. Still, Liz II roars; he wants Mar to sense his—ahem— superior equipment. Her nipples feel like snub-nose bullets on his black leather back. *Exciting!* But no chance for conversation: flies and mosquitoes can rocket to the back of an open mouth.

Highway 1 (westbound) is glens, gullies, nooks, brooks, picnic tables. The two spy signs that read, "All spring flowers must go!" (Like *Youth!*)

At the Look Off, Mar unfurls her picnic: cheese and ham sandwiches, Coca-Cola for her, ginger ale for Carlyle (his full, *royal* name), and a small, frosted pound cake to serve as the birthday pastry. Carl perches the machine on its stand.

He plunks at the green park bench, across from Marina, and gawks at goddess eyes that know all there is to know about the human body—if not by touch. He remembers the cold day when she brought him peanut butter cookies and elongated herself sinuously upon his sofa. They're alone together *again.* And she's so prodigiously ripe. In this Eden. Carl imagines her body naked under the wind, under his face, as his hands slide free her panties. The thought has him sitting stiffly—as upright as an apostle.

Carl thanks Mar for the repast. She asks him about his art.

O! That voice! Honey-coated lemon! Goin down sweet in mine ears!

Flattered, Carl lists the plastic virtues of the model bombers, motorcycles, cars, and the train sets he's assembled meticulously and oil-painted dexterously so that they mirror—in miniature—the full-size originals. He's sold several to collectors. Carl shows off—again (for the umpteenth time)—his helmet, a work of applied *Art*. He tells Mar that he'll draw her next. She admires (again) the fine flames flicking back from the face. She feels a cool smouldering within. To be a model—supine or prone—but with a moral excuse for her amoral flexibility!

(Marina's studied *Anatomy* as a nurse, but the corpses permitting her dissection or discernment are always white. But Carl, in his *living* art, is conscious of Negro beauty, Negro physique, Negro physiognomy, Negro elegance.)

Tender, pale apple blossoms blush as four eyes close and four lips close up. Carl gotta lean cross the maple picnic table to effect the kiss. He stretches. The kissing's good. Fresh-cut pine scents the air. Stirred, bees tumble from flower to flower. *Honey here. No lie.*

Sunlight showers Carl as he lowers Mar now gently, as if he's got her down in a baptismal pool. Gallantly, his black leather jacket will protect her white cotton skirt from grass stains. His heart is steaming full-throttle; still, he rightly expects her to check him before he can roam his hands over her flesh. Instead, she finds her knees, and perches, looking up at him, and puts up a hand, halting him before he can topple or crumple upon her. But her right hand doesn't rest on his chest. It slips down, hesitantly, but not accidentally, and she emboldens herself and shocks Carl by unzipping him. Carl fears he might climax at once. Marina's hands, knees, and (necessarily temporary) smile are shaky, but she proceeds to grant her gift. Carl closes his eyes. His voice falters: "Mar, don't; you don't have to."

Weirdly, at this triumphant instance, when Carl has the nurse-to-be, *bourgeoise*-to-be, on her knees, misgivings cloud his mind. Any sex act between them will be heavenly, but Carl would like Mar to be committed to him, by official ink or precious metal, so that he need not fear her applying her sultry ministrations to another male human.

But Carl's hesitation is thwarted when, in addition to his exposure to her mouth, Mar applies a vigorous—if by-the-book—manual stimulation. She jerks him off as if he were a bull, a science project.

Despite his sharp odour, her worry at his cleanliness or lack thereof, Mar thrills at her hands-on command of the man. Yet, Mar's manipulation of Carl—literally—leaves him feeling a waste. Her forwardness bothers him, despite his *Pleasure*.

For her part, Mar had figured that any other intimacy could jeopardize her health and reputation. She won't risk either for Carl, for who knows how he'd view her if she got pregnant?

But, in Carl's view, her deed is a *pissoir* act, not his *victoire*. He's not *had* her.

Suspiciously too, Mar has ready a dainty serviette; she wipes clean Carl's organ, even as it begins to curve down. Her conception—her plan—has proven immaculate.

So, Carl's climax marks *Sorrow* and *Regret*. Contradictorily, Carl deems Mar no longer 100 per cent virginal, if still—cynically, hypocritically—"intact."

Carl lies beside Mar on the springy turf. Murmurs ensue. He could right now roll atop her and grind her ass into the grass, giving their affair some true, Adam-Eve lineage. Instead, they doze. She rests her head on his belly. He wonders if the moment is Edenic, after all.

He feels arousal again as soon as he sees the wakened woman smile. She senses his refreshed vigour, but Mar stands, smiles, and buckles her watch about her wrist again.

• • •

2 p.m.: They hustle back to Halifax. Wind grumbles as Carl cleaves ninety miles in scorching chill. Mar wears his jacket on the return, so as not to be too cool as they attain the top, two-passenger speed. She grasps Carl with the anti-gravitational hold of a ballerina.

Back in Halifax, after the fast, cool trip, the sun soon sets them sticky and hot. Carl crosses the peninsula, back to the Miramar.

At her door, disembarking, Mar grants Carl an amiable kiss. Three-thirty p.m. is a bright inferno. Instantly, a car pulls flush across the street from the couple; its strident horn blasts, swivelling their heads.

Carl sees a white-suited, tony black man, an obvious foreigner, glaring out a rolled-down window, his scarred face resembling a ventriloquist's dummy's square-lined mouth and jaw. The stranger yells, "Marina, we got a date! Who's this chap?"

Mar breaks away from Carl. Sheepishly, Carl asks, "Who's he?"

Mar shouts across the street, "This is Carlyle Black. We're best friends. Today's his birthday." Mar studies Carl: "Leicester Jenkins is a medical student. He's from Grenada. We've taken a class together."

Carl feels sick: *I don't like that you've suddenly got all these friends.* He imagines Mar on her knees before Leicester.

The M.D.-to-be rises from his late-model car, a green Cadillac convertible (the exact same model as Martin Luther King's snazzy auto); sunlight jumps from the verdant metal as atomic-age photosynthesis. His suit is dollar bills repurposed into silk. He greets Carl; his handshake is steel, but his smile projects a billboard's trickster gloss: "So, you're a birthday boy! Congrats. Marina is so generous with her time—as charitable as the nurse that she will be. But now it's my turn."

Carl frets that Leicester—a man with no-nonsense, Malcolm X glasses and a cool, Sidney Poitier grin—is tutoring Mar in sex tricks. *Detestable implication!*

Mar is all smiles: "You two should be friends. Leicester, Carl's the smartest person I know."

Leicester asks the mean question: "What's your field?"

Carl can't say, "Nuclear physics." He won't say, "Linen cleaning and baggage lugging."

Mar rescues him: "He's a motorcyclist; he's been everywhere: Montreal, New York City, Boston."

Leicester slaps Carl's back: "I see you've a quality bike. Maybe we can trade for a day: you'll drive my Caddy; I'll take your cycle. Mar can take turns riding with us both."

Carl loathes Leicester for calling *his* Marina "Mar." He feels now might be the time for him to serve Leicester a two-by-four length of wood—to strike the dolt in the ass. Or just splash his gloved knuckles into Leicester's cologned, mouthwashed, and blandly sweaty face. Instead, Carl's *Revulsion* evaporates into mere, dutiful *Distaste*.

Mar revels in attracting the attentions of a good-lookin Med student with cold cash and a Cadillac. Perhaps she could be Coretta Scott King, a reasonable helpmate to an above-average man, rather than a tan doll straddling the rump of a motorcycle. Yep: she got options.

Marina kisses Carl on the cheek: "Happy birthday, again." The action is chaste. But Carl recalls Mar's hand frigging his member and his member jigging in her mouth.

Leicester smiles and clasps Mar's hand: it is a friendly gesture, not necessarily that of a lover. Nimbly, she is gone to his side to sit in his car and purr away to some velvet event. She waves at Carl. He wants suddenly to kick Liz II into the gutter.

Carl senses Mar has treated him like a jerk. He has literally been jerked about—and on his twenty-fourth birthday, too. The solution to his woe is as clear as the strength-inducing feeling-emotion of the engine again roaring at his crotch. He will not hesitate.

• • •

Carl zips toward Muriel: his dependable, "bottom" girl; fundamental lover.

The thought of Muriel is an electrical surge from his spine to his brain, from his brain to his groin. The memory of her peppery atmosphere is already pepping his lungs and prepping his sex. He thinks, *Marina sins with her clothes on, but Muriel sins with hers off. She goes as naked as the wind.*

He arrives at that ramshackle tenement, wood-shingle fossil from Queen Victoria's era of widowhood, and clatters up creaky, musty stairs. The outdoor reek of pepper, as Carl approaches Muriel's cinnamon beauty, melds into her room's pungent scent of ginger.

She clasps him: no reluctance. It's his birthday, after all.

Hers are diabolical caresses. Her lips go everywhere. Her ale is citrus; her fish is softness. Soon, that rickety property—her bed—shakes as the candle flame shakes. Muriel is giggles and gasps as she falls upon Carl and he thrusts upwards. They act chummy, clammy lovers. Then snooze together, their natural, lonely-hearts sex fluids oozing.

Carl dreams: Mar is naked and plastering her gold self with a rainbow of paints as she undulates against a blank, hanging canvas, thus orchestrating smears that resemble a life-size Rorschach test. Her teats equal small but pointed brushes as she presses her writhing body all over the canvas as the Miles Davis Quintet spouts blue trumpet and black sax from a radio. Every few minutes, Marina pours a different colour of paint over herself, then gyrates against the now soaking, dazzling canvas. Carl grabs hold of her, thus slashing colours all over his clothes. He tells her, "I'm an artist." The scene shifts. Carl and Mar lie together on a plush, pink bed in a pink cave. Mar yells, "I protest!" So what? Carl pushes apart her legs—bullishly—and thrusts himself to the heart—the crux—of the matter, and she is moaning as he, groaning ecstatically, awakes, pleased that he has finally asserted himself— though uselessly—in a dream.

After his accidental nap, Carl hauls on clothes and stops at Muriel's WC, to scour the pepper reek from his penis and his backside. But it's almost as gritty as Snap, practically impervious to soap.

He repairs to Liz II, but takes a jaunt, east to Gottingen and its *macédoine, sans-culottes,* razor-cut-up, and odoriferous folk; its Babel of French, English, Yiddish, Italian, Greek, Chinese, Soviet, and Dixie dialects; plus the off-colour tongues of sailors shit-faced drunk. But no respectable woman is out at one-thirty a.m., who he might try to seduce, or dragoon, and so Carl zooms back to 1½ Belle Aire Terrace. Solo.

He could have, he should have, he would have, he can have, he shall have, he will have brown-skin Miss White. At last! *If she's truly still pure.*

Well, *Romance* has as many angles as a woman has curves. To succeed at courtship, Carl frets, he gotta be an optimist in Hell.

• • •

Muriel is pliable, for she can't demand the simple-simple *Respect* that Marina, a *bourgeoisie*-bound nurse, expects. Muriel is fuckable: she's a maid. Nor is the equation false. Negro gals who work as white folks' housekeepers get fingered—literally—as casual sluts, subject to manhandling, digital insertions, thumb-and-index-tweezered nipples. After all, a white husband can silkily bribe his black maid and pump her up with a child, much lighter in shade than her other children. Or a white lady's spouse, brother, or son can just trip the maid, tup her, and next romanticize dreadful *Rape* as "drunken *Rapture*," thus exonerating his ass.

(Carl swears no wife of his will be a maid. Her place will be at home, caring for *his* children. She'll not suffer *Coercion* perpetrated— or private *Rape* sheltered—by the Caucasian wallet. Being a black husband, he'd want to avert, in *his* household, the sullen silence that'd greet the arrival of a white man's whelp gobbling up already niggardly stores.)

Carl'll save one woman for wife, take others for playmates. At least until he can more-or-less settle, i.e., accept the ball and chain of *Monogamy*.

Yet, Muriel is more his natural spouse than is Marina. The alliance of Coloured maid and Negro railway worker befits their shared class. In contrast, the congress of Negress nurse and black (Beat) biker is a page torn from *Porn*'s shiftless scenarios.

Though her employ seems elementary, Muriel's life is complex. A magnet-black woman so magnetically lovely, Muriel's black *Beauty* flouts Renaissance aesthetics. European propaganda says "big bones" signal unsavoury fat, that dark skin is blemish, that curly wires of Negro hair must be pressed and straightened, that a flat nose is ugly, and that a capacious bottom signals *Sloth* and *Lust*. Muriel notices this *negation* of her physique in ads that parade Aunt Jemima and Mammy as icons of *Mirth*. Likewise, movies project blonde dancers and brunette starlets as the apogees of *Femininity*. Occasionally, the brown-skin Josephine Baker or the beige-skin Dorothy Dandridge is touted as an *almost* beauty queen.

Yet, Muriel knows that men—white and black—see her *Beauty*. She is a woman who, waiting for a trolley and dressed demurely, will get propositioned to party with an anonymous white man—and his buddies—for a few bucks. Nor is she unaware of the spectacle of Dr. Fullerton eyeing her derrière as she stoops to wash or dust items in his home. More than once, she has caught his ruddy flush in colour and quavering fluster in voice as he recognized that she caught him, staring openly, *lusting*. Nor is she oblivious to her attraction to black men, albeit working-class, just like her. While some are locals, others are West Indian—or Negro Yank—sailors, thirsty for drink, hungry for excitement, hankering for company.

Muriel is thought no rival to white middle-class women or well-schooled black women (like Marina) in winning a man's affections. Yet, she is their greatest threat, for she has no illusions about men ("they're pigs"), nor about her marital prospects, should she refrain from coitus (as Marina is striving to do) until Mr. Right materializes, as blue-eyed as Jesus and just as supposedly capable of miracles.

Ironically, by vaunting Marina over Muriel, Carl is wishing for someone "better." But Marina can classify him as precisely as he classes Muriel: he's okay for now, for some thrills and some laughs, a snack and a show, or a sip and a puff, but not for the role of a baby-making, child-rearing, day-and-night companion.

Open to various proposals, Muriel maximizes her chances for scoring an engagement ring. She could (1) escort—um, comfort—a white tycoon; (2) undertake an impromptu coupling with a snappy Negro gent; (3) play happy hostess to Coloured sailors—Wessindians from the Caribbean or Jack Tars from the States. Because she has no illusions, no *Romanticism*, she can allow a man the romantic illusion that she be open to his *Seduction*.

Friday, May 29

After his birthday and Marina's abrupt fall from *Grace*—by pleasuring Carl, then rushing off with Leicester—Carl must see Avril again: she don't seem restricted or reticent or hesitant or hypocritical in any way. Together, they're black leather and white silk—or iron and chrome. *Maybe, baby?*

She calls; he prepares the arsenal—wallet, cologne, the hard-to-come-by condoms, tie clip, cufflinks, etc.—while he whistles along to calypso, the black-bottom balladry of Trinidad, by Lord Invader: a carnival study in high-fidelity sound. Carl peers into the mirror, not the dark glass of James the Apostle, but the looking glass of a dark-complected James Dean.

• • •

8 p.m.: Carl trolleys down to Barrington at Spring Garden and enters the lobby of the Capitol Theatre. The red and gold interior resembles a dwarf fairy-tale castle, suiting the South End and its gold bug, humbug, Victorian-era capitalists, still preferring Ricardo to Keynes.

Here's Avril: dame all dolled up. They're in public, but Carl's gotta kiss her cheek, ogle all her glamour. She's in a black top and a beige skirt, plus a beige beret and a long, white, all-weather coat.

They catch *Frankenstein 1970*. The Monster is as dehumanized and as inhumane as a beast. Its face shakes em up. But Boris Karloff, as Doc Frankenstein, is scary because he looks just like Prime Minister Diefenbaker. His character fashions new people by knitting together organs and electrifying bones.

(But *Coitus* is the better way: each infant is only a new Frankenstein amalgam of parts of the dead.)

Carl and Avril exit onto the street. As Carl inhales her perfume, he also sniffs chocolate whiffs from the Moirs factory just blocks away. The chocolate is disorienting; the perfume is persuasive.

Carl reflects on the divisions between his buds and bros (bankrupts) who patronize North End Got'gun Street, and the old-money WASP mountebanks who patronize South End Spring Garden Road. The class divide traces the lay of the land, with the old fortress of Citadel Hill, a grassy armoury bristling with cannon, splitting the statue-less North End and its rough workers from the statue-overrun South End and its Richie Rich retinue. The fortress hill also truncates Gottingen, forestalling any bastardizing intercourse with Spring Garden.

Avril pooh-poohs Halifax stigmas of *Class* and *Race*. She's a plantation landlord's daughter, outta The Most Powerful Nation on Earth (alongside the Union of Soviet Socialist Republics, lest we forget), now studying for *entrée* into a lab-coat profession. Being Mississippian, her world is only oysters Rockefeller and Eisenhower fallout. Still, she's enticed by the posh manner of a Coloured biker with an *Encyclopaedia*

Britannica vocabulary—so unexpected in a dead-end enclave like Halifax, the Alamo of the North Atlantic.

Avril's black heels (sheltering nice, pink toes) click along the sidewalk, telegraphing (Carl prays) a sexual intent, an ideal underlined by the flow of her breasts forward and her backside upward. Her perfume wafts lemon and lily, thus warding off the eve's otherwise chocolate and mackerel scent. Sassy smells: Carl can't stroll beside her and not crave to be *inside* her.

The impulse is, actually, mutual. Carl's poise, his striding step, the black leather jacket polishing the night, his burnt copper skin that she suspects might just taste like caramel, all please Avril's four alert senses— sight, smell, sound, touch: the census—account—of the man.

The mild, starry night, a periwinkle and *azzura-negra* sky, with its colliding accents of cocoa and Chanel, is promising as the pair strolls, now arm-in-arm, up Spring Garden, heading for the Lord Nelson Hotel at the cross street of Park. The squawks of raucous seagulls and the warble of dusty, dirty pigeons serenade their promenade.

They shan't enter the hotel together. One block away, Avril tells Carl her room number. Carl will hang back, then pick up Chinese food to "deliver" to her room. They both chuckle over this ruse—though they rue its necessity.

They kiss, and then Avril canters on ahead of Carl. Her tilted nose and the white mouse fur of her April coat saunter toward the hotel.

Carl repairs to the Garden View Restaurant to order egg rolls, chicken chow mein, chop suey, and sweet-and-sour spareribs: takeout. He knows Avril will have U.S. whiskey at the ready. *Boy, is he ever ready!*

Thirty minutes later, playing the eunuch Uncle Tom, Carl steps into the ritzy hotel, passes under the lobby's lustrous chandelier, approaches the mahogany-panelled front desk, and tells the officious clerk (who is so prejudiced that he doesn't even look at Carl) that he has an order of Chinese to deliver promptly to Miss Beauchamps. (Carl mispronounces the surname deliberately as "Bow-champs" to seem even more a poor, illiterate Coloured chap.) The gent sniffs that he'll call Carl a bellhop, but the "boy" pleads, joshes: he "really need dat tip, boss." The clerk grants Carl egress—to extend him *Charity* (the cat's paw of *White Supremacy*).

Now, Carl stands, glimmering, before the polished brass elevator doors. He smiles at his doubled, brass self. The doors open; he ascends— uplifted—to the seventh floor. The rise equals a hike in income—or the heightened esteem he'll feel if (no, *when*) Avril hikes her legs to welcome him. At Avril's door, he raps seven times—*da-dadadada-da-da*— rhythmically, rapidly.

When Avril opens the door, she's invisible at first, for she is standing behind it, to up his suspense and eagerness. When he sees her at last, he hath *Joy*: between he and her nakedness, there's only a midnight-black nightie (a filmy cloud of chiffon nylon from Frederick's of Hollywood) that glorifies her incandescent skin.

Carl sets down the Chinese takeout and scoops up his Mississippi angel, his Vargas pin-up. Her kiss smoulders with whiskey. The queen bed awaits a bumblebee. When she falls against him, he smells sweetness akin to Peek Freans' biscuits.

For Avril, too, this dusk means *Liberation*. If she was once the prisoner of a KKK fairy tale, in which black men and white women meet and fuck—and are executed if discovered—she now feels the pleasure of choosing a man for herself, one necessarily superior to those scoped out for her to marry, back in Natchez, Mississippi (fictitious locale of *Show Boat* and true location of a mass lynching).

The two kiss deeply. Carl notices the white stucco, the mahogany furniture, the brass fixtures, the indigo and gold wallpaper, all the monarchical touches of the royal-welcoming room. Still, the contrast between Avril's lodging and Muriel's rancid, ratty hole is pungent: whiskey versus boiled cabbage; soap versus wet newsprint; perfume versus pepper. How sweet to lie with a woman who knows her value in the world—*cos she be valued by the world.*

Carl slips a hand south, to sweep away fabric and to finger, gingerly, Avril's slit. He kisses, nips slightly, the creamy prow that's each breast; suckles each supple nipple until each pink tidbit is stubbornly straight as a mast. Avril feels a dark thumb press against and slightly indent her sex; she swoons.

Now, her nightie's off and lovemaking on. Furious—like Casablanca clutching at Gibraltar. There's no top limit to their desires. Avril accepts Carl's pivotal direction, to turn on her belly and lift her bum. An incriminating smile reveals her teeth as sweat drips from Carl's face onto her ass, and she moans, "Oh God oh God oh God," sounding awfully like a church lady.

Thus, Rilke's "two solitudes" kiss. For Carl, this night redeems the trauma that was his youthful study of the *Lust* and *Rage* exemplified by the black Mr. Paris and the white Mrs. Naas at Italy Cross. Avril also fulfills for Carl the doomed wishes of all those poor Dixie Negroes who got strung up, with their dicks cut off and stuck—like drooping cigars—in their mouths. This night, Carl's a combo of Nat Turner and Nat King Cole: simultaneously natty and a dastard.

Avril's panting is a scorching tempest. She believes her sweat, right now, is the most honest gift she has ever allowed herself.

After: the moon pours its light onto the bed, where the pair snooze, chaste in restored nightie and uncloseted hotel robe. Carl is cast iron next to Avril's chrome. She snuggles herself into his arms. The Solid South gone molten.

• • •

Carl's got safes: he can do it again safely. Does he ever want to! Muriel and Mar are frustrating, and Laura's afar. But Avril's playful girlishness and funky wit grace mature, confident *Womanhood*. She's not a frisky little flirt. No, she's simply *not* Mar. Nor is she as depressing—or as depressed (because she's *not* oppressed)—as Muriel. The *Surplus Value* of white skin renders her freer to be careless, to be experimental, to be spontaneous, to be—*golly*—a female beatnik. *Herself.*

Yet, Avril scorns the icy chivalry that places her in an Untouchable caste. As a Mississippian, Avril's heard that solemn drawl bout "pro-tek-tiiing whyte woo-mun-hoood," that code that lets white men reserve to themselves select brothels, where Coloured girls work shoulder-to-shoulder, on their backs, with white ones, while Coloured men are forbidden any contact with any.

Too, Avril suspects she ain't the only Dixie deb to pass a chain gang and witness Negro men, half naked, sweat showering their tasks, and to wonder about the power present in those iron-coloured, bull-muscled torsos. Thus, Carlyle be her case-study Negro.

Avril's dark-complected eroticism would get her tarred and feathered down South. Worse, her suspect interests in Russian literature would see her branded a Commie. (Cf. Nancy Cunard.) Truly, she loves Pushkin, borscht, Dostoevsky, caviar, Tolstoy, vodka, Pasternak, mink, Fabergé, the whole shebang. Given her predilections, Avril—a descendant of displaced Acadians, anyway—is lucky to be in Nova Scotia and at Dalhousie (she says "Da-lousy") University, and taking nursing and Russian—and taking (to bed) Carl.

Carl lands, in Avril, a woman who also adores classical music (Shostakovich and Sibelius), art (Picasso and Warhol), letters (Mailer and Nabokov), and who can speculate about geopolitics (West and East Berlin, and "Naw Leens" and "Joe-jah"). Talkin with Avril, Carl don't need to drop his g's, dot his i's, and cross his t's. Even if he do. Sumtime.

Still, Carl is not the simon-pure Negro that Avril lusts to try. He's for starters, not for keeps!

Carl's oblivious to Avril's true mania. She is *his* Darlin Naas (the *belle dame sans merci* of Italy Cross), *his* Liz Publicover (his junior-high crush), and even *his* adult version of the red-haired, hot-lipped harpy who'd jumped on his lap on the Halifax trolley ten years back. *Yahoo!*

Avril knows Carl's sweet on Marina, but she slights it as puppy love. Yes, Mar'd make a fine trophy as a Coloured wife, but she's nothin special *qua* woman. Avril's sure that Carl needs a real lady, just as she—Avril—needs an unambiguous, unadulterated, *black* man. Coal-coloured in groin, iron-firm where it counts, mustang-wild in the clinch, mustard-tang in odour.

Too, Avril deems Mar a hoity-toity hypocrite. She suspects the goody two-shoes is enticing Carib peacocks (studs masquerading as students) and promising em more than a good-night kiss. In hope of a hyped-up white wedding in Ocho Rios or May-he-co.

Yet, Avril desires Island Negroes less than she does the Yankee version—though so, so, so bleached out in Nova Scotia. The West Indies gents are sophisticated, brash, bold, elitist, and *Race*-proud, if also (*Episcopalian*) *Anglican*. Hailing from Coloured-run proto-nations, they see themselves as equals to whites—or *superior*. Surely, they do better than most Canucks because they have more money, more knowledge, plus more panache, and are closer to unadulterated *Independence*. While a Canadian woman could bestow the gift of her citizenship upon them, they could bestow upon her a coveted middle-class status, complete with servants, either in Canada or back home in Barbados, Jamaica, or Trinidad. In short, their psychological health does not require seduction of white women. In contrast, for Avril, the ecstasy of sleeping with a Negro American (or Canuck) derives mostly from the *frisson* of putting to bed a taboo.

So, Avril relishes being with Carl. With him, she be part–artist's model, part–motorcycle moll. When Carl peels off his denim or light wool trousers, then cotton briefs, she views lean, tense mahogany and burnished bronze. His groans and moans echo rumbling, earthy machinery—what arranges her ascension. *Peace!* But never enough!

Sunday, May 31

Restless after the joys of clandestine lovemaking with Avril, and curious about how he'll feel about seeing her colour-and-class opposite, Muriel, Carl decides to exercise a *Playboy* prerogative and zip over to see the maid. It's Sunday; as Baptist Youth Fellowship president, he should be in church. But he wagers that Muriel won't be. So he pours himself into his blue jeans and black leather and kick-starts his purple and chrome machine and rolls over to those peppery, curry-scented quarters that corner Maynard and Cornwallis.

Carl brings along his paints because he wants to ask Muriel to pose for him while he limns her portrait. If he's honest with himself, he'll admit that painting—*Art*—is an extension of his basic interest: to whore and wine. From a Christian perspective, Carl knows he blazes so much with sin, his black leather duds almost glitter. If only he could see *loving* as being more than a game, see coitus as being more than a woman's subduing unto his own satisfaction. Like quicksand, he empties himself into ladies' laps but remains as self-contained as an hourglass. And yet, *Intercourse* is the concourse to *Love*, he doth believe.

Carl does find Muriel home and kisses her as if she's his one-and-only. She's thrilled—in part because Frederickson Dent is again away, aboard his ship, and out-of-the-picture. It's tricky for Carl to set up his paints and canvas in Muriel's kitchen, which is more a nun's cell than it is a garret. But there's a wedge of light in the window over the sink, and Muriel's lily perfume accents the gleaming, sweet-sweet chocolate of her chassis.

So, Carl paints Muriel, depicting her sunlit crowning as a virtual Madonna, pinpointing lips like sanguine strawberries. He asks her to unbutton two more buttons on her filmy, white cotton blouse, to bring out better the contrast between her dark-lightning cleavage and the ivory cloud of her top. Muriel smiles coyly as she acquiesces: she knows that Carl is intrigued by her measures, the S-swish of her curves, the most mystical algebra to his paint-by-numbers aptitude. Indeed, Carl's brush swoons to bring out the full beauty of Muriel's breasts—two Moirs chocolate-box *bonbons* cupped by pale paper.

Muriel is pleased, yes, to be the subject of artistic focus—not just in the snapshots of casual parties, picnics, frolics, fairground jaunts, and holidays, sometimes picturing her, *qua* maid, in the precincts—or on the fringes—of Dr. Fullerton's household, where her image as family servant—if subversively sexual in her uniform—is background asser-tion of the clan's upper-middle-class position. Today, she sees herself in Carl's eyes as *Beauty*, consecrated by paint, elevated by light, as if his canvas were really stained glass. Her familiarity with *Art* is limited to the reproduced *Mona Lisa* and *La Maja Desnuda* that Fullerton, M.D., keeps in his home to signal his safe, domesticated sexuality. As a "Negress" model, Muriel disturbs and upsets all the European protocols and Caucasian aesthetics—*perfectly*, as Carl sees.

Carl now knows that he can picture Halifax as an unpicturesque

Avignon, a mirror Naples (scuzzy, lurid). He wants a Haligonian *Harem* the colour of Neapolitan ice cream: Negress, Caucasian, Indianess. He can envision himself canvassing sparks of oils to display Haligonian Negroes as transparently colourful as Neapolitans. His master will be the *crème-de-la-crème* Rockwell—namely, Rockwell Kent.

(Kent's inking of Boccaccio's *Decameron* is sculptural, stressing right angles and straight lines. Yet, his women are dramatic: Their breasts are not merely round, but circular, throwing the encasing straight lines for a curve. The disconcerting aspect of Kent's nudes is that their heads seem canine, their faces masculine, and their limbs mannequin-stiff.)

Carl asks Muriel if she can feel his brush as he figures her on paper, *with sympathetic magic*, simultaneously stroking her face. She answers, with a breath, "Yes, oh yes," trembling at the silky feel of the invisible bristles.

After an hour, while church bells chime through the Sunday noon, heralding the closure of the Lord's Morning, the end of services, with all the various denominations flocking and scattering from their respective portals of *Confession* and *Redemption*, Carl reveals his portraiture to Muriel, who is *affected*, just as he has prayed. A hand caresses a back; another brushes a knee; a bold palm cups an ass.

Muriel squirms laughingly out of the embrace, the squeeze, and switches on her hi-fi. The sudden, secular music is amenable to Carl's touches; it conducts and it ameliorates. It's doo-wop cruising bluesily from the speaker. It's the blues of New York and Detroit and Chicago, imported by black magic locomotives to Halifax. Now, The Platters are crooning, not at all blasphemously, "My Prayer," and soon two faces sweat in a snuggling clinch, while Muriel keeps one satisfied eye on her satisfying portrait.

Roaring back to his digs, Carl ponders his Friday night with Mississippi's Avril and his Sunday afternoon with Scotia's Muriel. He figures that Avril can take portraiture for granted, that there's a Richard Avedon—to be paid (of course)—somewhere in her future, while, for

Muriel—and Marina and Laura—there's no James Van Der Zee (the Harlem photog) to show off their beauty, to preserve it for ogling *Posterity*. Such could be his—Carl's—role, and the benefits and pleasures incalculable . . . Carl smiles, and a mosquito smacks his upper front teeth.

· · ·

Over some six weeks, May through July, Avril and Carl lie-down-as-one some two dozen times, twice per meeting. Avril—the daughter of April, of Bolshevik April—yearns for Carl as much as Carl loves indulging her. How she revels in the work of his ebony transfixing her ivory, with dark hairs marking the moment at both ends. Going to meet Avril, Carl's step is jaunty; he swaggers. To hear a white woman, a student of human reproduction and an acolyte of Pushkin, converse avidly with him about his pet topics (classical music, world politics, *Art*), and then go avariciously—after kissing, petting—to bed is miraculous to Carl. Avril is a *Playboy* pin-up without staples and without scruples. Too, Avril's purse buys ale and vodka, wine by the case, and it lets her encase herself in lacy, racy lingerie. Carl is suckled by her amplitude (bust and butt) and sucks down her plenitude (drinks and kisses). *Sincerely*—as the McGuire Sisters sing—Carl's never felt, with a woman, *freer*.

But Avril craves to try a gold-standard, unqualified buck, a dude untainted by Christian mores, a man who is all Moor, always Moor, and nothing less. She wants *Fornication*, not just dirty, but muddy, sloshing juice and stink. A spurious Dixie stanza haunts, spurs her on:

> *In the evening, by the moonlight,*
> *Juanita loved her old black Joe.*
> *Man or horse? She couldn't say quite.*
> *Sighing, she didn't need to know.*

DETOUR

The only thing to do was to go.
—Jack Kerouac, *On the Road*

TRIP DIARY

Property of Carl A. Black,
1½ Belle Aire Terrace, Halifax, N.S.
(If lost/found, please return.)

Saturday, June 13

Corkum shows at 8 a.m.: Liz II is ready. I dress hastily, eat, say, "So long," to Muriel, passing by. Off at 9 a.m. sharp. Like Jesse Owens, racing. Mileage reads 1,492 (or magic #7).

Truro by 1:15 p.m., Amherst at 2:55 p.m., cross the Nova Scotia–New Brunswick border at the Tantramar Marshes, skip through Sackville, parade past Gothic-style Dorchester Penitentiary (jailbirds always inhabit monster-movie castles), on to Moncton. There at 3:55 p.m. Not bad time. Stop for rain. Not too long.

(New Brunswick is a realm of saints—St. Andrews by-the-Sea, Saint John, St. Stephen—all along the Fundy coast. Too bad the saints be impotent and the Devil vigorous.)

Exit Moncton for Salisbury, Sussex, Saint John, then St. Andrews by-the-Sea, and next St. Stephen; cross the Canada-U.S. border here. Exchange Her Majesty's nickel beaver for the President's silver eagle.

Highway 1. Roll coastal from Ellsworth to Belfast. Silvery-green forest fronting green-silver sea. Pick up Highway 3, to Augusta, Me. Weave among silvery birches. Ceaseless rain. Hear the lilt of leaves under the rain's light rhythm. That's "Me." *Free (again) at last!*

Hit Augusta at 9:45 p.m. E.S.T. Put up at Ralph's Tourist Home for $2.50. (The guy who runs this place uses a 1958 Cadillac Fleetwood hardtop model for a taxi.) Look out the window, all I see is framed oblivion. Beautiful nothingness.

The motel is scrupulously—conspicuously—clean like the scene of a gore-and-guts homicide that the murderer has set to rights. The tap drips a remorseless Morse. Water is as "hard as nails"; the rubbery soap grudgingly sloughs off its cleansing film. (In the shower, the water strikes like wet fire.) The bed is suspiciously soft. Once the lights are off, I worry a cockroach troupe will invade to claim whatever crumbs my snacks have deposited in the sheets or on the floor. Improbably immaculate, the room's also distressingly shabby; the carpet is worn out almost to the soil beneath the floor, and the cigarette burns are practically peepholes, including an odd one in the shower curtain. Well, the radio works: siphon enough music into the room that I, somehow, sleep. Notes scurry—if not roaches. The Flamingos: "I Only Have Eyes for You."

In Maine, I buy ready eatables: big roll of bologna, some canned fruit, nuts, a half-pound of pepperoni. Can't stay in most Maine hotels and motels. (One Maine postcard shows a flock of white sheep and one black one. The slogan? *You's in Maine.*)

Number of miles totals 1,552. Travel 500 miles plus in one day. Try to make Washington, D.C., tomorrow. Hope rain lets up. Gas costs $3.98.

Sunday, June 14

Shave in cold water. It ruins smooth skin. Face copies a coral reef!

Exit Ralph's at 8:50 a.m. Weather awful. Keep off turnpike until free of Maine. Rain pastes clothes to body. Rain's my raiment. Visibility nigh nil.

Make New York City at 7:45 p.m. Traffic snarl up to New Jersey Turnpike. Cross George Washington Bridge and hit 8 congested lanes. The glamorous, terrifying, canyoned labyrinth of Malcolm X Town! But, yessiree, N.Y.C. has the sun! (Spy X on TV: Redskin Muslim in a natty, mohair suit. Surprise chic for a "hatemonger.")

Leave Manhattan at 8:20 p.m. Like MacArthur said, "I came through and I shall return." Good weather past Hartford, Connecticut. Flood of rain yesterday; now sun. *La fleur de mon désir.*

Monday, June 15

Washington, D.C ., at 12:50 a.m. Poet Pound's ex-prison is fog or bonfires: a faux-Monrovia (Liberia) surrounded by a faux Vienna (Virginia). See bronze horses *et* bronze eagles. Imperious. Bellicose. Imagine desperate bigots staffing lynch mobs. Streets carry the stink of sewers, the stench of earth, the odour of bones.

Room in a Coloured hotel—The Dunbar (after Negro Poet Dunbar)—on 15th Street between U and V Streets, NW: for the usual Negroes bent on fucking, it's no more than a place to take a woman. (Night manager offered me one, but I said, "No, thanks!" *Virtue* by necessity, sadly.)

Draw blind against sight of polka-dot-dress tarts lounging under street lamps. Gaudy mosquitoes. Unhealthy whispers. Sordid guffaws.

Toilet exhales yelping funk, strong enough to stun a rat. Yet, a book rests atop the john ledge: Pound's *Selected Cantos*. Newspaper page, torn out, reminds us Emmett Till's papa got hanged at Pisa, while cellmate Pound got sprung.

Quit hotel at noon. Try to find a decent tourist home: economic, non-erotic.

The Capitol's a mosquito mosque. (They're thick, hungry, curtaining the Potomac, that miasma.) Inside the dome, politicos bawl like brats: clandestine sodomy. In its corridors—as on the obedient radio waves—asinine, asphyxiating speech. Ghastly stupidity is aired, so long as it's "anti-Communist." Fascism masks as *Schmaltz*, *Kitsch*, glitz. Overhead, an arrogant copter clips twixt the White House and Camp David?

(America displays a Tiffany grace: sprinkle feces with diamonds, and who won't buy? Here sacred cows and golden calves alike are struck dead, strung up, and stripped to bone. Tombstones double as tables, desks, even beds.)

Check out motorcycle dealers. Change oil. Meet two Colo(u)red mechanics. They have clean bikes, yes, but their shop be grimy, greasy, oily, smelly!

Cop cars throng this white marble capital. D.C. is part-prison and part–liquor-distillery. The channelled dust of Pennsylvania Avenue mocks every statue.

Nigh The White House sits a black ghetto. Pig Alley and Goat Alley—rat-traps and cat-houses—run, stinking, catercorner to The Rose Garden. Ironically, Benjamin Banneker, Negro astronomer, planned this city. His use of grids, circles, and triangles recalls Byzantine Istanbul. But cockroaches chip away at the marble.

Go to Bethesda, Md.; see dealer Miller. His fine BMW shop includes a spectacular, white R50, with a 5-gallon tank. In effect, a cop chopper.

Thunder through Vienna, along Gallows Road and Old Gallows Road. See only diamond shops.

Lunch at a French restaurant whose chartreuse advertisement features the *chanteuse* Mistinguett, her cinch'd waist boasting a bunch of lime-green Champagne grapes. Sip a cocktail that exhibits "a spirituous orange and caramel bouquet." It sure do!

Back to D.C. Pass down M Street, bound over Rock Creek and enter Georgetown, home of Mr. & Mrs. John F. Kennedy. (Sen. Kennedy snagged an LLD from The University of New Brunswick in '57. So, he's an honorary Maritimer . . . Why I like him.)

On Wisconsin Avenue, near the white and gold, Greek Temple-like Farmers and Mechanics' Bank, note the abode of Missy Anne,

Tarot Card Reader. Who'll be my wife: Marina or Avril? (In the shop window, a trapped brown moth beats its wings frantically against a copy of Robert Graves's *The White Goddess*.)

Go to a white tourist home. Feel funny there. Not served in restaurant either. I make like Jesse Owens. *Scram!*

Am almost ready to rejoin pimps and prostitutes at poetic Dunbar. Instead, a Negro postman directs me to a Colo(u)red lodge at Constitution and Tennessee Ave. N.E.

Go there. Arrange with the lady on duty—a buxom sphinx from Virginia. Place is just like The Dunbar, except you take your own woman and pay for so many hours. ("Not painted ladies, but venerable," the "elderessa"—*60 et* sexy—says.) Considerably clean, though, it is, with working radio and TV in the room: radio chained to wall; TV bolted to the floor. One way to rivet attention! (Pun!)

The postman arrives in his car, wanting to show me the sights. I say, "Thanks, anyway." His name is U.S.-Negro-typical: Maurice Johnson. A lean, charming, white-haired gent.

Washington is a washout. Glimpse "Dirty Tricks" Nixon exiting the Supreme Court. Likely not for the last time.

Tuesday, June 16

Zip to Virginia Beach, Va., two hours south. Pass spine-tingling greenery. Geography with room for mirage.

Cross snow-white sand. At the ocean fringe, bright bikinis splash—by the dozens—into the white-edged, blue water. I eye through dark sunglasses. *Nice!* Combers stroke the shore like brushes on a snare drum.

Picnic on the beach. Dine on meat, cheese, ale. No excessive draughts of ale!

Mauve, ivory, rose, aquamarine, lemon, tangerine are popular pastels here—as if each colour has cream added, to render brilliant, harsh, original tints soft and velvety, as if bleached. Here, both black and white get reproduced as tan.

The Negro paper carries this poem: "Your sparkin eyes / Be diamond mines. / My mournful heart / Feels like someone's / Squeezed it apart . . ." Marina!

Wednesday, June 17

North to N.Y.C.—Gotham City. White wool clouds don't hinder the sunset.

In at 2:30 a.m. See a house fire. Piano falls, blazing, from window. Pianist jumps. A smash hit.

Reprimanded by cop for going wrong way on a one-way. Check in at Sloane House at W. 34th Street and 9th Avenue. Mile gauge reads 1,645. Gas bill = $2.34. Oil = $1.12.

Dream of Mar: Her brown hand splayed over her bare belly between black-lace bustier and white-lace panties so sheer I can see her pubic hair. (Legal in N.Y.C. since just last year.)

Morning news: Dolt electrocuted himself while trying to wire up high-voltage to exterminate rats. The 61-year-old Greenwich Village artist was found dead next to a 380-volt cable and metal spikes jabbed into his bathroom floor. No rodents were fried. *Jolting!*

(In New York, radio is the people's parliament. Only act more popular than bugging God with prayer is begging fools for cash.)

Off to U.S. Post Office—for stamps. What an edifice! Paid $8 for 4-day parking at garage across street. Man there remembered me from last year. (Not many Canuck Coloured cyclists here!)

Orchestra ticket for *Music Man*: $8.50. Also, Standing Room Only ticket for *My Fair Lady*: $3.45.

Macy's prices are high. Items are priced above those at smaller stores. Spent $52, and still didn't fill gift list. Did buy haberdashery for myself: my fashion passion, I guess.

See large party on at Rockefeller Center. Jukebox blasts jazzy chaos. Ginsberg's *Howl* as interpreted by Howlin' Wolf.

To the Museum of Modern Art: 75¢ admission. Hours there. See works by Picasso, Lautrec, Gauguin, etc. Some works look spectacularly absurd, but intriguing. Lunch at the Museum's Tea Room. Chicken, apple pie, ice cream. Fine meal @ $2. I swear I'll show Avril my art.

Visit a rubber ware show at U.S. Rubber Co. building. See process of making condoms: life savers. Inspiration for "lays." (Pun!) Buy a few. (Never enough?)

En route to theatre, stop outside the Rivoli (where I'd seen *South Pacific* last fall). Watch celebrities arrive for the world premiere of *John Paul Jones*. See a tall blonde—can't make out who she is. (Marisa Pavan?) See a crowd out to see (France's) Brigitte Bardot in *Mam'zelle Striptease* and (Quebec's) Lili St. Cyr in *Josette from New Orleans*.

(Burlesque is Film Noir as Romance, eh? Strippers always attract an audience, which seems bizarre, for female essentials never change. But different women wear what they got—reveal what they boast—differently. One woman's asset is another woman's tease? Explains all.)

To Imperial Theatre in time for curtain: *Jamaica*, starring Lena Horne and Ric Montalban. Superb! Sadly, the house ain't packed. Too bad: the magic of this musical comedy exceeds my descriptive capabilities. Bought *Lena Horne at the Cocoanut Grove*. Like buying Belafonte crooning of the Caribbean. (Memory of Dear—Gone or Strayed or Lost—Dad.)

After, Broadway is lousy with cops and bogged down by limos. Gay atmosphere: this city is so shiny that its condemned killers must positively glow in their electric chairs. New York is like Halifax: a bad town for good women, but a good town for bad ones.

Read about Negro rapist Goodfellow. Being walked, flanked by two jailers, across Sing Sing prison yard to his hot date with electric chair, Goodfellow suffers lightning strike. He got incinerated—yes, but ahead of schedule. His guards, handcuffed to him, died of shock.

Meet a young singer and husband—from Head-Smashed-In Buffalo Jump, Alberta! Only in N.Y.C.

Walking to the Apollo Theater, see Carnegie Hall and The Met. (Watch Rudolf Bing serve coffee to a long line of Met patrons. Opening night: *Tosca*! The big shots parade.)

Eye flicks at the famous Apollo Theater on W. 42nd Street: *No Sun in Venice* (Roger Vadim, 1957) and *Fire Under Her Skin* (Marcel Blistène, 1954): French and sexy. No flim-flam. Couples act out obscenities, ass over heels, hand over fist.

Thursday, June 18

Write/dispatch about 10 postcards home. Breakfast in Sloane cafeteria.

Meet a student, ex Hong Kong, nigh Red China: Bob Soong. Nice guy. Good chat—geopolitics and the humanities. Also meet a Negro Pennsylvanian who studies. Wondered if I did too.

Sunshine on and off in morn. Later, overcast and rainy cool. Tramp in chill and damp.

Hike down the tip of Manhattan—through The Bowery, Greenwich Village, etc. Visit Cooper Union Museum: fascinating articles on display. Old objects—from huge urns to small antiques and sketches.

Survey the Lionel (train) display rooms on E. 26th St.: felt "transported." (Pun!)

Go up the Empire State Building at dusk: a grand view. Dusty light. 3/4 light. Next, spy almost intolerable gaudiness of neon. Elevated levels of luminescence.

Dine at The Taft. Order a supremely delicious avocado salad (salted and buttered), followed by tea-smoked duck, kept moist by a pleasantly dry red wine (1959 *Château Leoville-Las-Cases* "Grand Vin de Leoville du Marquis de Las Cases," of Saint-Julien, France). Could drink this wine all night. Next, ogle Zahara on the hotel's belly-dancer stage. She cavorts without prudery. What top-drawer, costume lingerie! ("Nothing makes a woman more feminine to a man.")

Back to the Apollo. See *The Way Out* (1956): Gene Nelson's acting is phony. A German film, *The Third Sex* (*Das Dritte Goschlecht*, 1957), lives up to my expectation: patently disgusting (if true)!

Buy a frankfurter from a cart. Muse on third sex: reality? Back to Sloane at midnight.

Friday, June 19

Dawn sun opes mine eyes. Breakfast in cafeteria. Regain Liz II. Away by 9:35 a.m.

Proceed to F.D.R. Drive, cross bridge to Long Island. Find Port Washington easily. A Coloured man on a black Harley gives directions to Butler & Smith.

En route, I visit Ghost Motorcycle: a fine set-up, busy. Owner's son,

Sal, is a swell dude (like dad). Sells me a chrome headlight cheap. Gives me a free BMW T-shirt.

At Butler & Smith, ask about R60 to R69 conversion. Find it's "impossible, impractical, and altogether out of the question." (Good buddy Sandy MacKay will have to stick to his Harley! Anyway, as a machinist, Sandy can modify it further; he already gets 100 mph at 7,000 rpm. He's a rich man's son, could just live off the old man's portfolio, but bikers respect him because he dirties his hands, tinkering, retooling, repairing, etc., acting a truly "Popular Mechanic." Sandy doesn't care if all anyone ever sees of his machine is the "ass-end," for that means he's ahead and they're behind. But he's not usually a show-off or daredevil. Never as immaculate as his income could permit, his hero is Howard Hughes—the millionaire with a mechanic's brain, even designing a "cantilevered" bra. When I dreamt up the Halifax Motorcyclists logo—a variation on Goodyear's, save that a winged wheel replaces the winged foot, it was Sandy who footed [pun!] the bill for all the letterhead printing and fabricating as a device to be affixed to leather jackets.)

Cross Brooklyn Bridge. *What a span, man!* (Whitman didn't write *that*!) Take steak dinner at Cobb's Corner restaurant at 45th and Broadway.

Go to the Majestic Theatre; see Bob Preston and Barb Cooke (who lost her voice shortly before the end of the 1st act; replaced by her understudy). *Music Man* thrashes *My Fair Lady*—perhaps with a black, wasp-like, riding crop!

Buy lovely gilded earrings. For Avril. *My Sin* fragrance. For Mar. The identical perfume for Mom.

See *Look Homeward, Angel* at Ethel Barrymore Theater on W. 47th St. A Pulitzer Prize winner. Thoroughly enjoy it: brothels are always merry! Occupational necessity?

Subway to 125th: Amble Harlem. Gaze at the Harlem River.

Drop into the Apollo Theater. See finest Rhythm and Blues show EVER. Lewis Lyman and the Teenchords, Larry Williams, "Baby" Washington, The Pastels, John Bubbles, The Hines Kids, and Ed Townsend. I drowsed through 1 or 2 numbers, but they were all cool, man! A gas to absorb with the all-Negro audience. *Exciting!*

At Sloane round midnight. Slight rain tonight. Milky light.

Saturday, June 20

Up at 7:30 a.m. Breakfast at The Y Cafeteria. Pick up souvenirs on 34th Street.

Exit garage at 11:15 a.m. So much rain, it jointly massages and savages. 1,654 on the mileage gauge. Roll through the suburbs—pampered hinterland of Gotham City.

Meet two Jersey boys heading to Laconia, N.H. Happy when they ask me to lead. (They weren't sure of the way; well, neither was I.)

Put rubber to asphalt; snap into wind. Pass *every* luxury car: working-class revenge! Nice to roll from city to city in a train of bikes.

Introductions at a station. (Spend $1.95 on gas.) Shake hands with Frank Glass and Dallas (no known surname; it's not "Texas"). Frank is a runty, taciturn guy with a rat-tail hairdo. Dallas looks as fit as a moose, but his words stumble round his smokes.

Weather is sad. Gusts of water stream down our backs. Clears up as we near Laconia. Only a steamy fog as we enter town. (No fog smothers mountains.)

Rendezvous at eatery on Main. Have fantastic stew—and hot, butter-slathered biscuits. Plus unprecedented Presidente beer.

Later, Frank, Dallas, and I find a rooming place—a sorry property: $5 for 3 people. Not bad price-wise, but the room reeks of disinfectant and bug repellent.

We share beneficial alcohol. I undoubtedly seize his Jack Daniel's from Frank. An indubitable drink. (Better than Dubonnet, eh?)

Dallas shows off photos of Venice, Italy, last January: The city was icy with snow. Spires and statues glittered with diamond frosting. Canals were frozen solid and the trapped gondoliers were complaining. Usually black, the gondolas looked albino. The piazza's pigeons pecked at snow-frosted bread crumbs.

Next, Dallas hands round poontang snaps—"better souvenirs from Europe." Frank blurts, "If it was me, I'd wiggle it up and down, side to side." Dallas shows off the rubber in his wallet: "Guy's gotta be careful in copulatin."

Hit bed at 11:30 p.m. Bone-tired, dog-tired, just plain tired. This night, fireflies shed more useful light than stars.

Sunday, June 21(!)

Dawn is bright and early. Had a hard time gettin covers last night, what with Frankie and Dallas hoggin all the blankets.

Breakfast in town. My N.J. friends meet a couple more of their N.Y. friends today.

En route to the train station—now also a motorcycle shop—Ez Walcott overtakes me: "Sure good to see a face from home, let me tell you!" Unexpected meeting. An old Haligonian pal, Ez just got out of jail on a Sedition beef. Circulated cartoons—in Jamaica—derogatory of Prince Philip.

At the station, we check out bikes on display and buy A.M.A. memberships. I join AGAIN and receive a silver belt buckle. Then, Ez and I snap many photos of the assembled bikes—and of various motorcycle clubs (pointedly, patently, *not* gangs).

Then, Ez and I go into the motorcycle shop to chat with sales-girl Cathy (Fearon)—a sad, weird, superbly beautiful, tall, black-eyed blonde, with ice-cream-smooth skin. Flower-child farm girl. No wonder the shop carries on considerable commerce. (The pungent machinery of the display bikes out back, oiled, running smooth, hypnotizes.)

Behind the counter, Cathy wears a tight white T-shirt and ultra-tight black shorts. Her face gleams honey; her limbs are gold.

Ezra asks her for a kiss. She gives him a candy cane.

She tells me my teeth are "lovely." She says she'll think of me (or, really, my teeth) often.

Our four bikes dodge rocks and trees, down a long gap to the highway. I lead the boys back to town so we can gunk our machines for free at a local service station. (They nickname me "Blast Off" due to my speed and "punny" wit.)

After gunking our bikes, we start to wind up Belknap Mountain to see the sights and view a few races. (The mountain's murder for an unwary rider.) We're in time for Laconia Motorcycle Week, to view the machines competing at the Gunstock ski grounds.

We huddle, hunker, on the edge of an enormous forest, pure miles and miles of mosquitoes and trees. A swallow, just one, swoops past. Fill our canteens, scooping water from a hillside, gin-clear stream. Swig chilled, honeyed drink. Swallow.

(Dallas hands round another dirty snap. We all think no doubt about Cathy: how pretty such a scene could be.)

Over at Belknap, BMW put on no grand display this year. But the Ducati people show some spidery machines—Italian grace.

The lightweight races seize us. One guy, out in front, suffers a humiliating spill. His bike swishes on still-wet grass. The operator jackknifes into the air, but lands—uncomfortably but unhurt—on his butt. He stands, staggers, wobbly. (Can't help mourn last year—Mactaquac, N.B.—Mack's death.)

Later, in a big race, another fellow crashes—in almost the same place. Metal sorely, brusquely, rips his body. Cracks his noggin gainst a rock: almost pokes an eye out. (The injured man's oozing skull summons the helicopter ambulance. It sashays down, plucks him up.)

Belknap's races underway at 1 p.m. 100 miles go first—because of storm clouds. Exhilarating contest: Dick Musson (BSA) leads for many laps, only to find an empty track, which lets Bear Andrews win.

During the race, a press photographer snaps 2 or 3 pix of me in my aviator sunglasses. (Must catch tomorrow's local newspapers.) Like all journalists, he's a pudgy alcoholic, but with alcohol-polished, brilliant white teeth.

Later, a series of ills—the plug and the clutch acting up, Frank losing his knapsack, Ez going to get his—splits us. We regroup, but Frank and Dallas decide they'll sleep outside with their hometown friends—even though pouring rain is due.

(I won't sleep out in these elements. Too easy to either drown or wake with pneumonia.)

Ezra agrees to stay with me in Laconia for half of $5. I'm glad of that, but I'll leave early, to start for Halifax.

Farewell to Frank and Dallas. Last supper is at a restaurant.

Later, the rain is black, the night is black, Cathy's eyes are black, her hair is blonde. I do not recoil from such gold. (After the cascades quiet, light-grey clouds scuttle before a white moon in the brilliant, black night.)

147

Monday, June 22

Ezra's snoring when I wake and leave. Quick gait to the garage at 8:30 a.m.

Am shocked to find the gas tank cover off, the steering clamps loose, and a bolt loosened off the front generator cover. Maybe the oafish, beer-bellied, cock-eyed mechanic schemed up sabotage? Maybe he's a hillbilly Klansman? He fixes up everything quietly though, no explanation, and I quit town at 9:30 a.m.

To Bar Harbor, Me., then cross on the ferry to Yarmouth, N.S. At first, I see only a streak of blue beyond hills. Then, suddenly, the Atlantic widens into a world. Then, I'm back in Canada—parochial Europe. Elizabeth II—unspoiled monarch—beams upon Liz II and I.

List of Articles Purchased in the U.S.A.

2 Girls' Bracelets	@ $1 each
1 Girls' Bracelet	@ $2
2 Perfume	@ $5 each
1 Letter Opener	@ .88
1 Bottle Opener	@ .88
2 Plaques (N.Y. State)	@ .98 each
3 Belts	@ .79 each
1 Belt	@ .59
1 Box/Handkerchiefs	@ $1
2 Rubber "Heads"	@ .99 each
4 Sets of Earrings	@ $2 each
1 Stuffed Toy	@ 3.98
2 Cartons Cigarettes	@ 2.50

1 Cushion Cover	@ 1.49
3 Boxes/Chocolates	@ 5.27
1 Box/Lollipops	@ $1
5 Tie Bar & Cufflinks	@ $1 each
7 Pairs/Socks	@ .39 each
1 Metal Crucifix	@ $1

TOUR III

My wrong, my wrong, my most grievous wrong.
In which comes this beauty.
— ROBERT DUNCAN, "IN MEMORY OF TWO WOMEN"

Friday, July 10

Though Carl is squiring Avril about, and aiming to keep the tryst secret, he's turned up at Muriel's premises (on spurious premises), severally since his U.S. trip. Now, he and Muriel are dubbing each other "boyfriend" and "girlfriend," but guardedly, casually, because each knows that the terms really mean "bed buddy, occasional." Still, Muriel's more serious about this nomenclature than is he, for Carl desires other women—Avril before Laura, and Avril before Muriel. He yet hopes to ram Mar—if possible, to secure her, and then marry her—but other women must do service in the interim. Cognizant of Carl's plays, Muriel knows he'll never engage her own fine self for a wedding. So, she needn't show him *Loyalty*.

In due recompense, then, this night, Muriel's minuscule apartment becomes the port of choice for seemingly—in Carl's jealous eyes—dozens of bull-bodied, snow-uniformed sailors in Halifax on naval exercises, as it is for Fred Dent, whenever his sugar-and-gypsum *Sunflower* docks. Muriel calculates her marital prospects as superior with a Wessinjun or a Yank sailor than with a fly-by-night, smooth-talkin Scotianer, motorin— yessum—a getaway bike.

She's not wrong. Black fellas surfing the Atlantic's white tufts are more amenable to marriage than are Coloured guys manning the iron horses with their moonlit wheels, always riding off. Railwaymen like to keep two families. Sailors are more honest: adulterous, yes, but not biga- mists. Except that, when they choose to disappear—like Locksley Black— they vanish completely. (Cf. Tom Wingfield in *The Glass Menagerie*.)

Truly, once the Yankee ships float in, Haligonian Negroes run short of women. Problem is, the Americans spend money like a government. Their smiles are chrome; their chewing gum is platinum. All em know "Slackers" be a stack of gaily painted, wood-frame, three-storey-high whorehouses, a clapboard Venice-on-th'Atlantic.

So, Yanks treat Halifax like Whitman treated Tennyson: as an entity requiring a good beating, a good airing out, and then a re-education. They cast themselves as heroes who burn through cash, not as Ku Kluxers who burn books and torch "niggers."

Suddenly, North End Halifax is seasoned with old salts and pep- pered with U.S. Tars. Craving a meal ticket to the Great Republic, Haligonian chicks flock to the pubs, but first stow their panties at home. Carl guesses this situation suits Muriel: he wonders how many sailors have already seen her backside and the soles of her feet.

Muriel's rooms are prohibitively cramped, due to the nightmarish horde of sailors—dark, drawling, brawling, and drunk—pressing into her rooms in their dress whites. (Their salty speech and sugary uni- forms complement the reek of pepper out the Schwartz smokestack.) They hog the kitchen; they horse about in the bedroom; they tomcat in the hallway. NATO just means "Negro Americans Take Over."

Muriel's viral flirting guts Carl's heart. So many sailors stagger about, their giant hands clutching their humongous, Tom-of-Finland crotches. Carl tries to be as raucous as the gum-chomping, tobacco-drooling, Coke-gulping Allies. But his pedigree is more Halifax than Harlem. Though Carl reveres Yankee culture, the funnies and the flicks, he knows that Superman is a Canuck (not Nietzsche's hero) and that America's Sweetheart—Mary Pickford—is a Hogtown pixie. So, it ain't credible for Carl to kowtow to big-spending, big-talkin Negro lugs. He likes wielding his own big words—that dictionary vocabulary—so he deems Coloured Uncle Sam lingo a lot of bigmouth cuss. They're almost as incomprehensible as Newfies and have the same disconcerting habit of pronouncing *Eisenhower* as "Icin' Whore."

Saturday, July 11

This night of jitterbugging June bugs, black insects creepin bout fluorescent-incandescent concrete, Carl cruises to Cornwallis Street Muriel, but finds her apartment and her entire building clogged wall-to-wall with whitewashed-uniformed Negroes—just like last night. Every single Tar in Halifax seems to be droning and moaning in Muriel's tiny rooms, as if her apartment is Harlem shrunk down into the bell-jar-size Kryptonian city of Kandor.

Carl fakes cool, but he's totally cheesed off (as he tells himself) that Muriel's attractin such questionable Bros. & Co. Worse, in his eyes, she's nastily provocative, wearing a white cotton top sheer enough to show a white bra, which is itself sheer enough to allow two nipples to poke teasingly through the fabric like two tasty macaroon tips. She hasn't dressed this way for Carl's peepers, but rather as a tonic for sore Yankee eyes, to persuade them to quit sweethearts back in Chi-Town or L.A. or Harlem, and to invite her, instead, to see "the stars and bars"—the stars of Hollywood in the bars of Manhattan. Carl watches her smear cherry-red lipstick on her lips. *Damn!* Her eyes are coal-black, coruscatin diamonds.

Muriel senses Carl's upset. He tries to hide it, but he's a miserable actor. His smile contorts to a blackface grimace. He's as fang-mouthed as Othello facing Desdemona in their Cypriot bedroom. If Muriel acts Shakespearean, she's either Cleopatra or Lady Macbeth, those strategic seductresses, survivin "by any means necessary" (to quote ex-con X).

Despite the throng of U.S. Coloured guys lookin on, cigarettes boogyin in their choppers, their hands hoistin beer bottles or slappin down playing cards, Muriel stretches out her arms to beckon Carl to her. The Yanks figure Muriel means sumpin to Carl and he to her, but they couldn't care less: "Any port in a storm" has been a true statement since Christ stomped down the waves of Galilee.

Carl accepts Muriel's embrace, but he's angry, jealous, haughty. Muriel tries to kiss him playfully. But he wrenches himself out of her arms, sucking his teeth but still trying not to appear flustered before the Yank phalanx. He fails in that effort, for he—very ungentlemanly, very uncoolly—pushes Muriel, brushing her aside, then goes bounding down the squeaking staircase with its shaky banister, clattering down two storeys, two steps at a time, as yet another taxi, ferrying more sailors, zeroes in on Muriel's ramshackle pile.

Deliberately crunching too-slow June bugs, relishing the splattering of their blood and bile, Carl exits. He inhales fresh pepper from the Schwartz warehouse. It is his equivalent of battlefield gun smoke. Sneezing but invigorated, he jumps onto his June bug–black, peacock-purple, fluorescent-chrome machine. He hears Lola guffaw at some moose-coloured man's pungently blue parley, all "effin" this and "effin" that. The dude's cussin as loud as a priest atop an altar boy. Carl bristles; he fears the sailor be laughin at him. His German engine thundering, he roars off, his Scotianer heart roaring. *Battle stations, mate!*

In crises like this, Carl is sure he loves Mar. She'd never cause him such heartache, *he imagines*. But what if she's been *nursin* "Doc" Jenkins?

Sunday, July 12

C arl's worry over Muriel's possible sluttery gets justified, or so he figures. Visiting the USS *Valley Forge*, the vast anti-submarine warfare support aircraft carrier (which has helped to ejaculate many of the four thousand cocks-o-the-walk now striving to inseminate every Non-Aligned female in Halifax until July 16), Carl encounters one of Muriel's U.S. pals.

He'd gagged at the harbour's raunchy stench as he clambered aboard the expansive ship. He noted where the carrier's open-bow design had caused her to incur heavy damage in heaving North Atlantic seas last January: waves had broken over her forward flight deck, ripping away part of her port side. The wreckage be cleared now.

Aboard ship, a Coloured seaman—Toe Joe—recognized Carl. Toe Joe's uniform flagged his surname as Washington. Black-to-the-bone and electric in his eyes, the wiry, rock-jawed man saluted Carl: "Carlyle, you's one helluva dude. Tried my damnedest to pull Muriel, but she told me square, 'Carl be my man!'" Toe Joe slapped Carl's back: "Got quite a gal there, Carlyle. No skin off my ass to say it!" He grinned, saluted again, maybe mockingly, and swaggered back to his duties.

Carl wanted to feel flattered by Toe Joe's statement. But he distrusted this news as much as he distrusted Yanks in general and West Indians in particular. He was now convinced that Muriel's legs had criss-crossed Toe Joe's extra-broad back.

So, Carl felt like kickin in Toe Joe's Jap-war-crook-branded mug. But he knew that a brawl aboard the atom-bomb-laden ship would be suicide for him, even if he lived. Better to grin niggerishly and haul ass. So, he did.

Sides, the Negro Yankees were known to stick razors in their shoes. You'd challenge one to fisticuffs, and—*shick, shick, shick*—you'd lose your eyes and your nose: two out of five senses gone in one tussle. Or, if the spat occurred in a bar, broken glass would suddenly splinter jagged into your face (all this troop got as many scars as tattoos) and you'd sway as if drunk. Or if the fight shook up a shack, expect a hammer to crack your skull or a saw to be struck—stuck fast—into leg muscle, as if a leg were a log. Martin Luther King is into *Non-Violence*, but these seamen, by definition, can't be. They've spent their lives battlin cracker cops and kamikaze Commies. Their singing is that of choirboys, but they fight as dirty as cowboys wielding rakes, battering down a cow. Some of em are Korean vets, with flame-thrower-charred lungs and bayonet-slashed faces. *Look out!*

Night: stiff lights melt Dali-like in the water that, beyond McNabs Island and Eastern Passage, tracks the Atlantic's sprawling dark and glare. Carl imagines the U.S. sailors trading limericks about Muriel. He gets low-down blues high up in his lungs:

Moon is big and silver—
A death-head in the sky;
The moon's too big and silver—
A white skull way up high:
If you won't tell me you love me,
Baby, I'll tell you goodbye.

Translation: His head conjures a *Harem*; his heart succours a brothel. To have many lawful wives, rather than several furtive lovers, that'd be *Heaven*.

• • •

Frustrated by his suspicion of Muriel's *playgirlism*, Carl paces a brooding constitutional. He don't wend home (where he's left Liz II) straight off, but crosses Park Avenue into The Commons and drifts diagonally, still within the dark North End, to head north up Robie—the spine of Halifax.

The city's slim harbourfront is a flood plain that suddenly rises up to terraced streets, and then rises again to the vast plateau of The Commons and the North End. (Hulking in the central harbour, the USS *Valley Forge* is an island dwarfing Georges Island.) Moving west, the city ascends to the ridge and plateau defined by Windsor Street, then descends to the Northwest Arm and the adjacent plateau of the Bayers Road plaza (bowling alleys displacing trash-strewn alleys). West of the Armdale Rotary and northwest toward Rockingham and north to Bedford, the city rises again into hills. Africville—the Coloured, seaside village—is tucked under the northern slope of the city that descends toward Bedford Basin.

At North Street, Carl veers east past the radio tower of the Maritime Telegraph and Telephone Company, where his mom, Victoria, has telecommunication, elocutionary employ (thus replacing soap flakes with coiled wires), and steps smartly down to Belle Aire Terrace. Smells of stove oil mix with the grease stench of bacon and eggs slapped down in a heavy black iron pan (excellent for true domestic murders too). Or there's firewood hissing like gossip. The tang of woodsmoke hovers over all, makin neighbourhood coochies seem smouldering, tantalizing.

His zigzag perambulation reminds Carl that Halifax is a city divided into Upper Crust and Burnt Bottom, between ass-kissing attorney and cock-sucking sailor. Turning left onto his *ulica*, Carl looks east, down North, and sees the four-year-old Macdonald Bridge beckoning suicides to drown their sorrows in the dark, seething Lethe below. He gotta feel for such sad souls: they lack—clearly—a van Gogh–style, movie-star-Kirk-Douglas-affirmed *Lust for Life*.

• • •

Carl wishes he were better-fisted. He recalls visiting Pow-Pow Prevost on May Day, for a haircut, yes, but also to catch the London vs. Patterson bout on TV.

Survivor of a U-boat torpedoing that sank his merchant ship, Pow-Pow's feet got badly damaged in the fray, so, he clicks about his tiny studio on crutches. He allows only the precise intelligence of scissors and clippers going about their business of slicing through knots and naps or cleaving parts into skulls, or unravelling whatever is untidy. His shaves and cuts mimic strafes and bombings. On May 1, Pow-Pow had his telly on.

Carl saw two shadows, one Negro, the other Brit, trade blizzards of punches in a snow-white ring in Indianapolis. The crowd was a flat field of grey hats, cigar smoke, white shirts, black suits, black ties, plus black and white faces. Greek tragedy ensued. Bloody fists rushed to batter London. In the eleventh round, "Pretty Boy" Floyd put Sir London down—*smack*—onto the canvas. The punch was like a karate kick: London's legs flew up as his head hit the hard ring surface, and a dark liquid ejaculated into air. A sheen of mud. The drift of Patterson's fists had hit London like a buzz bomb striking the City of London. Carl didn't think that London heard the blast inside his head until he was being counted out. He became ruins—like yesterday's newspapers. He looked as stunned as if he were watching Malcolm X escort Jackie Kennedy to a Las Vegas bordello. The Negro barbershop cheered on Patterson lustily.

If only Carl could hit a Fred Dent or Toe Joe Washington or Leicester Jenkins just as hard! To keep Mar and Muriel *his*—in his corner *only*. *Reserved!* Though he hath Avril . . .

Monday, July 13

Carl loathes sharin Muriel with other men. But, she *must* share him with other ladies. Them be his (would-be) *Harem* rules.

Squaring off with B.W.I. Fred and U.S. Toe Joe, set to prove that he be *The Man*, Carl summons Muriel to his place. Her visit means one thing: drawers droppin down.

Carl's groin twitches and jerks with anticipation. He tidies up. Oysters slide from tins; crackers shake from boxes; beer grows frosty in the fridge. The man has he-man expectations of Muriel: Me *Tarzan*, you *Princesse Tam-Tam*.

Nigh midnight, she shows. *Gee whiz*, but the girl—*my gal*—is vehemently voluptuous. Off falls her pink summer jacket. Carl beholds white lace trimming a shipshape self. He sure as heck doth feel beholden.

Muriel resembles a mahogany-complected "Eskimo" doll: a lady with a big bust, straight black hair, big eyelashes, and plush lips. Magenta fingernail polish gleams from the tips of her digits, so ten look twenty. She is hard to resist, impossible not to desire. Free of the jacket and her magenta sandals, every time she moves, Carl glimpses intense-gold-licked skin. Simultaneously, a spindly filigree of gold runs up his living room walls due to the single candle shedding light.

Muriel reveals that Mr. Dent has set sail this very afternoon. Her left hand wafts no ring.

"A drink?"

"To start."

"The usual?"

"Yeah. Muddy champagne!"

Carl pours down iced, dark rum. A hot kiss.

Muriel demands, "Is Marina as good to you as me?"

Carl snaps back, "What bout Freddy 'Ever-ready'?"

"He's almost dead to me. I treated him like gold; he treated me like dirt."

Carl heard that "almost"; it echoed like *never*. But Muriel is molasses candy, sticking hot to him.

Carl doesn't ask about Toe Joe Washington, the back-slappin Tar. No, he puts Tommy Edwards ("It's All in the Game") and Perez Prado on the hi-fi, plus the refreshing rum bottle gets set on the coffee table. Muriel sashays into the bathroom and emerges in a sheer black nightie that she's (smartly) brought along. Carl can see but not hold (yet) just bout everything. *Wow!* Her cigarette smoke is as slender as the tie that Carl removes.

Soon, Muriel is shimmering as the candle canters low. She means to forget her long-gone sailors, those fickle suitors. Carl's fickle. But he's here and *hers*—right now.

Carl kisses her as rum burns in their bellies. Her hands clutch his head, his shoulders, his manhood, as if to baptise him in marriage to her. Then, Muriel's weeping and clutching him, telling him how lonely she feels.

Carl suspects that, like a feral cat crazy for fish, Muriel's consumption of men has made her a little mad. He holds himself, shamelessly, *blameless* for her woes.

But candlelight eliminates clutter. Two tongues wiggle and wriggle as one.

Later, Carl hits Muriel with a slug of whiskey. She sips. She asks him what he wants. He lies. "You."

(He admits *Truth* silently: *I don't want a wife; I want a non-stop parade of belly dancers.*)

Now, Carl walks Muriel home, seven blocks south, sauntering from North to Cornwallis. Their trek is quiet: She holds his arm. Lovers getting their breaths back. Then, she poses a test.

"Carl, why doncha take me to a flick tomorrow night?"

Carl is pleased to deny her: "I'm taking Marina to the movies."

"Why her and not me?"

"I have feelings for Mar."

Muriel retracts her arm, strikes a buffalo stance: "Don't mess up your prayer sessions with the Sunday school teacher!"

"I'll try not to let that happen."

Now, Muriel asks, pitiably, "Carl, we have something serious, don't we?"

Carl delivers false hope: "I've never said that I don't like you."

"Okay, then, take Miss White out. But don't have too good a time."

"Don't worry yourself."

The pair parts inhospitably, with callousness from him and *Calumny* from her. Muriel feels despoiled and discarded. *Uncle* Tom, *Tricky* Dick, and *Dirty* Harry seem awful pleased to plough her sex and ply her sheets, but that's all.

When she sees Carl stride away from her, not even proffering a good-night kiss, Muriel suspects it'd be better to see the backs of all men—from a distance. Tears spring up, but she be the daughter of Bessie

Smith and Ma Rainey, a woman born to blues: she can be bruised, but never broken. Her own mother died scrubbing the toilet of a rich white man (likely her father, maybe Dr. Fullerton). Still, *she* got born.

Back home, Carl thinks he likes Muriel because he likes taking her from Bajan Dent and—also—from the Yankee Tars. He loves Marina: but she half teases, while Muriel pleases all the way. Carl opens a sailor-left-behind-copy of Henry Miller's *Tropic of Cancer*. (*Oh, to be Henry! To have June Miller on her back and Anaïs Nin on her knees!*)

Forget such analyses—or diagnoses. Carl can't spurn Muriel. He can have her—lots—but Marina is nearly as remote as a glass-encased trophy. Laura is flighty: she flits into town, then flits out. She might call; she might not. She counts as a conquest, but she's out of sight, out of mind. Mississippi's Avril Beauchamps is still just-for-fun, really great fun. Muriel is, paradoxically, equally frustrating and dependable.

For her part, Muriel despises Carl's instability, his immaturity, but she likes Liz II. The bike brings heat. It melts thighs open. The machine's more trustworthy *and* more thrilling than is Carl. She loves having the wind comb through her hair: it is as enlivening as liquor after a day of washing white people's linen, clothes, dishes, cutlery, pots, pans, glasses, and bodies. She feels fresh clean again after the sordid looks or filthy words or actually dirtying hands that she fends off all day. Astraddle Carl's seat, she feels she sweeps through the streets or down highways as if she's a movie camera, taking panning shots along the way.

Carl cares little, of course, for her feelings. He is oblivious to his treasons of *Love* (which are heartfelt) and his treacheries toward women. *Betrayal* is the natural outcome, he wagers, of *Betrothal*. He exhibits a puritanical scowl, but it is not up to him to represent *Virtue* in a community where it is—as it is *everywhere*—*always* more theoretical than fact.

Carl presumes that lovemaking is superior to romancing, and a whole lot more honest—as well as rapid—without the necessity for continuous entanglement. He's a Coloured man trying to negotiate a white world that wants him to be a safe, smiling servant, and black women who want him to be a respectable husband and a responsible father, raising clean children in a paid-off house. But what if he wants to be an artist? To escape the railway? To live more like Picasso and less like a preacher? What if he doesn't want to be merely middle class, married, monogamous, and mortgaged?

Sunday, July 19

M uriel telephones Carl, asking him to visit. He hesitates, for the suspense. Then he says, "By all means, I'll drop by. In a jiffy." Then he gripes, "I haven't heard from you for almost a week. Is Freddy already back in port?"

Muriel pleases Carl: "Fred's been trying to get me back. But I don't want him. I'm calling you."

He conjures their previous pleasure. Carl tells Muriel, "I'll bring a nightcap."

"Please bring rum or wine. I think I've the flu."

Her statement shocks Carl. He fears the ailment is code for a Coloured woman who is *in trouble*. If so, who's the culprit?

"Lemme drop some rum by you; you can make a grog. No socializing till you're shipshape."

"Yeah, okay."

"I'll be by. *Ciao*."

Carl runs the rum over, plus honey. He bounds up the dark steps to her door, but he don't stay: not to be compromised . . . In the harbour, darkling ships fade in and out of fog.

Friday, July 24

C arl's phone jangles like a banshee: "Muriel's fainted and lost pints of blood."

Carl guns Liz II over to Cornwallis. He clatters up the pepper-steeped, boiled-cabbage-reeking stairs. Lola unhinges the door, yells, "You did Muriel a fucking wrong!"

"Shut your foul mouth! You're not helping matters!"

"Black men are shoe-squashed shit, worth less than tripe is to dogs."

Carl regards Muriel, *my darling*, on the floor, a white tea towel reddening between her legs. Unconscious now, she'd been moaning for help. The oozing stain exhibits an oxblood dullness.

Carl opens her blouse and sets a pillow under her head. She awakes. She's so weak, so woozy, she can't even groan. He snaps open the fridge, takes out milk, sets it to her lips to sip. Some of the milk dribbles white down her dark chin; the blood—twixt her licorice-tint legs—trickles red. He figures—worriedly—that Muriel's suffered a miscarriage.

(But whose once-upon-a-time child is—*was*—it? His or Fred's or another's?)

Carl dials an ambulance—the first thing weeping, useless Lola should've done. O whirs and clicks; the operator answers. (Carl almost expects to hear his mother.)

The cherry-topped, uncheering but screeching, vehicle speeds. White men in white uniforms—resembling soda jerks—leap out and slide the white-sheeted Muriel within. Carl rides with Muriel—*my girl*—in the back. (Her complexion's a pastel purple, and she complains of headaches. The medics mask her: oxygen intoxicates, like ether.) At the Victoria General Hospital, Muriel is admitted, and Carl tells her to "Get well soon."

(Is it relevant to say, "I love you"? *He does*. It's true for that moment.)

Back across the garrison peninsula, this saltwater, Atlantic outcrop, Carl lopes. The sky has an odour of yellow and a colour of rain. Appalling clouds smoke. Afternoon sobs. Was Muriel's bleeding the extinction of his lineage? Another human starting—and ending—as slime?

Outside Muriel's rooming house, adjacent to the Schwartz spice warehouse, neighbours stand under biting mist, trading news about Miss Dixon's "accident." Carl feels as self-conscious as a headline. *Sorrow* racks his ribs. He weeps as if wounded—sharply—in his heart. He hopes he weeps also for Muriel, and *their* presumptive child, his stymied *Fatherhood*.

Carl smells the salt and tears and pepper in the Atlantic-born breeze: the calculated aroma of *Grief*.

Back at his place, he hammers rum. Alcoholism proves a subtle Catholicism: he gets drunk, but he don't give a damn.

• • •

Life is as harrowing as a miscarriage. Carl's learned *this mantra* by mishap.

Recall January 1959: A woman in Arles, France, suckling her infant, loses her head when she leans out from her train and into the path of an oncoming train. Her infant, instantly an orphan, still nursing contentedly, sucks in heedless mama's milk with headless mama's blood.

The last the London, England, optician sees: the robber's scissors penetrating slickly, simultaneously, his eye sockets.

Closer to home, fire incinerates the Dalhousie University Theatre. Also up in flames goes a *papier-mâché* miniature Venice. No fireman can play Othello (not even in blackface) and save the representative republic. No, they play Nero: their equipment can't wash out this inferno.

• • •

Life is as harrowing as a miscarriage. In June this year, a Hollywood stunt pilot's body is chipped from a California glacier. He likely crashed in 1932, while filming the aerial finale of *King Kong*. Since then, scattered biplane parts have surfaced, but only now have mountain climbers found a goggled and helmeted head, disgorged from the ice. The man's whole body, well-preserved, is now being exhumed from the thousand-year-old glacier, where it's been encased for twenty-seven years.

Pursued by RCMP in Alberta, two thieves dive into a pile of horse manure—fertilizer—and suffocate. When they decay, no one is able to separate their stench from that of the animal waste, and so their bones are spread over the fields, along with cigarette lighters, eyeglasses, dentures, belts, boots, and bits of rags.

A century-old Coloured man in Mississippi, born into slavery, shocks everyone by awakening in his own coffin, and sitting up calmly, a bit stiff, and asking his "mourners" for "a whiskey and a woman." Emerson Dickinson was at his own wake, for, having been found cold and limp some days before, his death had been pronounced. A widower for some decades, the "deceased" fathered his youngest child at age seventy-five with a woman aged thirty-five. He's known to love his moonshine. When he sits up in the coffin, Dickinson startles a forty-year-old cousin, who drops dead instantly, thanks to a massive heart attack.

• • •

After Muriel's miscarriage—that *subtraction*—Carl feels a deep, sharp *crisis* because *Life* that he could have sponsored—or overseen—is gone, and he sees that he faces again a treadmill of pursuing quarrelling woman after quarrelling woman; some dismissive, others disagreeable. What's the value of his testicles? Just two hanging bags of dirt?

Smoking is a waste of breath, but smokers leave behind, at least, ashtrays full of cigarette butts. What of *Fornication*? Aren't offspring the proof—the catch, the capture—of *Pleasure*? Carl looks at himself hard: nothin to show for all his fornicatin . . .

• • •

Feeling still nervously culpable for Muriel's loss, Carl rides to Cornwallis Street African Baptist Church for the first time in months. Where Grampy Waters once held forth. The occasion is a funeral sermon, one that might rekindle his own *Faith* and also help him mourn the passing of Muriel's, and maybe *his*, "child"—tissue half-animal and half-syrup. (Carl never names the failed being a "fetus": too *clinical* a term. *Whoever* this *other* was.)

Rev. Ignatius Map's sermon re: dead Edward Dawson is hot enough to raise up Hell. *Maestro* doesn't praise or defame Dawson. The unpainted cadaver, already entered into *Eternity*, exudes a sallow majesty—a sand-drab modesty.

174

Dawson is dead because he tripped and struck his head on the sidewalk outside 160 Harvard Street. The talk goes, "Eddy tried to jump over his own feet, but crossed em up. He crash down like rotten timber. His forehead got a big gouge in it; his nose got mash flat. Ed's big head look all dents and holes. Blood gush out all over the place—from more than one place."

His face vertically scarred by a razor-blade fight in a Bermuda divinity school (over the yes-or-no issue of *Circumcision*), the bulbous-nosed preacher lets his elegy hover overhead, dusting off the deceased's life, polishing the gleaming bits. But Map also admits that "Br'er Dawson" had flailed within Satan's grasp, "torn by the crooked talon of Bacchus and ripped by the painted talon of Jezebel." Frankly, "when ya die, censorship dies too. Then, *Truth* blazes as bright as God's love or Hell's flames.

"But Eddy wasn't hopelessly lost in drink—nor was he morbidly trapped by perfumes. In the beginning, and at the end, Christ was there; His salving *Mercy* was there—never ineffective and always on time . . .

"All of Dawson's herein before-mentioned sins, whatever their number (some known to us, but all known to God), are hereby erased, reduced to zero, because his name is in that sweet *Book of Our Lord*, He who holds the pen and checks off the names of His Believers. He has whited out the tally of Ed Dawson's sins.

"If we can count his sins now, it's because there'll be no more. What about *you*? Your sins are still countless—and there may be yet innumerable others before your uncountable breaths reach their end . . . Count on it!

"You need to consider your own *predicament*, your own prospects for Heaven—or for that Other Place . . . *Sainthood* gotta be your striving!

"The laws of man are full of spite and bile, but the grace of God is a salve and a sweet. The *Law* spit on our Lord and hammered Him to a cross. But the *Love* of God brought Him striding out His tomb. Don't you want—and need—that *Love* and that *Mercy* too?"

The congregation moans, weeps, hollers, screeches: "Lord, have mercy! Mercy!" Yells: "Pity, Lord Jesus, pity!" The black-garbed choir sways; folks swoon.

"Our brother, *our blood*, is ours no more. His body is—like all of ours—a mess of dust; it will be a womb of worms. But his soul is *happy* to be alive with Christ Jesus!"

Rev. Map is so intense, he is sweating and spitting as he orates and illustrates. Th'assembly gasps, shouts, claps, hoots, and just gets excited, ecstatic, or cries out, at the most pitiful or most poignant moments in his catalogue of saints and sinners (almost naming names), and striking fear into some hearts (and loins and bowels), and arousing desire for salvation (if it's not too late) in those of others—the monotonously sinful.

Map's words assail the church. He be all pep and pepper and smarting pounce and bite: "That sugar-face, big-foot, fast-talkin *Deceiver*, yessiree, Master Devil, Mr. Justice Satan, Doctor of Philosophy, Doctor of Laws, and *Doctor of Divinity*, got some of you bamboozled. You think you're livin well: but you're already in Hell. You think you're goin to Heaven, but you're already sixty thousand feet under: that sky you think you're seein is only buried turquoise.

"Some of you think sin is just a little itch, a touch of a fever, a small cough, but nothing to cloud over your life, your career, of . . . *glitter*! I'm commissioned to tell you, that little bug you have, that pain in your backside, that ache in your belly, well, brothers, sisters, that there's your *Mortality*. And after your precious, proud flesh is finished, I say, after the doctors are finished, after the morticians are finished, after the lawyers have read out the will and the tax collector gets his cut, and after your loved ones stop grievin and start partying *again* [shouts and amens from the assembly], why, then, you face the Judgment. Are you ready?

"Listen up, brethren and *sistren*, you're followin the Devil, all delighted, and drunk, deceitful, dulterous . . . Oh, yes, I know! You livin high up on the low-life, or gobblin high up on the low-down hog. It won't be a pretty vista to see you get flung down, screamin, into the abyss of flames, while Satan just grins and tee-hees.

"In Hell, blood lights up everything. Each corpse is ooze and pus and rotting flesh. Your pearls are maggots and your halo is flies. Down there, you'll become *nostalgic* for freezing wind and Arctic snow. You'll miss January a lot!

"The Devil is the Deceiver. Don't you know that? His ugliness is precise and his treachery is clear. When he is right, when the Devil is right, he is *self-righteously* erroneous. When he is wrong, he does wrong *religiously*. He's an artful hypocrite, quotin scripture left, right, and sideways, to trap you into *Destruction*.

"He take a woman, and he use her til she be *useless*, brother! He take your *lust tools*, man, and smash and mash em up with disease.

"People, good people, pay attention! Satan is a chameleonic zebra: black with blacks, white with whites, a Tory with Tories, and a Grit with Grits. He tries to hide and dissemble—just like a rat or a roach. But you know the righteous saints stand out bright as day from ye evildoers.

"Let's hear some music to drive the Devil out and beckon Christ on in." A berserk organ pipes up. "It's a grave, grim error *not* to fear the Lord.

"With the Redeemer at your side, you can cakewalk through the catacombs; you can lindy-hop into Heaven. Otherwise, Paradise disappears.

"Brethren! Sistren! God has given you this very day to set down your burdens and take up The Cross, to mend what is broken, to repair what is ill, to displace night with shining sunlight, and to cease your vain yearnings. Take it! Do not confuse Jerusalem with Gomorrah."

A fanatical crooner—a soprano—lets loose spontaneously, and every note is pitched high, piercing head and heart. She seems bent on lifting heavenward the congregation by the power of her lungs alone.

The ravenous drumming of hands on knees and of shoes on wood backs this instant, ingenious spiritual.

Carl thinks: *Humanity is created by* Lust *and motivated by* Greed. *The desire to fuck and the desire to feast outweigh the fear of* Disease *and the fear of* Despair.

At the close of Map's fire-breathing sermon, sixteen white-robed black saints are baptized. Surprisingly, the water doesn't boil when a few of the suspect candidates are dunked in the pool behind the pulpit.

If he has lost—in Muriel—a son or daughter, Carl wonders where that tiny spirit has winged, based on the putative parents' sins, up to God or down to the other place. He wishes he could know.

Friday, July 31

Eager to view the parades and cannonades gracing the Royal Visit, Carl works only a half-shift, from four to six p.m., at the CNR station. Just laundry and luggage toting. He'll join thousands saluting the Queen and *Il Principe* (Philip) today. He's added a pint of oil to the machinery of Liz II. (*She was awful low.*) The bike contraltos beautifully. The wheels and engine growl wolves' vowels: lope, run down, track, wheel, lunge . . .

Although she didn't spend the Depression consuming Carl's brand of bread and jam (*two slices of bread jammed together*), Carl favours the Queen: she resembles another desirable brunette—Darlene (Darlin) Naas—who'd romped with Pete Paris in that stinking Italy Cross cod shack, years ago. Easy for Carl to compare Naas *and* Her Majesty and to note the alliance of their perfections: sugar complexion, black crepe hair, and cherry-cool, kissable lips. Too, the Queen's only nine years Carl's senior. Once he was old enough to understand that Elizabeth was the Dominion's Very Special Own Princess, Carl had to admire her pluck in the Anti-Fascist War, which he canvassed in the papers he dropped at Haligonian stoops. Princess Elizabeth could've been a Sadean heroine—tart and taut, likely ferocious at horsewhipping captured Nazis. Certainly, the monarch is more to Carl's elitist liking than is the brunette pin-up beauty Bettie Page. Nor does Carl ever forget Aunt Pretty's Royal Command Performance for the royal couple, and so Carl knows he's but two degrees of separation from the monarch. For reasons of persistent, long-distance *Affection* (crossing vast oceans of *Religion*, *Class*, and *Race*), also ineffably sexual, Carl has christened his machine after the monarch, thus connecting the German roots of the House of Windsor back to the makers of his motorcycle. The mischievous poetry of the nomenclature also supports his sense that he be "ridin the Queen"—metaphysically, at least. His steady dream is to jump up and down on Liz II, to tread down and throttle this palimpsest queen (quean), and slick swift outta any trap—*Economic*, *Racial*, *Romantic*, i.e., the clutches of *Error*.

So, shift done, Carl shunts uptown. He wades through whiffs of chocolate, the smells of diesel fumes, coal, and oil, and, wafting over all, the recalcitrant smell of fish—bleeding, dying, briny, and rotting—plus, in the auditory realm, the steady braying of ship horns and seagulls. He ends up moving with (occasionally *contra*) loyal thousands strolling to the Garrison Grounds to see Her Royal Majesty (the transfiguration of "The Black Dahlia") and His Royal Highness (the complexion of a crab, pinkish white, partly devoured). Carl pushes the cumbersome BMW through the crowd because he prays the real-life Liz II will admire the motorized Liz II—and *her* black-leather operator. He's mounted proudly on the big bike—just as Mounties jounce smartly erect on their steeds.

Upon arrival, Carl sees that the Garrison Grounds allot little marching space. He is so distant from Their Majesties that they look like toy trophies, borne aloft by prancing, high-stepping horses. (Carl thinks suddenly of Edward VIII—his unhorsed excellence when not mounted upon Mrs. Simpson, a woman who could pass for a divorcée in a *True Confessions* photo spread, with rectangles blacking out her eyes.)

Despite steamy fog, the event blazes rainbow colours. Togged out in royal purple, Canadian scarlet, and Anglican white, the royal couple disperses the fog and fades in and out of it—like the ephemeral brilliance of fireworks. The Queen's gems glitter victoriously, shaming the levelling, populist mist. Her equestrian cape fans around and about her tunic and about her horse's spine. Here's equine, no-shit *Dignity*.

The temporarily royal audience shouts, "Hip, hip, hooray," with raucous, Yank enthusiasm, especially when Elizabeth II furnishes any sustained smile. Her voice is like pebbles and glass—a tinkling, gravelly sound. Cheers volley up when Her Majesty ends one dainty sentence with an arch pronunciation of the Canuck, questioning "eh."

The pretty brunette Queen charms all. Her melancholy whiteness offsets the Prince's dreary whiteness. Disregarding, even disrespecting, the monarchical presence, pigeons squabble and dive among the crowd, mobbing any person nibbling bread or cookies. Carl hears doleful seagulls squawk. Some disrespectful gulls—likely republican partisans—drop guano willy-nilly.

The premier of Nova Scotia, the Hon. Robert Stanfield, heir to an underpants-manufacture fortune, appears in a black suit and overcoat, a black top hat, and a white silk scarf. His official speech *sounds* noble, but he fails to note that Nova Scotia, this spit of Great Britain, imports more liquor than it does teachers.

The Queen greets an elderly N.S. woman whose deceased father had saved the long-deceased George V from drowning on a fishing expedition near Sable Island. (This salvaging allows the royal granddaughter to grace Canuck stamps, coins, and cash.)

Then, after the obligatory salute—blank cannon discharging, their echoes thudding in every ear and chest—the crowd roars *lustily*, "God

Save the Queen," while Union Jacks and lovely, primary-colour Nova Scotian flags fan the fog. The royal couple dismounts and strolls amid elms and maples to greet their Canadian subjects, but steers clear of the droppings of the police cavalry, though a healthy stench hovers.

Suddenly, springing from the fog, one riderless horse starts—bolts with maverick speed, like a cross bull—toward the prince. A sharp-shooter acts. The horsey cranium cracks. A second bullet through the belly renders the stallion a tangle of guts. The creature splinters; it pan-cakes down, its four legs splaying flat. Blood lurches from the instant carcass. Some blood splatters the prince, but 90 per cent of the mess strikes scattered, falling citizens.

Carl can't help but recall the accident a year before that had seen a motorcycle couple with a horse, while his good buddy Mack had fucked his noggin with the hard-core roof of a car. The imperialism of the internal combustion engine had brought horses only ill will and bad luck. Today's attack was clear *Vengeance*. However, this observation is a metaphysical reflex. The reality is, Carl is, once again, face to face, so to speak, with ill-affixed bones and unfixable wounds, not only as when he had witnessed Mack's horrific demise last year, but also, only days ago, Muriel's abortive pregnancy, unnerving him to the quick. *Life* seems a movement of inescapable and insistent corrosion or collapse.

Protocol sees the Queen applaud the shooter, a parchment-bland face blacked by a moustache. Knight-like, but as pacific as a chess-piece pawn, he kneels to receive her public commendation. A gift of nomi-nal *Affection*. The naval cadet band strikes up music sounding like fog-horns. Cheerless, if blameless, the Royals appear.

To study Elizabeth II from the perspective of Malcolm X—if Carl could do so—he'd see that Her Royal Majesty's family is not unlike his own, housing *Adultery, Bastardy, Concupiscence, Divorce, Exhibition-ism, Fetishism*—the full alphabet of peccadilloes, if airbrushed by photo ops. But, first, one sees a circle of sweet children.

• • •

As he inches his machine painstakingly through the fracturing masses, Carl spies, in charged luminosity, Liz Publicover, his junior-high crush. He recognizes her instantly: she is, like Her Majesty (her image), of partial German Palatine descent. Then a pretty teen, now L.P. is beautiful. Carl eyes the brunette, her hair curled severely, her lips crimsoned. Forget the passage of nine years: Carl feels a surge—or shock—of *Affection* for L.P. well up deep within, electrifying his pulse and crackling his voice. He'd like to know—to sound—her thoroughly. Years, if off and on, he's thought of her—a giggly, happy girl in memory, who somehow smelled of milk and April grass.

Sighting her ringless, pale left hand, Carl has faith that Liz remains a Miss. He's ecstatic. Slender but busty, Liz sports a spring suit of pink skirt and jacket, a white blouse and cream pumps, but no nylons. No need. Her coal-black hair gleams; her sky-blue eyes ignite light itself; her lips are rubies. Cold sweat—the condensation of shyness—almost paralyzes Carl. But she calls his name.

"Carlyle Black—I'm so happy to see you! What've you been up to? Is that handsome motorbike yours?"

L.P. means to say that Carl is handsome. The motorbike is a diversion.

Liz's smile is royal, as is her being, which is as lyrical in movement as it is ethereal in presence. Carl blurts *Truth*: "I've thought of you often and hoped to see you again."

"I'm flattered. Why think of me? School was a long time ago."

"We were both Head Boy and Head Girl."

"A proud moment. Can't say I've headed anything since!"

"Whatcha doin now?"

As they talk, flirting (she unconsciously, he self-consciously), the Royal Visit fans disperse about them, thronging past each side of them like a stream parting before a rock and closing up again after. The

183

conversation begins to attain the calm of collegiality, amiability, the hallmark of *Amity*. But Carl's heartbeat is urgent.

"I keep the books for a lumber company back down by Lunenburg. For the summer. I'm here today to see the Queen and prince."

"Got anyone expecting you?"

Liz smiles mischievously. "You mean a fellow?"

Carl must find out: "As good as you look, I'd not be surprised if someone were waiting for you somewhere."

"You're flattering, Carl, but I face facts. I was a secretary in Montreal, but was too Lutheran for the Catholics and too liberal for the Protestants. Then, I went back to school, studied bookkeeping. I got ignored more than I got courted." A wistful look. "Now, I'm here to study *shelving* and retrieving books: to become a librarian."

Carl gambles: "I'm at the train station. Lemme get us both away from here."

"Love to." Unspoken is the *real* hankering.

Without being beckoned to do so, Liz swings herself aboard Liz II, behind Carl, her ready response surprising him most delightfully, and then he noses the BMW through the depleting crowd, vanishing like fresh snow at spring thaw. Carl wants to replenish lost time. The year that each ruled as Head Boy and Head Girl was less fun than official; they didn't socialize beyond school ceremonies.

Now, Carl would like to take L.P. down by water, to Point Pleasant Park (as Allowishus did with Muriel last December), to sit and talk. He wants to treat the Lunenburg cutie to boiled lobster and butter and generous mixes of rye and ginger ale.

Carl drops Liz off at the Hotel Nova Scotian, the railway hotel beside the train station. Liz has the weekend off. They schedule a sortie the next day.

Zooming from the station, where Mrs. Black may be entertaining Mr. Beardsley in an empty sleeping car, Carl envies yet the porters. They realize distinct benefits. A porter has access to pampered wives, women with time and bankroll to finesse clandestine escapades.

Carl thinks again about his mother, beginning to guess—perhaps— how lonely she had felt in seeking love, how humiliated she had been by her father, and how she had struggled—as Carl struggles—to establish a life in which there is love in the heart, a roof over the head, food on the table, and money in the bank. The last time he saw Victoria, she'd prepared him lobster—a special treat—and had offered to give him her still-new stereo because her "friend" Grantley had just bought her an even newer one. He remembered how physically bent she'd been—no better off than Muriel now—in having to launder and launder and launder to keep the lights on, the rats at bay, and five boys fed, clothed, and housed. Carl began to feel—finally—a smidgen of *Empathy*, the germ of *Charity*. Not only that, he realized, suddenly, that a coloured laundress could very well raise lawyers or artists . . .

Still, Carl is committed to his bachelorhood and admits to himself that he doesn't want Muriel as a bride; he lusts for their *wondrous Intimacy* (as he terms it). An added boon: Muriel's presence in his life prevents him from becoming overly besotted with Avril. Yeah, he don't want the *M-i-s-s-i-s-s-i-p-p-i* Miss imagining that his 'n' her matching towels will soon hang in his apartment's bathroom.

Having secured L.P.—rousingly—for the morrow, Carl decides to stop in at Maynard and Cornwallis, to see how Muriel is doing. Perhaps she's recovered enough from her hospital stay to favour a spin?

• • •

Round ten p.m., Carl—still clad in motorcycle-vivid black leather, swings by Muriel's. She's in; she's willing to go out. *My oh my*, Carl thinks, *but she's splendid*. Her lost pregnancy has left her a tad pallid, but she's still chocolate encased in silks. She slides her own black leather jacket over a white blouse and a red skirt; her lipstick glares as fresh as fire. *Fabulous!* He's delighted, too, that his portrait of her, framed, hangs regally above the entrance to her bedroom.

Glad, too, is Carl that sailors no longer plug Muriel's portals. Only Lola, who still seems upset about her friend's medical mishap, is lurking (or lounging) about, to scowl at Carl as soon as she glimpses his impish face.

Carl cuts his eyes at Lola. He remembers last winter, the booze-pudgy lady with her nose in Muriel's crotch, on his couch. Actually, this memory sickens him: "Muriel, let's go. Three's a crowd."

Lola laughs harshly: "Ya got that right!"

Muriel shrugs: "Let's go."

She glides to her door: she's always had a jiggly yet smooth-moving step, as if she's pacing a vacuum cleaner. "Lola, I'll be back in an hour or so."

What relief! To exit that volcanic, stuffy kitchen, that steamy bedroom, that sweltering bathroom, those three rooms of broke-back bed, unstable table, cigarette-charred night table, spark-jetting hot-plate, shallow sink, warm fridge, grungy toilet, grey-ringed bathtub, and cracked dishes, frayed towels, rusty cutlery, worn sheets, dented pots, stained pillows, and booze and bread and cigarette smoke and cabbage: to take Muriel for a jaunt, to inhale oxygen, to air grievances and salve *Discord*. Yet, Carl don't mind smelling the odours specific to Muriel's rooms behind the Schwartz spice warehouse. He's missed the unforgettable aromas that saturate her home, even as he now savours the milky, *bourgeois* aromas that halo Avril.

Carl plants Muriel on Liz II, and their patented, frank-talk, easy-going alliance seems reborn. There is laughter—hers—percolating as he takes a tight corner or opens up the speed to race down Gottingen, with all the shop window mannequins seeming to turn their heads to watch the couple (*strange word*, Carl thinks) pass.

The two clatter loudly bout the sleeping town. By and by, they stop on the natural fortress of Citadel Hill, the teat-round, casual drumlin—that high point favoured by *plein-air* lovers. From its summit, the downtown lights look like good-natured tears; the harbour—that squalid glamour, coloured red wine and molasses—gleams glumly. At the southeast corner of the slope, the Queen and *Il Principe* are retiring for the evening. At the southwest corner of the slope, cleaners are scouring the Garrison Grounds of horse carcass and discarded Union Jacks.

Carl hopes for a serious talk about *our situation*: he doesn't want to be coupled, but he does want Muriel to be his lover exclusively. Instead, the conversation turns to—*of all things* (Carl ponders)—"L.'s" and "F.'s," Muriel's preferred euphemisms. She asks, "Do you think I'm an 'L.'?"

"Honestly, Muriel, I don't know."

Muriel, decisive: "I like girls."

"But you and I've been—um—*friends* too."

"Say a girl stinks like a horse, I'll still ride her. I like girls."

"You've always got guys around you."

"Maybe I've just been slow, learnin how to discriminate."

"What about Mr. Dent? 'Ready' Freddy? What about *him*? What's that all about?"

"You vroom in, vroom out; he steamed in, steamed out. Lola lolls—and lollygags—and laughs and loves."

Carl's bitter disappointment borders on *Repugnance*. He'd *had* plans this night. Now, dejected, he ferries Muriel back to her pungent, murky rooms.

Yet, Muriel's sworn Lesbo predilection has both iced his desire *and* stoked it: he recalls last February when an almost *ménage à trois* almost transfigured his bachelorhood.

Muriel bades him wait. He sniffs the pepper of her rundown premises while still craving the peppermint of her kiss. One impulse is to retch; the other is to fetch her tight.

She trips lightly—Holly Golightly–style—upstairs, then glides back down with a novel: Gale Wilhelm's *We Too Are Drifting* (1935). "Tell me what you think bout this story bout 'L.' girls."

"Yeah, sure." His answer is noncommittal, but Carl kisses Muriel hard, intensely, to remind his ex-lover that she needs a man: *himself*, who also likely almost made her a mother.

Muriel feels Carl's tongue hard against her teeth, steely against her mouth. She senses his insistence on penetration, as if that had ever been enough. It's not.

"Carl, I'm interested in girls." She kisses him.

He feels kissed off. He shakes his head. His heart's volatile. He quits, goes, while Lola leers at him knowingly. His step on the stairs is a stampede.

Carl can conjure only one remedy to tonight's insidious upset. It's not to tuck into a book, and especially not one about "L.'s."

The lily-white, Stravinsky notes of Chanel perfume are more his style than is the black pepper and licorice of Schwartz. Or so he's convinced.

Saturday, August 1

Buddy Sun cometh up Belle Aire Terrace this morn to deposit, again, the milk bottles on Carl's doorstep and all the other stoops awaiting the milkman's sure trudge. The milk is so white, it's an avalanche in a bottle. It slaps whitewash gainst each decrepit house (twist of smoke out a crumbly chimney), making each hovel less grim, less grimy. Sunlight, lopin through glass, makes the milk look as sweet and inviting as ice cream.

Now, Buddy be a black man Carl helloes cause he likes his name. Some folks say he's Huckabuck's papa. Maybe. Anyway, he's a Buddha shape, a Zen hum. His shade is so deep dark in the flesh that he's the Sun come right down to earth, shoes kicked off (weather permitting), and buddy-buddy as Christ. All that molasses and butter that Buddy wolfs down grants him gyrations of fat, so he's a sight to see, trundling along, trilling, shakin in his one-horse cart, bringin the neighbourhood all that white light, liquid ivory, each dawn. His face shines even when he's moody, so most folks guess he's happy. He's not sad. All that nice sweetness in the bottle reminds him of white ladies he's glimpsin as they dash to doors in skimpy whatnots, to get their own breakfasts and coffee happenin. He can whistle; he's got a right. Don't matter what them Ruskies are up to, or who's black self be fryin in a Mississippi hot seat.

Carl thinks of Bud now, as brother sun be blushin the sky with licks of rouge, as if night's some dark-blue bruise needin healin. Come the sound of Bud Sun's step upon the stoop, the delicate *chink* and *clang* as the clean nourishment is set down as carefully as money gettin deposited in a bank.

As the white bottles are chuffed into place, dark smoke comes up chimney after chimney as the morning fires get going. Up, down the street, mothers or husbands are roustin children outta bed and off to play. And if they're too slow, there's a switch waitin for their behinds, right hind the stove.

Smell of oil or wood catchin fire. Some hand, dark or pale, sticking a tube of dry newspaper, already jetting back flame, into the maw of a stove, to conjure up heat just right for hash and bacon, eggs sunny-side up, toast, a mouth of milk or coffee. (*Integration* is a kitchen: a Stuart Ltd. May West vanilla-cream pastry consumed right along with a Vachon chocolatey Jos. Louis cake.)

Carl gives Bud half his mind, but the other half's concentratin on Avril. Went by her hotel last night, scooped her up like she was water to lap from his palm. She jumped on his bike straight off.

Carl leans now over his lady's back, that ski slope white as milk, as if he's a dark sun descending onto a plain of snow. Avril cries out, "Carlyle," moaning her impossible delight. Soon, too soon, Carl is pouring possible—*accidental*—generations into her bucking thighs.

Carl hears again Buddy clip-clopping his horse over the street that's more dirt road than pavement. Carl imagines Buddy's bulk movin right sure as he steps up to a door, then clinks down the two bottles, as white as the two tits Carl now suckles on as he and Avril snuggle into a snooze, what's left of sleep before he must up and ride to work, relinquishing the *Pleasure* he has just had.

Avril and he have taken no precautions—as usual. Carl seldom does; but, so far, no "friend" who's reported a pregnancy has claimed him as the responsible party.

Carl prays silently that *if* Avril ever files a similar report, she'll finger some other lad. He and Avril—like most Haligonian couples— take their chances.

What Avril thinks about all this, Carl can only guess. But he'd prefer not to worry.

So, his eyes wink shut after grazing upon her breasts again: such pink-tinged snow, such ivory blushing carnations. Her arm curls about his waist. *Love, Love,* his blood sings. *Not yet, not yet*, his brain broods.

The milkman's horse goes on. Buddy's song goes on and on. He's the Buddha of the blues. No lies. He's singin even when he's only breathin.

Look! The sun looms in Carl's windows facin east, but his curtains are clasped gainst its strokes. Avril's too tired to get up and wash out what she's absorbed of him. And she likes Carl's warm auburn colour against her hot white. Why should she move? And he's already asleep.

Avril thinks Carl's tender. But she's not keen to have a "brown papoose." A Deep South Catholic, she'd never been raised to want a Coloured chap or a motorcyclist. But, here she lies, a white Dixie student-nurse in a black Canuck railway-worker's bed. Avril snuggles closer to Carl, for the warmth. She drowses.

Buddy goes on his way; the sun follows. Halifax stirs; windows catch fire.

Once the lovers rise, wash, and breakfast, Carl will spirit Avril— surreptitiously—back to the South End, that section of Halifax closest to the South, that is, to swishy bullwhips and twitchy violins.

There, Avril reads among ivy, while Carl works at the train station, among *Envy*.

Carl appreciates someone like Buddy Sun—Br'er Solar—but Carl'd never blurt out such rudimentary blues. No, no, he'd rather whistle Sibelius.

Let Buddy shuffle his shadow along under the sun, steppin and fetchin dem milk bottles, an croonin dem historical black, lowdown blues. Carlyle Black will go his own way, *individual*, *liberal*, seekin *Love*— and satisfyin his *Lust*—as fast and far and wherever that big BMW can take him—whistlin into the wind, unto a woman (or women). *Gone*. Except that there's the memory of *Mortality*—for horses, men, kings (George.VI, *par exemple*), and babes hardly even conceived—and only that fact restrains his temptation to post-coital euphoria.

He has a date later this day to see L.P. To see how she "works out." He stores Muriel in the back of his mind, for he has Avril in bed. He can whistle on his ride southward. He *should* see Miss Publicover ("Public Over" or "Pubic Lover") later this date. To discover her fistful of letters, her stacked novels, her pale feet, her black blouse and silver pleated skirt, her orchid-bloom smile, her gaudy, turquoise eyes, her extraordinary lips. He imagines they'll fit well together, eh, like sliced pear and drizzled chocolate.

• • •

On this Saturday, August 1, the Queen hands fresh colours to the Royal Canadian Navy. Crowds applaud H.R.M. and H.R.H. ("Dark Prince"), both nonplussed by their encounter with the mad horse and its royal bodyguard–butcher yesterday.

The horse's death is folklore now, thanks to *The Globe and Mail* of Toronto running a gory, Goya-like photo: It shows the maniacal horse—Black Jack—its hooves in high dudgeon, people leaping from its path, blood lurching from the right of the equine head, and its belly spewing blood too. In the upper right corner, one can see the Duke of Edinburgh being spattered by the mad stallion's black blood, which had the effect of melting the fog.

Today, Carl bears dark sunglasses, sports life-like black leather, helms his huge BMW that snorts guttural vivacity. Upon leaving Avril at the Lord Nelson Hotel, he veers south and east to desultory, soul-corrosive *Labour* at the train station.

After his suitcase-lugging routine, Sambo mugging for tips, then offloading leprous sleeping-car linen and replacing the lot with bleached sheets (semen, blood, and crud laundered nigh—in patented Black style—to invisibility), Carl strolls into the Hotel Nova Scotian lobby to meet Liz. Not only is she ready, she's dressed so nicely that Carl can spy her flowery white bra showing delectably through her filmy white blouse (as if she's taken lessons from Muriel). Swell: she bunches up her long, white skirt to straddle the bike, and her legs glimmer silvery against the clean chrome, purple paint, and spanking black tires.

Today, this evening, Carl deems *fine* his life: Last night, he toured a pretty, but volatile, brown gal round Halifax; late night and this morning, he had a creamy, Southern belle in his bed. Now, here's another white woman, a girl who resembles the Queen, a girl with a Jayne Mansfield figure and a Katherine Mansfield vocabulary.

Carl sorties along Barrington Street. To their left is a red-brown, glowering lion, striding fixedly above an engraved toponym, identifying the Crimean War battle site, SEBASTOPOL, its head forged toward the harbour. Then, they exit the city. Carl skirts Africville (as usual), then surges down the Bedford Highway to pick up Highway 1—Evangeline's Trail of Tears—westbound, to reconnoitre Newport Corner, Three Mile Plains, and then Windsor-Falmouth-Hantsport. At St. Croix, the pair admires the 1935-erected water tower and hydropower station. They cross the bridge, where a miniature waterfall pours down with great energy and noise. (The Salmon Hole Dam looks like a water pail filled to the brim, but with a nick in it, and the spill from it thunders down into the cranky abyss that is the St. Croix River.) Wild roses flare and flame. A mint smell near the bridge. Carl remembers having toured Laura "Blue Roses" States through similar geography—and rain—back in May. A million moons ago.

All the way, Liz hugs tight to Carl's back. Her gleeful shrieks arouse him as he speeds past slowpoke tractors and horse-and-buggy contraptions (all claptrap, really, compared to the throaty eloquence of Liz II). He soars up and down hills, granting them both a split-second feeling of floating. Only the memory of Muriel's miscarriage and Mack's crack-up, the year before, could tamp down Carl's insurgent *Joy*.

The pair passes stretches of wild apple trees, wild pear trees, pines, spruce, maples, as well as farms, gardens, here and there a lake, a river, fields studded with strawberries. In the six p.m. daylight, they see guys felling timber; they hear saws screeching and axes thwacking. They roll past orchards, somehow cut from the woods, plus patches of green wheat, green corn, green beans. They see streams stoop down cliff faces. All is pastels—velvet colours. A Dominion Atlantic Railway locomotive and passenger cars, despite the clanking and the smoke, supplement the pastoral scene.

He stops at a picnic area in Falmouth, and Liz and he take seats at a wooden table amid grass studded with clover and strawberries. They chow down on baked beans, biscuits and butter, cornbread and molasses (all good, hearty food), and then have Coke and ginger ale. He knows it's not quite the same as his birthday date with Mar, that sexual *Pleasure* that unfolded in a glen a few dozen miles off, but this moment is equally Edenic, and maybe more *promising*.

Liz and Carl face each other, in the slowly dwindling daylight, and nine years of guessing and dreaming and remembering and wondering end. The two kiss and clench, non-stop. Away from small-size Halifax, with its—*to their minds*—small minds, Carl and Liz claim liberties. But this kissing passion is too new, too fresh, to make him throw down his jacket in a clearing, hang her skirt on a branch, and then let them have equal way. The picnic can't escalate to coitus yet. For the first time, they're together as man and woman. *Conscious of their difference and attracted to that difference.* But there is no time to do and try more than they do and try.

They return to Halifax *via* the twilight detour over to Walton, along the North Shore of the Minas Basin and Cobequid Bay, and then find Shubenacadie. They jiggle over dirt roads; on the paved routes, they pass trucks, cars, and the Acadian Lines bus.

Crossing the Macdonald span, they see, far below, waves striking and shattering each other like fragile dominoes. (What Carl and Liz will experience, they muse, shattering the bed.)

They reach the city in time to join a fresh crush of folks milling the North Commons, now lit up by Nuremberg Rally–quality flames. The royal plane cleaves through fog, cannon boom from Citadel Hill to honour Her Majesty's passage through Haligonian cloud.

On the dignitaries' platform, Lieutenant-Governor "Ox-Cart" Plow, in top hat and tails, orates into a microphone as press cameras flash: "I am honoured to have the privilege to announce, on behalf of Buckingham Palace, that doctors attending Her Royal Majesty, Elizabeth II, have confirmed that the Queen is expecting another child." Great cheers greet the honour accorded the city, the province, and the nation in being the first territories of the Commonwealth to receive and to relay this momentous news. Another horror-movie-strident rendition of "God Save the Queen."

The trim fighter-bomber wings smartly to ferry the pregnant monarch deeper into British North America: *her* realm. Only later does Carl learn that Her Majesty weeps, all the way to Quebec City, over the horse slain before her very eyes Friday. The Queen proclaims the stallion "spirited" and its destroyer "gallant."

Carl and Liz kiss again, to share their honest delight in the Queen's refreshed maternity. Yet, Carl feels a tinge of melancholy over the Queen's expectancy; her increase in heirs to the throne of Canada highlights his own solitary state, isolation, and his failure to amount to anything more, so far, than an impending deletion. Thanks to agility, if not God-granted miracles, he's thus landed on his feet—half the time literally—following his motorcycle spills. Yet, he's not stable: no settled career, no decided girl, no concrete *Faith*, no real direction. Perhaps Liz Publicover—L.P.—will prove the Long Playing love-of-his-life: to anchor him as much as he may buttress her.

• • •

Time to frog-march the bike back to 1½ Belle Aire Terrace in the fog that links the royal aeroplane to the loyal-always Haligonians now skedaddling—as if inhaling tear gas. But Carl has his hands on his handlebars and his mind on Liz, while she has her hands on his hips and her mind on the overnight hour(s) ahead.

At his place, Carl parks Liz II beside a picket fence, tosses a black tarp over the machine (thus blotting out her glimmering chrome), and pulls L.P. into his parlour. *Hallelujah!* To spy his one-time crush now pushing back on *his* cushions. Quick! He sets out Ritz crackers topped with Brunswick sardines and Brunswick smoked oysters. Next, he uncorks a bottle of white wine. The petite repast grooves down their gourmet throats while Nat King Cole's Spanish warbling swirls from the record player.

Liz is nervous but needing more kisses. She's had casual dates, curt flirtations. She yielded her virginity, five years before, to a freckled, boyish clerk with horn-rimmed glasses, a chap in a bookkeeping course, whose seduction gambit was to insist that if she didn't sleep with him, it was due to her backward, provincial prejudice against Catholics, or her

Anglo bigotry against "we French." She deemed this man, Eric Landry, a devolutionary mix of toady and bully, and yet, she—vulnerable in skirt and blouse and loneliness—had let him kiss her, fondle her, shred her panties. Liz still can't believe, half a decade later, that she'd let herself be laid like a floozy in a storage room of a business college. It'd been a peculiar affair, for she felt no love for Landry, only pity, and she was relieved when he, finding her more stoic than sexy, turned his attentions to an incoming typing student, mousy in style, but capable of biting, rat-style, a-bed.

Due to her inexperience with "*les types, les gars,* the guys," *Trepidation* trembled Liz as she stepped into this single Negro's apartment and buttressed herself, legs crossed, on Carl's sofa, with music in the air and wine fast in her belly. She hasn't been—still isn't—sure she's ready for more than kisses and conversation, and maybe more conversation than kisses. She'd like to get to know Carl—this man of pimento loaf, Tabasco sauce, mariachi trumpet–croon and mescal mystique—better before letting him *know* her—in the biblical sense. *Maybe.*

Yet, to her, Carl is singular—and he was one of the few lads who'd intrigued her at school. Back then, she'd viewed Caucasian as white and Coloured as black. Plus, everyone from her parents to her teachers to her church had inveighed against "*Race* mingling." But, in Montreal, in *La Belle Province*, it was not unusual to see dark chaps with pale "Pepsis," or sleeping-car porters with striptease dancers, or small-time crooks (all with switchblade-carved faces) escorting fancy, silk-clad call girls. In Montreal, working-class Negroes and working-girl Frenchies constitute everyday couplings.

So, L.P. is curious about Carl—not as a Coloured, but as a *man.* She worries about how pleasing a pearl was *that* Othello to Desdemona's eye. She prays Carl's big vocabulary cloaks a big heart.

She mustn't chance pregnancy if she will keep her bookkeeping job and her looming, come-September *Library Science* entrée. Nor does she imagine *Marriage*. But the wine and her will work their won-ders, and she uncrosses her legs and lets her bottom sink back into the sofa and settle plush against the cushions. The moment is underlined, underscored, by silk.

Carl knows his interest in Liz is mixed with *Lust*. *Ce soir*, he's more Don Juan than John Donne. Plus Liz is entrancing. Hypnotizing are her heady scents of eraser and pencil, ink and leather book covers, a blend of aromas like milk and wine, that is to say, the scents of *Trust*. Her aroma hints that Liz is bookish, if not a bluestocking, and quite avail-able. Carl imagines her body as a library of silk, such priceless skin, soft volumes of flesh, illuminated.

Carl kindles four candles, and he and Liz chat while the tapers burn low enough for the wax to gutter. They jest about their time in grade school, the strict teachers with pinched faces and arch tongues, the class jokers and schoolyard toughs, the teeth-grinding irritant of chalk squawking or caterwauling across a blackboard, or the punish-ment of the strap whacking an upturned palm, sizzling pain into the skin. They remembered their shared triumph as Head Boy and Head Girl: again, their two heads meet in open-mouthed, tongue-filled kisses. Mating.

Whatever her intentions have been, and however honourable in her own mind, Liz feels herself falling, literally, under Carl, as his hard weight thrusts against her, and then his hand is tugging gently—but insistently—at her blouse. But she retains sobriety to grab his hand and hold it; to tell him, "Not so fast . . . Enjoy the kiss. Imagine the rest."

Carl accepts the restraint; his advance relents. They right their frames and straighten their clothes. The candles are out, and Liz whis-pers, "I like you lots, but I'm not ready for more."

Carl laments: he thinks he's hearing a repetition of Marina's hesita-tions, if not outright *Prudery*.

Kissing her hand, and again her willing, willing mouth, Carl asks

Liz, whisperingly, to wait. He rummages in his bureau until he finds, among his underwear, one single, precious safe. He returns to Liz's side, but keeps the condom—daunting purchase—in a pocket.

The wine is translucent, ushering off, with candlelight's aid, resentful darkness. Light taps molten roots in four eyes, whenever they are open.

More kisses. Silent elsewise, Liz pants. She won't wait, now, after all. Carl bends back her head for another kiss. It generates others. Refreshingly.

All's *Easy Listening* as they kiss. Again Carl's hand explores Liz's tight, creamy blouse, white lace buttoned to the neck. He puts his hand on her waist in *ownership*: he feels Liz's dark hair like a horse's, her softness, and her white-seeming heat. Then, they wrestle; off come hindrances, fabricated inhibitions; the gospel goes up in smoke. The condom gets put into play.

Loving is Carl. He's making love with Liz, no fuckery. Yet, he also luxuriates in the *Black Macho* realization that he's just had Avril, in the *same* bed, this *same* day. This fact stokes his passion. He's had—is having—today two white women in succession—as if he's gone from the young Queen Victoria to the nubile Queen Elizabeth.

Carl has to keep reminding himself that Liz is Liz and Avril Avril so that he doesn't commit the heartbreaking crime of confusing the women's names. But *Triumph* throbs in his veins; he is rampant—in his own private bedroom, civil rights revolution. Tonight, Hugh Hefner is more his liberator than is Martin Luther King.

Climax—or climaxes—felt, Carl zooms Liz back to her hotel. They agree to meet again and keep on meeting, whenever possible. *Is Liz my best white woman, better than Avril?*

Possibly: Marina is for marriage, Muriel for relief, but Avril allows philandering that's *first-class*—from the chandelier in the Lord Nelson lobby to the Yankee whiskey in the lordly hotel room. Because of Mar's memorable birthday gift of "hand-and-mouth resuscitation," Carl sees her as less a lady. Despite his late surge of *Tenderness* for Muriel, Carl knows he'll never wed her, for she is a maid, and now a Lesbo to boot. As for Avril, she's a likely *Hausfrau*, but any marriage between them would be a version of Masters and Johnson. Each would bear, not a halo, but a sex-race mystique. As for "Blue Roses" States, their coupling had been commendable, but she is literally a *distant* memory. Finally, Miss Publicover remains unproven—save for this evening's single instance. More—ahem—*experimentation* is mandatory.

If no lady suits Carl yet, fine: maybe he's not doing too shabby after all for a railway plebe, a Coloured guy, with only Grade Ten, and a shanty-street—though well-appointed—apartment. In this Jack-Tar-coastal, hillbilly-interior province, he's emerged—courtesy of Liz II—as a Negro prince: D.H. Lawrence–discoursing and T.E. Lawrence-imitating (*sorta*).

But as soon as such *Triumphalism* rears in his head, he remembers Muriel's (and *his*) miscarriage, how vulnerable she was, and irrefutably female, and needing *someone* for succour and amour. Indeed, *Eternity* is unthinkable outside of *procreation*, which mustn't be thought *recreation*. Otherwise, the would-be chevalier remains a vulgar centaur, and, soon or late, a drab nullity, rather than a chivalrous, courtly man—father, husband. Besides, the libertine—with gold-plated, ironclad heart, silver tongue, and copper-bottomed ass—is so mixed—brassy—an entity, he is a constitutional fraud, an unsound being, of no firm strength and no sound faith. Are Carl's own values Bohemian (artist) or Baptist (middle-class and moral) or "black" (to quote Malcolm X)? Or does he manifest a volatile combo?

• • •

Carl's put off reading Wilhelm's *We Too Are Drifting*. He's amazed that Muriel—a maid—is reading; not only reading, but commanding *him* to read. A book bout subversive and subterranean (says Kerouac) San

Francisco. Shipped to Halifax by what strange *sister*? Or sailor. A man named Alice? Or a woman named George? *Curiouser and curiouser.*

The *grisaille* novel, Carl discovers, is a grisly drizzle of Lesbian desire in Frisco—all chill and fog and ocean and hills, with trolleys rolling here and there, sliding along like steel roaches. Carl wagers that Muriel favours the novel's Haligonian atmosphere. Even the Golden Gate Bridge is just a longer—*not* nobler—version of the Macdonald. Actually, Wilhelm's novel dramatizes *Decision*: who to acquire, who to jettison. Carl still disbelieves that Muriel is a woman who likes to suckle on women. Thus, he reads *We Too Are Drifting* as an extra-gloomy off-shoot of *True Love Confessions* comic book. For all the novel's chatter of coffee, cigarettes, and clouds, he sniffs out, in its flat-chest heroines, a lemony bitterness that could be rescinded, he thinks, if the right penis (*his*) could flush out each frustrated, feminine tract.

Carl throws down the book—its serene muddle. He deems it poor reading: *Can't see how this novel can be art*. He prefers the sweaty trysting in Beeline books. Nor does he credit that Muriel, *once* his *woman*, should feel *manly* toward other women. He promises himself to return the mias-mic novel and then deliver Muriel *the best night in the world*. Then, he laughs to himself to realize that his jealousy over Fred Dent and Toe Joe was all in vain: Lola Brown be the true recipient of Muriel's affections.

But Muriel's attitude differs. For her, the first modern Lesbian novel in English, which has passed her way—by sassy sailor and toss-ing ship—from San Francisco to Halifax, reveals *Desire* uncomplicated by threats of disease, pregnancy, bastardy, and smegma-smeared, piss-reeking, and wart-callused dicks. A Negress maid with a Grade Three reading level, she's now the fan of an ethereal, arty story about privi-leged white Bohemians in dust-bowl, Okie-overrun California. The tale hath opened her eyes to the feasibility of gal-on-gal *Romance*.

Then again, Muriel's suffered too much as a man's darling, the toy of every would-be Coloured Casanova to set anchor in Halifax and pound his way to her doors and then into her drawers. She's gotten *nought* for her troubles but failed pregnancy, a loose reputation, lonely nights, and even "love taps" from vile lugs. She can see that a caring alliance—a tender rooming—with Lola carries no pangs or pains. Moreover, Lola—married once for ninety days (like a prison sentence)—is pleased to feel loved and understood—and to reciprocate.

As for Carl, he should remember Wilhelm: "Poor little leaves, we too are drifting, someday it will be autumn." Surely, he feels just as adrift as gilt, *august* August leaves, leaving gilt, *august* August leaves.

Not that his psyche's in need of a grilling—a third degree. He's—transparently—a Negro male, of automatic *suspect* status in Caucasian, British, European, North End Halifax, Nova Scotia, Canada, North America, the Occident, "The Free World." He's *suspect* because police treat him—at face value—as a suspect. Then again, the tonality of his personality is soft speech but hard-hearted behaviour, for he's never wanted to be vulnerable—in affection—since he was a rat-braining boy in his mother's barn. Even so, his one anchor is his job—which is his employ because of Mrs. Black's employ as Beardsley's belle. So, even in terms of this mooring, Carl is patently adrift—just like August leaves. *Autumn be the slum of Summer.*

Friday, August 21

Carl chums about, times, with one Negro biker, Ervin Johnson, twenty-one, dubbed "Erv the Perv." Erv dwells by Preston; downtown be to him as a foreign country is for a migrant worker. Both railway employees, Carl and Erv share tastes in "cutie-pies" and "cupcakes." But Erv's a talker, not a reader, and more a doer than a talker. Carl deems him an A1 punk with B-movie looks and X-rated slang. In contrast, question marks—grappling hooks—snag and snarl Carl's fancies. Erv's voice is gung-ho, gritty, a sort of boozed-up blues. He's Frankenstein's Monster—blacked up. Razors rinsed in ice water hived his face bumpy; his eyes look jumpy. So pockmarked, maybe he filled in for the bull's-eye at a dart tournament. Vulgar as a bugger and lewd as a prude. So? He be a routine prick: "Got a nickel? I'll show ya the Queen's beaver!"

Given his *de facto* split (tantamount to a fiasco) with Muriel, Carl's extra proud of bedding Avril, and he boasts about his score in a phone call with Erv: gee, now Erv's hot to meet the gash. Carl talks up a dance at the Olympic Gardens.

Carl's read Shakespeare. He's as suspicious of Ervin as Othello isn't suspicious of Iago. Still, he's not suspicious enough. For his part, Erv knows that his sable skin cuts the female eye sharp when he's decked in a scarlet suit. He aims to please: he dress for *Success*.

The pals cycle from Belle Aire Terrace, west to Robie, then south to Cunard, then west again to Hunter. In the August evening, Liz II flickers like viscous liquid. Erv wheels smooth his Indian machine, tricked out with a radio and a cigarette lighter.

At the Olympic Gardens, Erv shimmies sly as the Eden snake. The lads guy through a swamp of cigarette smoke, the reek of rum and tobacco and ale and sweat and cologne, sliding along as graceful as bikers-gone-hoofers can. The dance hall is as dark and dramatic as a cinema—and just as unhygienic. Reddish cigarette ends light up faces, demonic, that are soon shrouded in pope-electoral-quality, white-blue smoke.

Carl means to show Avril, again, his gumption, his suavity, his undeniable class. But Erv, garbed as alarmingly crimson as a fire engine, twists as gaudy as a dervish. He likes to focus a lady's eyes on his bullish thighs, his Elvis-pelvis, swivelling and pivoting hips. Carl envies Erv's natchal, instinctual movements. He say to his bad self, *Shucks! Rightly so.*

Carl spots Avril. *Hey!* It's no technique to grin, to reveal auburn gums and ivory teeth. Avril looks sheer angelic—a collegiate, Nabokov nymphette, swishing a black pleated skirt. A wineskin dangles from her swan-white, swan-lean neck. Meeting "pluscious," very chic Avril, Erv don't hesitate: "Ooh-whee! Here's Venus in velvet and Lana Turner in looks! Carl, ya gots a swell lady here!" His head tilts back, striking a limbo pose. Erv chortles *Glee*. His feet glide far, farther apart, then snap back—a paramount, James Brown move. With every syllable he utters, his feet and hands seem to *cha-cha-cha* in lyrical, eye-catchin rhythm.

Avril blushes—just a little. She welcomes the Lana Turner comparison, except for the sullying matter, a year ago, of the slaying of Johnny Stompanato—Turner's lover—by her daughter, but it's unlikely Erv has that nasty situation in mind. So, Avril extends her hand for a kiss. The mouth brushing the back of her hand is hot. She exhales: "A pleasure." Susceptible is she to a show-off's jive.

Erv ejaculates, "Carlyle!" He slaps Carl's back: "Mind I beg yer charmin lady for the slow dance?"

Although *Jealousy* churns his guts as badly as *Lust*, Carl won't appear churlish. He mimics Austin Chesterfield Clarke's Griff. He smiles: "No gropin the goods!"

Erv licks his chops. Here's a humdinger chance to steal the white meat. To put the pretty lady to some pretty uses. *Stick her ass in bed tonight, kick her ass out tomorrow.*

Avril is ecstatic. She leaps up, pulls off her wineskin, hands it to Carl. To dull his anxiety, he takes a long swig. Gulps dark sweetness: Manischewitz concord wine. *Can it kill the honk at the base of his throat?* Sweet wine rams and reams his gut.

Erv steps on the dance floor with this sultry *Fraulein*. Erv clinches her, and there's no flinching. He's as bold as *Atrocity*. And Avril's plump curves jiggle and jounce just right.

Playing? The Platters' prize waltz, "Smoke Gets in Your Eyes." Carl eyes Avril and Erv. The two clench in tune and tempo with the ballad. Mississippi curves into Nova Scotia's arms. No: Nova Scotia—peninsular—pierces Mississippi's broad plain. Erv's right hand slides deftly up and down Avril's spine, lingering even at the sweet spot atop her ass, before palming again the length of her arching back, as their hips mate and their legs mingle in smoky ingenuity. Avril feels tingly; Erv feels kingly.

Olympic Gardens is as steamy as a Turkish bath. Carl pants—real *Anxious*—second-to-second. Erv starts kissin on Avril like he's a gourmet sittin to a banquet. *Provocative!*

In every corner now, there are duets of couples, petting, all bunched up, sometimes hunched over. The hall is basically a wall-to-wall stag party, tremulous as electricity.

Carl figures he should intrude, interrupt this waltz. But such would be uncouth or uncool; he don't wanna seem too enthralled by—or possessive of—the Miss missy. He chugs wine; a crazy calypso limerick pops into his head:

> *There once was a virgin quite green,*
> *Whose beauty was nothing obscene.*
> *Asked how pretty her legs,*
> *Said she, "That's a question that begs,*
> *A look at what lies in between."*

Carl's heart ticks like an Algiers time bomb (in a French café *right now*). He eyes Avril's waist, so voluptuous that *he* likes to drape his arm upon or grip solidly with his luggage-enlarged hands. But now he watches Erv cup Avril's backside, to measure—treasure—her *fundamental asset*. He can't think straight. He sees Erv already atop Avril. No, the moment is not that bad, but it's worse than he likes. Yep, Erv's deviant hands lock onto Avril's hips as if she's a glass of rum. Those mitts even flirt with the lady's bass cleft, and—*afore*—with her sizzling aperture.

Carl sees Avril's April-albescent face cuddled under Ervin's October-ochre chin. He can't believe that a Dixie intellectual who reads Dostoevsky can hanker for Erv, who only reads playing cards. Carl should cock his fists, run at Erv. He's on the verge, but Erv'd be hell to fight. The man resembles a cherry-red-jacketed lawn jockey; but hitting him would be like punching the side of a house. Carl elects to set his matinee-idol face as hard as a case of constipation.

Now, Avril likes the feel of a different black-boy-body, one that's like licorice in red wrapping paper. A male refuge in scarlet velvet. She can already picture Erv's coal-black truncheon, his inordinate blackness, his manifest manhood. In Nova Scotia, she holds a licence to make love that Uncle Sam don't extend to Uncle Remus and Betsy Ross. Though she savours Carl's politesse in discourse and finesse in intercourse, there's much to be said for a man of few words, and his name just might be Erv.

Formerly, Carl's cast Avril as a classy lady—educated, elite. Hard to find and good to keep. An elegant chassis. But *Elegance* is all that's left when *Romance* is left to movies, magazines, and novels. Too, Carl has presumed his *charisma* exceeds other Coloured men's "beastly" magnetism. Yet, tonight, Avril's philosophy will prove rearguard, when she's on all fours, taking a Socratic position in response to Erv's most pointed and penetrating assertions.

Carl fears now that tragedies unfold just like comedies, just more rapidly. His venomous *Animus* is as strident as stink. So, he decides: *I still have a chance with Mar. Mustn't blow it!*

• • •

While Avril relishes a salacious prospect, to screw down Erv, and is already salivating into her panties, Marina arrives with her escort, her beau presumptive, Leicester Jenkins, M.D.-in-progress, green Caddy in the parking lot. Carl ogles Mar. He's jealous over her now—just as he is over Avril. Plus, he looks idiotic: Avril's wineskin lassoes his neck. Carl tears off the deflated, flaccid vessel and tosses it upon a chair. Now, he must look *cool*, because Mar looks so darn delectable. Carl wants to press her to his face, ribs, pelvis, thighs, and legs. He worries: Has Leicester also probed the wonders of her lips and tongue?

Mar senses Carl's discomfiture. She'd guessed how far Avril had taken her introduction to *her*—Mar's—man, and had heard rumours about a white girl the black milkman serving 1½ Belle Aire Terrace had spotted. She's also seen Carlyle's Liz II near the Lord Nelson Hotel, at odd hours. She—Mar—is still *virgo intacta*, but not one iota naive. She'd guessed that a motorcycle ride had made Avril Carl's "human bicycle," to be ridden and pumped by him as much as a Southern wanton could want. Now, Mar hopes Avril—sister nurse-to-be—will suffer a comeuppance. Seeing Avril battening like a *b-i-t-c-h* on dirty dog Erv, Marina spies an "out" for Carl and an "in" for herself: she tells Leicester she'll dance next with Carl. Leicester harrumphs his inept disapproval, but then seeks out a ginger ale. En route, he'll survey the hall for any available poontang—easier had (and taken) in Halifax, N.S., than in Halifax, U.K.

The Orioles warble "Crying in the Chapel." Mar moves as lithe as a ballerina. Her eyes glitter; the light spanks upon her white pearls, white pumps, white dress. Her hair, hot-ironed straight, brushes her shoulders, and Carl can feel his hot breath, kissing at her brow and nape. During this welcome miracle of waltzing Mar, Carl decides Avril is no more his Godiva, but a *zorra*, all cunt and no *Conscience*. Carl throws invisible daggers at Erv and Avril: that his brain allows the conjunction establishes the new coupling. *Sho nuff*: Erv's got the hoochie-coochie plunked down on his lap, and his left hand's squeezin her rump while she titters; his hand be mashin Avril's bottom soundly. Her tits jitter agreeably—as if she were vaguely nude.

As Carl dances with gracious—*and* luscious—Marina, he thinks, acidly, *The Devil take Avril*. Mentally, Carl crosses Avril off his list of viable lovers. He exhales relief: no more need to sneak about the Lord Nelson Hotel playing delivery boy.

Avril finds Erv refreshing: He's as straightforward as an erection. No qualms. Also, no chat. His literacy begins and ends at *I*; his numeracy is "a 1 and a 2 and . . . 69." Erv's scooped up Avril just by cupping her ass. No, he's not hubby material. His role, in her life, is to tom, to dick, to harry.

Carl's hot with devil-may-care bravado. *Let Erv swerve Avril to the Lord Nelson and see just how adept he'll be, in his Santa Claus–crimson suit, facing a purple-faced desk clerk, to finesse his way cross Avril's threshold and ingress Avril's snowy drawers.* Carl prays that Erv'll get slugged in the kisser or bounced out the hotel on his keister, but Carlyle'll not humble himself to fight for Avril. He's already decided she's dog food.

To Avril, Carl seems a morbid jerk. *If* he cared for her, he'd strive to keep her—not let another Negro claim her by massaging her butt. Too, Avril thinks, *Carl is deluded to imagine that Mar is, in any true way, a real woman capable of giving a real man pleasure.*

The dance ends at eleven p.m. Mar waltzes back to Leicester's purring, sumptuous Cadillac, while Erv offers *gallantly* (Avril's term) to motor Avril to the Lord Nelson. Avril accepts: she wants to try riding Erv's machine. Interpreting Avril's comment as a sly *double entendre*, Carl scowls, sucks his teeth, and turns his heels away, to let his back void her existence.

Sober in his upset, sombre in his anger, Carl commences a lonesome, midnight drive. He can hardly wait to get away from *everyone*. The whole Dominion has let him down.

Observe: The highway lunges, spiking darkly—like wine stabbing a throat. Carl's headlight leaps whitely. The bike swishes easily like a snake. He tucks into a seaside nook at Lawrencetown Beach. Atlantic surf brays against sand, shells, and stone. The Atlantic's silvery turmoil squatters away against the sand. (As starlight pricks, apple-blossom-tinted froth shines like wet steel sunlight.) His sour tears scorch and sear.

Friday, August 28

Curious *Consequence*: Carl enters the Sunrise Café and, shortly, Laura States follows; she sits across from him at his booth. She wears a flared skirt—a crinoline. It's white, as is her blouse and linen jacket. Her shoes are clear plastic. Her purse is red. She says she's heard that he and Marina have had "a lovers' quarrel." Carl guffaws at the absolute *Absurdity*. Laura is glowingly beautiful. She sets a small brown leather suitcase on the floor.

"I've been trying to call you."

Carl smiles: "Here I am." He's not seen her for months. "Why not come up to my place?"

"When?"

"Tonight—late."

"First, I'd like another ride, please."

Too happy to oblige, Carl leads Laura to board his "pretty machine" (as she says), and they're off, dodging potholes and the crazy-ass dogs that chase and bay after anything on wheels. This bolting about jolts Laura constantly, so she's shivering against Carl's back most rivetingly. He can feel the lady is deliciously curvy; her *couture* is decorous, delicious, sexy.

All too soon, the ride ends. Carl suggests a flick. Off they go.

They take in *Lonelyhearts*, starring Montgomery Clift and Myrna Loy, playing a journalist and a newspaper editor's wife. Afterward, they exit the Casino Theatre and nip over to the Ardmore Tea Room, where they sip peppermint tea "to ward off the chill of the breeze."

Carl wonders just where Laura has planned to bunk this night. He can't help but feel sorry for—and protective of—her. After all, graceful as she is, she still rocks that only slightly disguised limp. Her suitcase looks flimsy. It also seems to cry out for shelter. Naturally, too, as he remembers their last meeting, last May, Carl feels *Desire* stirring.

Carl leads her back to 1½ Belle Aire Terrace. But he's bothered about that suitcase: If Laura hasn't *planned* to stay with him, *where* had she planned to stay? He doesn't ask, though, for fear that she will then want to go *there* (wherever *there* is), and he prefers her *here*, where he should like to have her—if she is so predisposed—again.

For one thing, Carl guesses, *Avril's likely enmeshed, undulating under Erv.* Now, he don't wanna feel glum or despondent about the lost lover. At hand is no trivial *Consolation.* Laura's delicate white skirt shimmers gold in the candlelight.

Until two a.m., the pair sits up, sipping ginger ale and munching nuts, molasses cookies, dates, raisins, and figs (last-Christmas fare). Unflustered, they talk of old times and the last time they'd spent such a good time together—all night too. (Carl recalls that, the next morning, she'd given him pound cake, homemade, brought with her from Three Mile Plains. The frosting alone had made his eyes close in rapture. Serving him while wearing one of his shirts, her ivory legs had shimmered golden in the dawn.) Carl recognizes that Laura is as sweetly domestic as is Marina, who'd also brought him "bakes," back in March.

They kiss. First with lips, then their mouths, then their arms and hands.

Some twelve blocks south, Avril is, as Carl imagines, embedding Erv. In light of that truth, Laura seems even more impertinently desirable.

She breaks away from the tumultuous kissing. She wants to know how Carl feels about her.

Suavely, Carl answers, "Amn't I provin right now my eminent ardour?"

He hopes this rhetoric mollifies Laura now. If she schemes on pillow talk later, well, his quick snoring should pre-empt the operatic—irritating—female demand for *Reassurance* (which is, Carl muses, the *raison d'*être for the entire *Romance* industry: flowers, chocolates, perfume, cards, lingerie, jewellery, plush toys, drives, tourist travels, etc.).

Thus, *Kissing* displaces *Discourse*. The two break at least one Commandment, if not more. Carl is with "Blue Roses," and he's not at prayer. (*Immorality* takes by snippets what *Morality* seizes whole.)

Soon, the pair baptize 1½ Belle Aire Terrace *à la* the Song of Solomon. They make it home.

• • •

Carl is not so magnanimous that he can let Erv go unscathed in luring Avril to his Indian motorcycle. Carl's *Vengeance* exploits a fine circumstance: Erv's boss—and his own—is Grantley Beardsley, that regular companion of Mrs. Victoria Black's sleeping-car sleepovers.

Carl chooses to coax G.B. to cut Erv's work hours so meanly, his ex-pal will need to subsist on a shitty brown bread, beans, and molasses diet—or sell off his glamorous Indian bike. *To serve him right. Maintien le droit!*

Power is available to those willing to acquiesce to its damaging utilities, if not willing to seize it for themselves. (Beardsley has always said, "CN needs a Mussolini to force it to operate a strict schedule.") Thus, Carl had his audience with unwholesome, unscrupulous, unlovely G.B., who did slash Erv's hours from twenty per week down to twelve. Erv now works three days instead of five. Better still, Carl's picked up one of Erv's shifts. G.B. is magnanimous in this shuffling of schedules. He won't pry into the reasons for Carl's request. He knows it has something to do with rivalry over a woman: good enough. His reason for cutting Erv's hours is, first, to remind all his Negro underlings of his power to better or ruin their lives; second to create a sense of obligation in Carl—above and beyond the never-spoken fact that Carl has his job, in the first place, due to Beardsley's first place in Victoria's bed.

Thus, thanks to Carl's Orwellian word in Beardsley's Machiavellian ear, Erv's soon thumbin rides to downtown Halifax from godforsaken, wind-whipped, rock-and-a-hard-place Preston. Carl exercises Beardsley's influence in his own favour.

(One reason why Carl motorcycles his dates about is, if he courts by train, taxi, or foot, he be subject to G.B.'s inquisitive—and acquisitive—eyes, sizing up Carl's gals, trying to transform their sexual inscrutability into private availability. The motorcycle allows a quick getaway from nosy Beardsley, drooling Beardsley, eyes-bigger-than-his-stomach Beardsley, as well as from envious, vigorously ugly, Caucasian [im]potentates—like Messrs. Sparky and Studs.)

When Erv discovers that his hours have been cut, he begins to beat Avril, to thrash the cash outta her. He rips open her blouse to steal whatever she might think to stash in a bra cup. It is not long before she decides to call Carl, sobbing quietly about Erv's manhandling of her, her mollycoddling of him. Carl spits, "Good luck. *Ciao.*" And hangs up.

• • •

Raised in a barn and set to work in a zoo (the white kennel and black lab-rat cage that is the railway), Carl could only view Avril, at first, as having committed the unpardonable Caucasian sin: not of confusing all Negroes as disagreeably, unanimously, the same, but of choosing to rank one as superior to the others. By electing Erv as her lover, on the gutter basis of brawn—or sexual ferocity, frequency, and vile depravity (coat-hanger whippings, Sadean buggery)—Avril had cast Carl in the unlovely position of having been bested, and in the domain in which his mirror and his yardstick said he should dominate. Little mattered now, the aubades and albas, the dawn songs of tender lovin as Buddy Sun came along, croonin, settin out the firm white breasts of milk bottles, then cloppin away. No, Avril was no longer April and spring and blossoms, but October and Halloween and dead leaves.

But now Carl's lost his first white female, the one whose sex first flared his nostrils and made him churn pepper twixt twin sugary flanks. Thus has ended this *ghetto libretto*, this *historieta perversa*.

However, Carl doesn't consider that he allowed Toe Joe and Freddy Dent to pester Muriel into coitus; nor has he gone after Leicester for his licentious urging of Marina to *Vice*. The reason for his stayed *Vengeance* is not his virtue; it's his powerlessness to cripple sailors and castrate male students.

Nor does Carl recognize that his sexual envy against Erv and Avril is just as atavistic as was that of the Italy Cross men who pursued Peter Paris, wanting to lynch him for having stuck his black dick in a white fishwife's coral sex. Carl thought his anger rational, but it sprang from his wish to best Erv and bust Avril.

Avril is astonished that Carl can be so callous; and she's terrified that Erv can actually put his fist in her face and his foot in her ass. But she is so accustomed to Negro *Servility*, of the enforced Mississippi variety, that the disregard of one Coloured man and the degrading attention of the other has unnerved her, almost to the point of dementia. Given the cranky mores of the Coloured Baptists of Nova Scotia, she now sees a return to the landscape of banjo-serenaded lynchings as a *progressive* move.

Carl is used to hardening his heart. Too bad for Avril? Impossible for her to worm back into his good graces? Well, if *Remorse* is eating her soul, Erv is still lapping at her crotch.

Yet, Carl also knows that Avril was good to—and for—him, validating his art, intellect, and aesthetics, and even an ideal of racial egalitarianism. Thus, he can't lastingly accept that his ex-lover should become prey to a domestic dictator. So, relaxing his *Arrogance*, Carl calls Avril to state mollifying, mellifluous words: "If Erv ever lays a finger on you again, I'll sic the cops on the man." She sobs, and Carl says, "Take care." He hangs up. He hopes that Erv will stop using Avril as his punching bag, but not as his moneybag. For sure, if Carl ever dispatches the cops to arrest Erv, the man'll likely be shot—or beaten—to death: *Racists' Rules of Order*.

Back at home, Carl cracks open Hugh MacLennan's *Barometer Rising* (the preface to Ray Bradbury's *Fahrenheit 451*). Fog lays a vinegary musk smell over the city. The only relief is rain, coming in bursts and spurts.

Soon, this September, the Kenyan "Old Man," not dissimilar in looks to Nat King Kole, will land at the University of Hawaii. To crack open *Econometrics* and seed a bit of Kansas, mirror-image of Oz.

DETERMINATIONS II

Beauty cannot exist without revelation.
—Norman Mailer, *The Presidential Papers*

Thursday, October 1

S ummer wanes inexorably into October, and Carl can number the freewheeling days (and nights) remaining this year, for motorcycles and black ice quarrel over who has right-of-way. The past season was good, all things considered: Carl had a slight spill but landed on his feet. (To survive—brain, bone, and blood intact—achieves the Triple Crown of motorcycling.)

Liz II did not fail Carl all season; she'd performed admirably. But flesh-and-blood ladies were infuriatingly frustrating, for their crises were inexplicable, unpredictable, and, worst of all, contagious: a smash-up in one relationship seemed to damage others *via* chain reactions of gossip, disputes, and splits.

Thus, Muriel's serial dissatisfactions with guys—Fred Dent, Toe Joe, *et al.*, including Carl (though he'd never admit it)—propelled her (Carl *believes*) to Lola and to the insular sorority of Lesbos. True: Muriel almost did become a mother. But Carl is relieved that he never had to face fatherhood—or husbandry—with the scullion: to watch Muriel exchange her apron for a nursing bra. But as soon as Carl thinks *scullion*, he retracts it: Muriel could have been the mother of *his* child.

Marina just flits about, landing with Leicester for one date, then with Carl for another. Her once-only, out-of-character, pornographic act of May 20 does worry Carl, for he fears what Leicester may have made her do—perform—next, one-upping each "sexcapade" until Muriel was ready to lie down and spread em.

Avril *was* excitement—and then disappointment. Sporting was it to gad about Halifax with an ivory, gorgeous Mississippi debutante, and to tip-tup-top-and-tap her. But Avril's hots for Negroes matched Carl's letch for white ladies. (The moral? *Love* is blind, but *Sex* discriminates.) Too, Carl can eschew wooing Laura "Blue Roses" States: his romance with Liz Publicover is flourishing. Her revelry in conversation and joy in coitus and delight in the motorbike upon the open road, her refined looks and her maternal warmth, all mark her as qualitatively a fine wife, if he should decide on—*and* she accept—engagement. Because she hails from the vicinity of Italy Cross, she understands Carl's contradictory anger at *White Supremacy* and concomitant *Lust* for white females. Raised in a fisherman's house, she *won't* lord it over a railway worker. Besides, her McGill education has fit her to be a teacher or a secretary, the two occupations—besides the *de facto* nunnery of nursing—available to her this year (until she can complete her *Library Science* studies). So, to wed Carl would be Liz's statement of intellectual and social independence, though she doubts that she could be the stay-at-home housewife he'd want her, out of (Coloured) male pride, to be.

Carl should admit, *My loving has hurt women. Too much narcissism, self-hatred, lust . . . No wonder I'm utterly out of luck with Mar— and Muriel and Avril . . .* Snafus flummox him. He is abjectly unable to don Hugh Hefner's—*or* Elijah Muhammad's—silk pyjamas.

Round midnight, Carl finishes Hugh MacLennan's *Barometer Rising*, the novel about the explosion of a munitions ship in Halifax Harbour on December 6, 1917, wherein Bedford Basin exists but Africville does not, and two thousand people are killed. In the novel, Neil Macrae clears his name and ploughs Miss Penelope Wain—again. *Excellent.* Carl thrills over MacLennan's exposé of the explosion: a man running with a sliver of glass in his throat, blood spurting; a fish hook snagging a penis; a baby's head replaced by a doll's head. The worst images are the crippled dogs, half-burnt cats, and horses cut in half. When Carl puts the novel down and picks up Yeats's edited *Modern Poetry*, it slithers him into sleep.

Friday, October 9

Because they're "two peas in a pod," Carl's whimsy to drive to St. Andrews by-the-Sea, N.B., for a final motorcycle adventure this year (October 9 to 12), needs to include L.P. He dials her. *Boy, she is keen to go.* She needs but an hour to get ready.

Carl picks up L.P. at ten a.m. She's gorgeous—from her dark hair down to the toes of her suede, low-rise boots. She wears a wool sweater, a tweed jacket, plus slacks and gloves: in looks, she's every inch the arch librarian. She even sports a tucked-in scarf. Carl kisses her fully, hotly, at her open mouth. He studies again her Ivory Snow–detergent-model blue eyes. Chrome-plated is his *Desire*. His heart races; his engine guns. Laura slides behind and grips Carl shamelessly—unselfconsciously. In fluent sunlight plus summer-killing cold, he realizes, *So many others have failed me, but here's a woman who doesn't care that I'm Coloured, who sees me as a wonderful man, and a skilful lover.*

On this shadowless but shivering morn, the pair veers through frost-ready fields in spicy, gregarious light. They bike past pines— sullen green—as holy as minarets, but also pass rusty or stripped-clean orchards. (The vineyards are already in bottles.)

Like Castro riding out of the Cuban hills to seize *Power*, Carl motors Laura into Loyalist New Brunswick. They stop in Sackville, just beyond Nova Scotia, on the Tantramar Marshes, all green-gold, tufted grass and red-brown mud flats. They eat frankfurters as big as logs; their teeth shatter cake. They kiss tea. A train draws its comma after a phrase of marsh.

From Sackville, they bound north to Moncton, round Dorchester's castle-plagiarizing penitentiary, then swing southwest to Saint John. From here, picking his way around potholes like sinkholes and caved-in highway slabs, Carl negotiates the bad roads—the bleak, medieval roads of the N.B. barons of newsprint and petrol—until he meets the livid Fundy, alive, vivid. The wind-nibbled, wind-bitten bay looks like whipped cream. Two hearts surge at sight of the Fundy's undeniable energy, its fundamental force hurling fish and shipping before it.

Next, the motorcyclists zoom past apple orchards of windfalls still unbelievably crimson. The road stays radiant—even when they see a buckshot deer sunning itself on the roof of a fall-coloured, dumpy car. (Liz turns her head askance, aghast at the blood.)

Liz II works like a top. The bike hurtles along smoothly—like a pen nib pushing forward ink. The engine genie sounds cheerful—like a church choir abandoning gospel for doo-wop.

Take to Highway 1 west: at Musquash Marsh, witness geese ascending, honking, "Winter's nigh." Autumn columns of birds, over a lake, darken its blue clarity.

At Digdeguash, the bike banks left onto Highway 127. Now, the pair heads south, past Bocabec and Chamcook, to St. Andrews by-the-Sea, transient light directing.

When Carl and Liz come down into town, they roll along Water Street, bordering a river harbour tinted to mirror champagne and ashes. St. Andrews by-the-Sea is a heartland of motorcycles: streets bristle with glistening, spidery chrome. Many East Coast bikers have had the same idea: *Get thee to St. Andrews befo da frost thicken!*

At Passamaquoddy Bay, soprano seagulls screech. The beach, such as it is, fields red clay, red stone, and red sand. Still-blue water froths white and silver. The riders watch waves rattle and rustle among boulders. The dusk sparks a silvery, glassy blaze.

Turning back, Carl reconnoitres *Triq* Pagan, then turns left onto Royal Princess *utca*, a stubby strip that, paved out into the river, is, at high tide, submerged. (A drunken motorist, if he times it right, can park easily underwater, thus foreshadowing a certain U.S. Senator's navigation of his auto into waters at Chappaquiddick, Mass.)

At Adolphus *Strasse*, Carl and Liz leave the harbour and soar uphill to reach the Algonquin Hotel, the railway-owned resort. Carl steers left onto *rue* Prince of Wales, left again, and pulls into the front entrance of the south-facing, raspberry-pistachio-and-coconut (Italian *gelato* tints) painted, Tudor Revival, half-timbered lodge with its manorial facade. Like the oils of Edward M. Bannister (1828–1901), a Coloured man (and a Barbizon School painter Carl *should* know), the hotel redeems Bannister's natal land.

Check-in accomplished as easy as a fill-up, Carl snags a bay-view room: radiant with rosewood, warm with maple. The lovers look out over a slice of bay between fir-pine fringes. Carl remembers the Halifax hotel that he'd had to sneak about within to visit Avril. This rustic redoubt is better, partly because ingress is easier, and partly because his companion is better: that is, loving—*not* researching, quasi-anthropologically—Negroes. Or so Carl now defines Avril, forgetting they both delighted in a mutual discovery of *Difference*.

The couple decides to stretch their legs a spell. They stroll, hand-in-hand, to the seashore, despite the October—repeat of April—chill. Carl delights in seeing the gleaming swish of Liz's nylons when she hikes the tartan skirt she's changed into, to perch on a red boulder over-looking the bay.

Back at the hotel, sunlight is dwindling (*chances* are dwindling). Liz sprawls on the king bed and pulls Carl onto her for long, deep kisses. The twain merge like coffee and steamy dry ice.

Requisite ablutions are performed, clothes re-ordered, and Liz and Carl descend to the dining room. Both order roast duck with pear and sparkling wine.

Who struts in but Sandy MacKay. The millionaire machinist with his humming—no, hummable—Harley. His triangled beard makes him look sharp as a tack. He's stunned to see Liz P. and Carl latched—like honeymooners. Carl grants a grimace of recognition that relaxes into a true grin of biker camaraderie. Handshakes snake about.

Sandy's in town because St. Andrews is the nearest day's-drive des-tination from Halifax, and serves as this weekend's likely last, decent, cycle opportunity until spring. He prays that nothing will break down: "Mechanics here can fix anything but have a bad reputation for rust." He'd trust his own skill, anyway.

Carl invites Sandy to join the table, and the latter's much obliged: he agrees to ride back to Halifax in tandem on the twelfth. He orders fish and chips and blueberry pie and ale.

Beyond discussing details of the drives, there's no easy gossip. Liz chats up her studies, her fetish for book-cover leather, and Carl realizes that the phrase *Dewey Decimal* has never sounded sexier than when slipping past her dewy lips.

• • •

9 p.m.: Supper's squared away. Calvados—the result of carnal apples—is inhaled and imbibed. Then, "Tut tut. Good night, ladies, good night, sweet ladies, good night, good night."

Carl switches on the telly: only a foolish space movie. *Click.* Anyhow, Liz expects first-class entertainment.

Steaming, luscious showers precede showy, luxurious love. L.P. wears black panties into a milk bath: not for long. Then she's a white beauty in a black nightgown. She straddles Carl, her nightgown fanning diaphanous over his chest. Next, Liz's black-black hair splashes over white-white pillows. She's a Bauhaus nude—pure, silk-smooth globes and swerves.

After, Carl shuffles the radio dial: They hear "Crepuscule with Nellie" and "Stella by Starlight," and then The Spaniels crooning, "Baby, It's You," cross a frazzle of static. Music rises from Hamlet, North Carolina (John Coltrane's cradle), and Sweet Home, Arkansas (Henry Dumas's crib). Soon, the sultry stations black out under the moon.

Later, the lovers watch a late-night movie: Marlon Brando as the chic, anti-everthing biker in *The Wild One. He did a marvellous job*, Carl thinks.

Liz thinks, *Carl did a marvellous job*.

They fall into the blissful, beautiful sleep of lovers—limbs intertwined. *Almost* one.

Thanksgiving, Monday, October 12

C arl wakes to autumn's first snow, a profuse fall. He regards snooz-ing Liz: beautiful is her profile. He recalls her wet, radiant pelvis, her jostling rhythms. The last three eves, Carl's rediscovered Liz. He feels *enormously at ease with her. I'd be happy to be with Liz always.*

On Saturday night, the 10th, Carl joined Sandy to eye the Jimmy Hornsby vs. Joey Padilla bout. The unanimous decision was for Hornsby in the tenth round at Grand Olympic Auditorium (L.A.), a site almost as smoky as Halifax's Olympic Gardens. Neither Carl nor Sandy cared: neither had bet on the outcome. Rather, the guys drowned in boatloads of ale. Beer bottles, sinking, pouted at Heaven.

But Sunday night, last night, post-prandial and post-*Pleasure*, he and Liz watched TV. Carl gloried in a CBC staging of Arthur Miller's *The Crucible*, featuring, as Tituba, his Aunt Pretty, the star contralto in her first dramatic role, this turn in a political allegory based on the Salem Witch Trials of 1692. Carl deemed her "quite good—even better than the story." Gratifyingly, Liz agreed.

Now, in the snowy light of this dawn, Carl's pretty sure that Liz P. is present tense and possibly the future. Shortly, she stretches, yawns, opens her eyes, and reaches for her man. To capitalize on his presence.

The idyll ends too soon, but breakfast offers a last fillip: lobster cakes, then blueberry waffles with maple syrup, hot apple cider, a gallon of coffee. Sandy joins in, and the mood is good. For one thing, the warm soil is melting the snow. Fine driving ahead.

Even at the best of times (meteorologically speaking), roads twitch wicked cross New Brunswick. The province's asphalt is shivered to bits by trucks carting timber, lumber, paper, potatoes, and fuel, and by a tax base too dismal to make a difference. (Provincial elections never help. The Same-Old Party and The New-Old Party promise, "Better Roads Ahead," but, after each "win," the policy becomes "Dead Ends," "U-Turns," and—really, *apocalyptic*—"Floods.")

At noon, post-checkout, Sandy boards his big, hulking, hand-refined Harley: he grins toothily, leaps up and down, ignites the engine. Feeling envy for Sandy's machine, Carl does the same; he sparks the BMW to a thunderous start. The purring roar reassures him of his equality to the plutocrat. Liz slides on Liz II, clutches Carl. In tandem, the trio exits St. Andrews by-the-Sea.

Sandy guns his sky-blue Harley like a G.I. Tommy-gunning a Jerry. He speeds cheerily past Carl and Liz. A minute later, they overtake him: a repetitive relay is underway, and it's fun, but Carl's also nervous—he remembers Mack, the fatal accident of eighteen months back. Nor can Carl let Liz face harm: she's given him—is giving him—the greatest *Pleasure*, just by gripping him, then mashing her chest hard against his back.

Yet, the bikes race unhurriedly on the two-lane highway, minding oncoming traffic and skipping potholes. Speed is watchful—mainly—of the limits. The machines take turns passing each other: they sit parallel rarely—an illegal and risky manoeuvre.

The percolating percussion of Carl's well-tuned machine—his persuasive engine—thrusts him onward, repelling the wind. Liz P. holds on tight, accepting Carl's bearings, reflexes, weight, even the idea of his physical windbreak as a kind of cushion.

At Musquash Marsh, Sandy accelerates. He realizes there's no point in investing refinements—in design and power—in his Harley unless he can show off. Not to show up Carl, whose dedicated riding he respects. But definitely to *show*, and maybe attract Liz's attention: *So lovely a girl; so lyrical her style*. Sandy lunges ahead, but his bike hits a watery patch and mutinies. The front wheel gives a sluggish twinge; then the bike. Out it scrambles from under him, like a scurrying bug. Metal rasps, sparks. A shining crash.

Sandy strikes asphalt headfirst. Pink spray shoots off his skull.

Carl screeches to a stop, kickstands the BMW, and rushes to help. Helpless, Sandy's dying—in cold blood—this red October. Red gurgles from his head and mouth. Dispersed, blue metal congregates. Chrome pours into Sandy's chest; it spills from his skull. A welder couldn't put him back together.

Shaking, Liz screams and weeps, weeps and screams. Shaking.

The bitched bike lies on its side, pumping out bright oil, attended by a litter of broken glass and twisted-off metal parts. It's a Ferris wheel bisected by a carousel.

There's the unbearable impotence of a dead body. Silent as smoke. Peculiarly dark, just inert, bleeding, black leather.

Carl sees in Sandy's incredible, fast-action *demise* a reflection of Mack's, also in New Brunswick, a year and a half ago. But Sandy's crash is distinctly a mishap of his own hand; no collisions occurred except between himself and the road.

Minutes pass. The living motorcyclists hold each other and sob.

Carl knows he cannot help his riding buddy, save to shoo off crows—as if in a Colville painting, pairing transport and dark animals, mingling *Realism*, *Modernism*, and *Gothicism*. They're attempting to colonize cadaver. But, charitably, a dog scoots over, barking, cringing, then lunging, scaring off the carrion scavengers, to make them flinch from their tantalizing lunch. But the canine does lap up some of the brain blood.

Carl feels weirdly disassembled himself, to be recalling his art knowledge at the same instant that he is shooing cadaver birds from the grisly highway scene. Still, there's the memory of that living blood between Muriel's legs, and it accents his awareness that he's twice survived crashes that have killed a pal and an acquaintance, and also survived the potential baby that Muriel could not carry. As Carl stands, flailing at black-winged air, and, almost using the same motion, flags down passing motorists, he sees that his actual future is present: Liz—loving and supportive, respectful and encouraging.

Once ambulance and cops come, and Carl has given out his ID and explanations, and then is cleared of *Suspicion* and treated for *Shock*, he and Liz are free to leave the scene (an *al fresco* morgue). But Liz loathes cycles now.

Carl collects himself, steadies his nerves and stomach: he lives still. Thus, he calms himself enough to coax—cajole—Liz to straddle Liz II again. Slowly, shakily, she does so. Trembling, she holds Carl tight—like a vise—as the machine snorts and roars back to life. *Life!*

They pit-stop in Moncton to gas up, but hotfoot it to Halifax—the glitter of home. The harbour exhibits buildings dripping glass and steel, the city's liquid foundations. Liz hugs Carl, begs him to bring her to his place. She needs *Relaxation*. He delivers. How else can they *thrive*—psychologically?

First, wine comforts the weary travellers, as it has many, after crossing—by bridge—the cold waters of Halifax Harbour. (The guarantee of Heaven: to drink wine to drunkenness from a Communion cup.) They find they enjoy breathing—together, ever, ever deeply, more deeply. In concert.

Saturday, October 31

Halloween marks the fallback to Daylight Saving Time, but Carl is tricked by the change. He motors to the station by eight a.m.—an hour early. Better sooner than not. Today, officially, is his last at CN Halifax.

Beardsley has been unable to work magic, to keep his gal-pal's son in dough. Too bad: autos are overtaking trains as ways to whiz from Kelowna to Come By Chance; thus, pavement is displacing rails. CN is retrenching, "cutting fat and belt-tightening." Beardsley's already had to kiss too much ass to keep his own pay, pension, and perks. Despite his local swagger, he's still a Negro the CN bean-counters would love to erase—as if his black face explained all the red ink. All "Great Britain" can do is elevate Carl's name on the seniority list: he'll be among those first called back to work, if there's an uptick in train travel (likely round Christmas).

Normally, Studs Sponagle is rude, but today, he's nice enough to say that he'll try to convince Jollimore they need "a man" (Carl) in the

Equipment Room. Carl is thankful for this consideration. But he's not naive: *My only real hope is that Burl, who I've been replacing, will suffer a relapse of cancer.*

When his shift ends, Carl is bewildered about what he should do *to keep income a-comin in.* His only trade besides carting luggage and linen is . . . painting. But no Scotianer has yet made a paying hobby out of *Art*, and most would consider painting not a hobby, but as dreamin: gossip is a hobby; drinking is a hobby; but *Art's* a delirium.

Carl goes to see Liz, that black-haired, splendidly structured beauty. He motors to a residence nearby Dalhousie University, where Liz is now ensconced, to earn that *Library Science* degree. They meet and Carl blurts his dilemma: "I'm jobless; can't think what to do next." How to avoid a tragic lull in his income? He knows his economic warfare against Ervin has degraded his ex-buddy perilously. Terrible irony would be his degeneration likewise.

Liz sees that Carl could use mothering. So, over milkshake and tea at the Ardmore Tea Room, she prods him to see that his future could be in *Art*, in painting; so he should start. His triumphs and profits would benefit them both: she'd enjoy shelving catalogues of his art, while both would get invites to tony soirees at boutique N.Y.C. salons.

When their snacking ends, Halloween trick or treat—for tykes—is over. Freshly enthusiastic, Carl drops Liz at her apartment, then roars back to Belle Aire Terrace and begins, picking up brushes and paints, to advance himself by *making Art. Finally!*

• • •

Carl dusts off his Lincoln School of Art kit, ordered back in June, to ready his financial *Emancipation*. To go from proletarian intellectual to motorbike Bohemian; at last, to dump Halifax for New York City, Africville for Greenwich Village—to join the young folkies fuelled by drink, drugs, and dreams. But he'll take Liz—only Liz—along. (Unless Marina comes to her senses. He thrills to think that he might give *her* an ultimatum: "Come with me to Manhattan to be a nurse; I can give you America; no Wessindian can.")

Wanted: the aromas of pastel, watercolours, oils, even charcoal pencil and India ink and eraser. These materials are his new lubricants—not chain grease, not engine oil, not hydraulic fluid—to engineer his final ascent, fine-tooled emergence, *via Fine Art*, from a subpar, *Alley Oop* and *Betty Boop* existence to edge closer to the attainments of a Warhol and a Monroe: to be heralded as essential, historic; his ostracism from the finer classes and better people ended.

The flavour and purpose of Carl's enterprise: to design a mess of colours; to realize the loveliest implementation of visions; to finesse his crafting of sugary scenery, aping Disney, or to indulge deep, dark-ink cartoon "blues," following Poulbot's example; or to draft solid buttocks and impressive bosoms such as those visible in *Stag* or *Male*; or to paint well-sunned or "flesh-coloured" nudes in the style of Vargas; or to limn women part-geometry and part-gymnastics, as in the work of Rockwell Kent.

To commence, he chooses, on an assembly-line basis, to draft a bullfighter series. The sketches are copacetic: *I'll colour in the content so that it shimmers. Relief!* This work takes only a day.

Carl experiments by painting a rouge-tone *Still Life of Rosé, Beets, and Apples*. The canvas has the look and feel of rodomontade firewater. Perfect for any pub serving Caesar salad and light wine.

Next, Carl turns out four No.1 *Lighthouse* drawings. He executes them fast. Paint follows. Colourful *Sensibility* bleeds from blank nothingness.

Carl expects to improve his speed each time—without sacrificing quality. He breathes carefully as he squints at each line, each paint daub, to verify that the image in his eye is what his mind's eye conceived.

He feels cramps in his back, but nothing cramps his style. He feels just like he did way back on May 9 this year: *Now* is his *Liberation* from— or escape out of—restrictions and inhibitions—those double, demonic consequences of a lack of imagination.

His exhilaration increases daily as his acceleration in facility increases. Carl realizes that he has produced, is producing, fluid work for sale; that he can be liquid and affluent, as the impending wet of paint or ink achieves the charted illustration. Then, following each righteous execution—in his own eye—he can chug back wine, pretend to be Robert Graves on Majorca.

Carl's kitchen table bristles now with charcoal pencils, pastels, watercolours, and model-kit oils, all handy. For Carl, *Art* borders on *Craft*. This *Labour* requires a deft hand.

Carl recalls Leo Fennel. The old drunk's voice wheezes in his ear, instructing him how to proceed. Carl begins to whistle—even without the record player turning or the radio tuning in some song. This veritable independence is intoxicating.

* * *

Carl goes to the corner store and buys milk and bread—plus fried herring, onions, and cheese. Then he bags white wine from a Belle Aire bootlegger—to celebrate his ascension to *Art*. He thrills to see images leap forth from pencil and paint, according to *Imagination*, and the fine muscles of his dexterous, finessing hand.

Now, the fantasy of a painter's *Harem*—of models and mistresses, harlots and bluestockings—returns with a vengeance. To lay down Simone de Beauvoir—the chic French *philosophe*—and Barbara Shelley— the queen of British horror flicks—*ensemble*!

Carl crafts two six-by-eight-inch paintings: *Full Moon*. The picture features a yellow moon suspended in a turquoise sky over a river streaked with turquoise, yellow, green, and white. The crinkled tinfoil sandwiched between the cardboard back and glass surface makes each element shimmer. Carl's innovation is to use model-kit paint as his medium: its texture is thick luxury compared to ordinary oils. Plus, it's cheaper.

Sunday, November 8

Come five p.m., Carl bundles a few works in an old brown leather briefcase (a "Great Britain" castoff) and calls on four neighbourhood families: the Pleasants, the Downeys, the Crawfords, and the Dayes. He displays his works; he snags *instant* sales. Little gab needed. Folks' faces gather about his paintings, looking at each as if it's a mirror, an aquarium, or a home-ready vision of *Gloom*-disintegrating gold. Dollars waft Carl's way like homing pigeons. Folks eye a painting, their wallets or purses open, and crinkled, grubby, low-denomination bills pop up. Soon, the Queen is bent and beaming, multiply, adjacent his rear orifice. *Capital!*

Next, Pow-Pow buys two *Lighthouse* paintings, and orders two *Pals*—a sentimental, Norman Rockwell–category pic of a pussy and a puppy, lapping milk from the same bowl. The paintings will grace a wall where all patrons' eyes travel as their heads are tilted, pivoted, and clipped or "buzzed." While at Pow-Pow's parlour, Carl meets Gerry Clark, of Africville, who purchases one *Pals* for his Beechville gal. The copycat Queen is now swelling Carl's wallet as much as a babe is swelling the living Queen's abdomen.

Carl raps on Rev. Map's door. The minister hums and points and produces a five-dollar bill; he purchases Carl's *Autumn* painting (a tree florid in tiny rectangles of red, gold, orange, and lemon). The sale is transacted inside a minute, with no sermon voiced.

Carl slides through premature winter slush and frosty darkness to three homes, where four folks are in. He markets No. 7 *Full Moon* (deep blue water, yellow-white moon, purple hills, white-greyish clouds), plus *Church*. He clinches three sales—including one from the late police chief's widow, Mrs. Fox. Carl grins because he's outfoxed *Mr.* Fox by vending his Negro art to the dead cop's honourable, available widow.

Emboldened, Carl sprints over to Muriel's and Lola's. Lola orders a copy of *Pals*. Carl wonders if they spy a Lesbian subtext: all that lapping. (Well, pets *are* fetishes.) But his portrait of Muriel, still fronting her—or *their*—bedroom archway, is a perpetual reminder of his bankable talent.

Back home, totalling the accounts, Carl discovers *Art*'s earned him, in a few hours, after only a week's worth of work, the equivalent of a week's pay at the station. *Exhilarating!* His *metier* or programme—to pass from plain proletarian to *Beaux-Arts* Bohemian—is succeeding. Sweet lady Liz alongside, if human; under him, if machine. But granting support in either circumstance.

He rushes up Belle Aire Terrace to show Mrs. Black—his mom—how well he's done. She is pleased, and sits her *succeeding* son to a meal of well-spiced venison.

In the meantime, the number of U.S. dollars in circulation is now exceeding the amount of gold for which they can be exchanged. The greenback is no longer gold-backed. Now, Carl believes his art might be worth gold, not mere (toilet) paper currency.

(In one week from now, none of the above will interest the Clutter clan of Holcomb, Kansas. In cold blood, their murders will seep into black ink.)

• • •

Carl's popular aesthetic conjoins Norman Rockwell and the po' boy illustrator of Montmartre, Francisque Poulbot. He plies an illuminated, folkish pictorialism. He limns trees, churches, pets, bullfights, and coastal scenes (lighthouses, sailboats): his art is for bedrooms, living rooms, kitchens, and offices, not art galleries, at least *not* necessarily.

Anyhow, he prefers technique to theory, and talent to mere technique. So, a war scene features metal scraps like agitated garbage, heightened corpses (grimaces, leering skulls), unforgettable black horses loosing dense floods of scarlet, and tragic gestures of limbs nettled—crucified—in barbed wire. Always, also, there are archaic trees, denuded of leaves, even branches, mimicking stakes. The sun is outlined in charcoal and coloured a bastard mustard. Or Carl drafts an agricultural drama, a set of compound fields, or orchards, wherein matadors appear with spontaneous blades and bleeding bulls.

Let critics condemn him as campy: *Fine*, thinks Carl, so long as he's not homeless. Carl figures, *Most people are willing to pay ten dollars for my eleven-by-fourteen pix. But how can I churn them out faster?* His answer? A one-man factory. *Organized properly, I can produce two small paintings and one large one per day, and still have time, at night, to scout for orders.*

Here, innocently, Carl mimics the Florida Highwaymen, those U.S. Negroes who, tired of slaving for peanuts in cotton fields and orange groves, now paint and sell Florida seascapes—thereby escaping cracker bosses, redneck overseers, and KKK cops. Like them, Carl paints for personal-pleasure-and-private-profit. He adopts the aesthetic of *Stag*, whose ads tout a "Famous Writers School" that pledges commissions because "11,000 U.S. publications pay for fresh material." Indeed, he wants to *market*—like a butcher his cuts. While he paints, he auditions Arthur Fiedler and the Boston Pops Orchestra's *Classical Music for People Who Hate Classical Music*. This version of Sibelius's "Finlandia" conjures up rugged, stony, forested, and ocean-carved Nova Scotia: a theme for his *Art*.

As for the Bluenoses who buy his paintings, they see therein their own world suddenly beautified. The Atlantic Ocean now churns, burgeons, charges, with gold and white streaks startling the indigo and the purple; their churches look wilderness chapels, steepled versions of Christ's manger; their pets are symbols of fraternity; their lighthouses are transfigured, haloed crucifixes. They see in Carl's art the proof of their own experiences.

Thus, Carl now heeds Iago's Polonius-style advice: "Put money in thy purse." The sovereign looks sweet when her face folds, in Warhol-like multiples, into Carl's wallet.

Better yet, it's likely easier to date a lady: Who don't wanna be a model?

Carl is happy with Liz. But, now that he's marketing his work—and making a mark—he's beginning to imagine himself an honest heir to beatnik poets and cubist painters, and to regard the endlessly reproducing tribe of women as wandering *Illuminati* of the *Eternal*, or as soft, Pre-Raphaelite diamonds, all diaphanous undress and clear complexions, and comfortingly available.

Now, quite out of the blue, Carl receives a letter from "Blue Roses," asking that he visit her in Truro. She says she's ill. But Carl shrugs, figuring it can't be too serious, or she'd have said so. He ignores the letter. Too busy. *Another time. Another life.*

Sunday, November 22

Victoria summons Carl to a fresh feed of venison. He's glad to go, for he detects a new evaluation of himself—her single legitimate son—by her, thanks to his nascent reputation as a *Negro Artist* of Nova Scotia.

He scoots over to her parlour, and she sets down the steaming, spicy bowl for his nourishment and enjoyment. This is what she has meant to do—tried to do—for all her sons: to provide for their enhancement and advancement despite the humiliation of beginning so poorly and so anonymously in a barn. She congratulates Carl on his profitable concern but also tells him that, should he fail to keep the business going, she'll ensure that Mr. Beardsley finds Carl a fresh railway position. Carl protests, but his mother insists, "It's my duty to my son."

Only now does Carl recognize—with a spoonful of venison en route to his mouth—that it was his mother's bargain with Leo Fennel that got him his first art lessons, anyway. Victoria has sacrificed herself, always, even by arranging the railway job *via* Grantley Beardsley. Moreover, his brothers are proceeding, even succeeding: Granville has enlisted in the army and is stationed on the Suez Canal as part of the United Nations Expeditionary Force to help keep the peace between Egypt and Israel; Premiere is a music teacher in Edmonton, and Encore is a teacher at a school for the deaf in Calgary; Huckabuck has joined the Royal Canadian Air Force and is based presently in Goose Bay. Surely Victoria's labours and emphases on elocution and education have contributed to the "Black boys" becoming more than "black boys," as is true for Carl himself.

Carl feels in his gut that he's been unfair to Victoria, as he has been to Muriel (in particular)—that both his mother and his (once) lover have had to settle for dreadful arrangements to accord him maternal love in the first instance and erotic love in the second.

He tells himself, *To be sanctimonious is to be insane.* If *Understanding* is one charity, *Forgiveness* is the perfect kindness.

Marina phones Carl to come sup with her at the Armview Restaurant. She'd like to buy a painting "that I've heard so much about," and Carl's bemused by the sale. He's also curious about this woman, to see if she still hoodoos him.

Now a dirty evening—pallid, bleaching, drenching precipitation—swamps this dirty day. There's nothing to do but to do what must be done.

Nigh eight p.m., Carl grabs a few pictures and cabs over to the restaurant. Warm-hearted, Cape Breton fiddles throb from the jukebox. Santa and his bread-coloured beard abound—like a propaganda icon. (Santa's the capitalist version of Satan.)

Mar charms Carl. It's winter but she's wearing a V-neck, sapphire cotton sweater that lets him imagine the deeper V of her cleavage; and her bra could be from Frederick's of Hollywood, for her Sunday-school-teacher breasts now look like in-your-face tits—as if flowering from a corset. Hard it be for Carl to concentrate on a business pitch—his emancipating proclamation (about which he feels a tad guilty). But the samples delight Mar: she asks for two *Lighthouse* paintings. Personal *Enlightenment*.

Carl feels good: that she, the university-educated nurse, is purchasing art from him, a high-school dropout and ex–railway hand, seems to equalize the two. *Moreover*, he thinks, *my wallet has expanded so substantially, in a single month, that I can afford to be lavish—even more than usual when it comes to her*. Carl doubts that Leicester could offer anything but a boorish, *bourgeois* life: Naugahyde furniture, formaldehyde fornication, and Jekyll-and-Hyde duplicity—joker at *Gynecology*, jerk at husbandry.

Then, over cheeseburgers and fries (and ginger ale for Carl, Coke for her), plus the diabolically insipid tune "Jingle Bells," Mar shocks Carl: "I'm expecting."

Carl is flabbergasted. "Whaddya mean?"

"I'm going to be a mother—in seven months."

"You said that you'd wait; that I'd have to wait."

"I'm sorry to let you down."

"You let yourself down . . ." Carl is harsh. "What about all that crap about setting an example, about staying a virgin unto marriage, about finishing your studies?"

His anger is vomit—acid—in his lungs. Mar refuses to meet his eyes. He notices that his fragrant Xmas gift to her of Chanel No. 5 mixes with the odour of fried onions to raise a delirious, stomach-churning stench. Carl recalls Muriel's odoriferous quarters. Mar's clothes seem now just as sordid. The two women become a *picante*, sickening jumble in his mind. Carl's leather jacket feels tight, hot. The woman who personified *Virtue* is unworthy the deification. She was as compliant with Leicester's flexible postures as is her bottom to sitting. Carl wonders whether Leicester had to pry apart her jaws—like a horse's—or split her legs—like a hook does a fish's jaws—to use her sex. Or was it just real, real, fuckin easy?

"I'll be respectable. Leicester's betrothed to me."

"Well, show me the ring! How many carats? When's the wedding date?"

"We'll be married in Jamaica—at Ocho Rios."

"Where's your ring?"

Mar flashes anger now: "True *Love* doesn't need trinkets."

"Oh yeah? The Government of Canada will want to see all those trinkets if he tries to stay in the country as your 'husband.'"

"I don't like your insinuations."

"I'm insinuating nothing! I'll believe this news about your marriage when I read it in the newspaper." (Carl almost said *funny papers*.)

Mar begins to tear up. But an Arctic avalanche weights and chills Carl's heart.

"Why'd you invite me here? I can't believe it was to tell me this fishy story about a phony engagement and a make-believe wedding."

Marina begins to bawl: "Maybe he won't marry me."

Carl sits up. "So, Mr. Leicester Jenkins is a cad?"

"He won't set a date."

She's sniffling, but Carl is vengeful. "So, the hack doc flees Grenada, comes to Halifax, gads about, *natch*, cad in a Cadillac, spewin a lot of bunk, and you effin bunk with him, while standing up, Miss Goody Two-Shoes, in church and giving me the cold shoulder—as if I'm the bum. So, what am I supposed to do about your fix? You want me to go and hit Doc Jenkins, Maiden-Deflowerer, so he'll cough up a wedding date and a ring?"

"You've often said you love . . . me, and I know I've been slow to say it. But, Carlyle, honestly, you always were the man for me." As Marina speaks, her breasts lift up, with deliberate vigour, as she dabs her tears (a genteel form of *Sleaze*).

"Whoa, sister! When I wanted you, you wanted nothing to do with Grade-Ten-dropout me . . . I guess your *bambino* needs a daddy-o . . ."

"Muriel Dixon almost had a baby for you."

"As you say, *almost*. I've no obligation to her—and none to you."

"I thought you loved me."

"'*Love*' isn't love when it's past-tense. Find another patsy. Oh yeah, congrats."

"Carl, oh Carl, how can you be so cruel . . . so cold?"

"Well, Marina, you had the hots for a liar but were solidly ice-cold to me, who *did—past-tense*—love you."

Mar's refreshed tears splash into her mustard, but vinegar—saltily—her fries. Her sobs steep to blubbering, and so Carl acts. To preserve his samples from teardrop stains, he slides them back into his satchel; then, he motions for the waitress (who's eager to usher doleful Marina out the restaurant and into the truly tearful night), pays the bill, adds a tip, then takes Marina by the arm to help her rise: "We're leaving."

Marina sops her tears with a napkin: it disintegrates like Leicester's promises. But she heard *We* inside Carl's "We're." She wonders where they're going. Not for long.

Casino Taxi—the fast one—shows up. Car slides into the back seat beside Marina. Free of the contradicting odour of onions, her perfume, gone back to its Parisian roots, enchants anew. Carl directs the driver to 1½ Belle Aire Terrace.

Marina is startled and half expects, half fears, that Carl will prostrate her—take her vengefully—no permission sought. Her body feels very nearly a corpse. She considers jumping from the cab at the first red light, but also wonders if, by making love with Carl, she can salvage her situation.

Carl is contemplating *Molestation*: to have Marina, naked tits to his naked breast, and thrust into her hard enough to exorcise her lingering spell upon him and, better yet, trigger an instant abortion of Leicester's papoose. Her confession's enraged him enough to give her bod a *sayonara* drilling she'll never forget.

Once home, Carl commands Mar brusquely to remove her raincoat, bandana, scarf, and boots, and she does so. Not allowing her to finish, he pulls her roughly against him and kisses her hard. She returns the kiss and begins to moan softly in Carl's arms.

But Carl pushes her away; he barks, "I've wanted you a long, long time, and I'm mad enough to take you—to just take you. But I won't. Somewhere along the line, you decided to love Leicester and stop waiting for me."

"You never ever waited for me." Mar has one boot on, one boot off.

"You're right, Mar. I'm a natural man. Like Ecclesiastes says. You must be a natural woman?"

"I fell in love."

"Yeah. Too bad. Too bad for me. So, here's what we're going to do. You're going to call Leicester and tell him that you and I will marry. I'll take the phone to confirm it. Next, you'll tell him that I know everything, that your baby is his. Then, I'll tell him that his child will be put up for adoption—but by some work-home or a circus—and that we'll stick ads in Grenadian newspapers to say so. His name will be mud everywhere the wind blows."

"But I want Leicester to marry me. To raise our child together."

"Nothing is guaranteed that isn't tried. *Capiche?*"

Marina nods in acquiescence. Carl sees her as an obedient animal— if contaminated—at last. Carl hands her the phone: "Dial!"

His scenario plays out as Carl schemes. Leicester protests the threat that Carl and Mar unfold. When Marina hangs up, trembling, sobbing again, Carl holds her, and says, "Now give me his address so that I can go and encourage him further to keep his word to you."

"Carlyle, Carl, whatcha gonna do?"

Strange to hear the university student lapse into natural speech, Carl thinks.

"I'm a-gonna do what I shoulda done first time I saw his cretin face."

"Carl!"

"Yes, I will. Put push to shove. Prove misanthropic. You take a taxi home. By tomorrow morning, your engagement will be back on."

Carl, I . . ."

"Mar, Leicester's insolent, detestable rot. But he's still lucky to have you—or maybe you deserve each other? Now, go. Leave before I change my mind." Carl slides a lighthouse painting into Mar's purse. "A souvenir for you to remember me by."

• • •

Though Leicester Jenkins is a big man, six-feet-plus tall and weighing several dozen stone, Carl's first punch catches him unawares, staggering him and knocking free his glasses, as soon as he opens his door, in his silk slippers and silk bathrobe, to answer the call of "pizza delivery." The pursuant punches aren't surprises, but still stun and stunt im down, so buddy is on his back, flailing like the human cockroach in Kafka's tale. It's a grotesque subjugation. But Carl feels amazingly normal. Punches leap about Leicester's face. The two men are as detached as toilets but also just as intimate.

Leicester manages to croak, from a still toothful but bloody mouth, "You're upset cos I fucked your lil virgin, cos ya warn't mon enough." (The last three syllables sounded incongruously like "Rachmaninov," minus the "Rach.")

"Nope! Dope! Ya got *my* friend pregnant and now you're not man enough to marry. Well, I'll marry her and stick your child, girl or boy, in a circus."

Each of Carl's more-or-less Maoist blows conceives *Diplomacy* as

248

War. His aren't mock stings; they're intended to impart scars too stunning for even a doctor to explain. Only when Leicester's face is a gory shell does Carl leave off.

It occurs to Carl that his B.W.I. rivals—Leicester Jenkins, Fredrickson Dent, even Grantley Beardsley—are all spectres (psychological brethren)—of his long-gone Carib father. He taxis back home, puts on Mathis, gulps dark rum, sits looking at his fists. Weeps.

• • •

Life is as harrowing as an unexpected pregnancy. In June 1960, Mar will show up, in a Grenadian church, at the altar, in "blasphemous" white, her belly bulging. But as Leicester Jenkins is about to say, "I do," a tan woman, his *other* fiancée, shows up, her belly mirroring the frontal balloon that Marina bears . . . No words are said. Marina breaks from her plausible paralysis, slaps Leicester so hard his head twists upon his neck. She flees from the church.

To mitigate her *Disgrace*, to—in fact—undo it substantially, Marina will complete her *Nursing* degree in Montreal. She elects to become a secular nun—a spinster—dedicating herself to her profession, to have a distinguished career. She will leave Leicester's baby—her son—with her mother (the baby's grandmother) in Three Mile Plains, N.S. She will also leave it up to Leicester to determine how *responsible* a father he will be to his son. But he will become a doctor whose medical licence will be revoked due to criminal interference with a minor. For this same reason, he will be forbidden to see his son.

Also in June 1960, in Stratford, Ontario, a just-married bride, twenty-one, still in her ivory gown, will have her wedding picture taken in a park along a white-swan-backdrop river: Unbeknownst to her, however, the train of her gown, dipping in the water, will absorb so much of it that the dress becomes heavily sodden enough to pull her into the element—and down. Two men attempt rescue, but the dress is too weighty and the current too strong.

• • •

Carl's art sales soar. No longer just pitching art to neighbours and his (ex) railway colleagues, he's beginning to get buyers from the tourist trade, *Bluenose* souvenir shops. He's so popular that he's profiled in *The Chronicle Herald*, successor to the paper he'd delivered as a lad.

Carl's joy thrills Liz, and she is heartened that there is no woman interfering with or interrupting *their* (and his) pleasures (although she's ignorant of his dream of *potentially* seducing his models). Being at Dalhousie University—in that small world—Liz hears of Mar's pregnancy by a foreign Negro, and then of the man's mysterious beating, but also of the beatings formerly visited upon Avril by a local man, and so she is relieved that she and Carl have avoided the despair of one woman and the degradation of the other (the abstract nouns being interchangeable). Liz is utterly unaware of Carl's hand in these violences, direct or indirect. She anticipates, rather, his hand in marriage . . .

So impressed is Mrs. Victoria Black by her son's artistic commerce, he has now a standing offer to visit her on Sundays for supper. Better still, because Carl has a real business to mind—his art—he's no longer interfering in hers, i.e., her relations with Grantley.

Carl's talent is further affirmed, thanks to a letter from starlet Aunt Pretty, summoning him to New York City, where she's secured him a contract, at three hundred dollars per week, to paint backdrop scenery for Broadway shows, starting May 1, 1960. Carl thinks, *Hot diggity dang!* The job will prevent any return to the drudgery of Mr. Beardsley's CNR. It also means escape from the socio-economic *Waste Land* of Acadia, which sees Negroes kept in peonage, but ever so politely, with tea and biscuits and photo ops served up for "good behaviour."

Liz is supremely delighted when Carl insists she accompany him to Manhattan. She knows that the idea is tantamount to a marriage proposal, and, so, her answer must be a clapping, resonant "Yes!"

But Liz doesn't know about Pretty Waters's "P.S." to her nephew. It is frank: "I hear that you are seeing a woman. Black or white, doesn't matter: I advise you to *not* let yourself be trapped by romantic feelings for anyone 'down home' in Nova Scotia. New York is twenty times bigger, and so you have twenty times the choice of a lover—or bride. Here, nobody cares what you do, so long as you succeed. Remember: For an artist, *Art* comes first." (Carl recalls that Aunt Pretty gave her only child to a childless couple to rear.) "It sounds selfish, but it's truly sound advice. Nephew, do not make your mother's mistake of thinking that minutes—or hours—of baby-producing *Pleasure* is a pursuit. The *Vocation* of an artist is to create *Art*."

Carl rereads the letter severally, but hides its terminus from Liz. He knows that if he goes to New York, he'll want Liz to join him, lickety-split. To go from her fishing village to Greenwich Village; to go from Halifax to Harlem. To advance them *both*. He'll leap from earning three thousand dollars per annum—including tips (already *twice* the annual income of the poorest, *working* Halifax Negroes)—to accumulating fifteen thousand in Uncle Sam bucks, perhaps more. And he could paint even paperback covers on the side . . . And the models he could "audition"? *Tempting! Righteously tempting!*

Saturday, December 12

Dawn brings sad *Duty*: under a wet, rainy sky, Carl drives Liz II into winter storage at Corkum's Halifax Motorcycle Shoppe. He's sorry to store his machine again, but now that he's painting, he just doesn't cycle as much. Too, the machine's motor has to be taken apart to be put back together in the spring. Corkum has to get the grit out. The BMW has been on the road for seven months—not a bad extension of the season, by some eight weeks, anyway.

But as Carl assigns Liz II to her Christmas-until-Easter garage, he feels *Time* winging swiftly away, with no real accomplishment, on his part, to show. In less than six months, he'll be twenty-five, and not employed at anything that most Coloured folk would recognize as a *j-o-b*. He is better off scrambling to sell his art than ever he was to humble and whistle and grin to secure train passengers' tips. His relative economic independence is rare in Negro Halifax. He's so unusual as to be eccentric. Might he now try keeping a wife?

Certes: Carl likes being nominally single. From what he's seen of marriage, it seems a headache, heartache, and pain-in-the-ass. The idea that two psychologically distinct persons should be able to live "in love" all their days strikes Carl as being more *Mythology* than *Theology*. His coupling—or affair—with L.P. is as fine as it can get, he thinks. He worries that marriage would, in fact, ruin all. Yet, should she agree to have his hand, *if* offered, he feels that they'd succeed. No need to rush, though: better to get to know each other *better*.

Liz is ready. Privately, she thinks that Carl's belated, but explicit, split from Marina is the bravest thing he's ever done. Selfish, yes, are her reasons for this surmise. She believes that Mar was Carl's code for *Respectability* and *Conformity*, the helpmates of *Boredom* and the enemies of *Art*. She sees Carl for who he is, and he is not a man who can settle comfortably for a mousy nurse (even if Coloured), all tawdry lingerie in the bedroom and total hypocrisy in church. Liz lauds Aunt Pretty's initiative to line up a gig for Carl in "Gotham City," a place where Caucasian-Negro couples are almost normal (as projected in John Cassavetes's film *Shadows*). She wagers her *Library Science* degree can profit her in one of the supreme card-catalogue systems on earth. What an ascension: to go from chucking cod into South Shore barrels to shelving books in the New York Public Library. Too practical to be already eyeing wedding dresses, Liz will be firm—once Carl requests her hand—that they *must* marry before they head south to "You-Ça."

Carl would like to settle down. That age—twenty-five—which is soon upon him, says that he's already a third of the way to the grave, given *Life Expectancy* (though, as a Coloured man, he is being overly generous in this allocation). *Marriage* could debase the chemistry, spoil the biology, of his coupling with Liz. But Carl can entertain the risk, for he supposes Liz broad-minded enough to allow him a discreet flirtation with a model, to maintain his studio as a private, bachelor space. So long as *Art* wins them *Prosperity* tantamount to *Security*.

Monday, December 14

Grantley Beardsley lands Carl a six-month railway gig in Moncton, N.B. Carl accepts: to expand his art business, he needs a horizon beyond Halifax. Station-to-station sales beat door-to-door. For now.

Carl deems the move temporary: until Liz completes her *Library Science* degree and they can both remove to New York in the spring. He knows G.B. can replace him quickly once he gives his notice.

So, come New Year's Day, 1960, Carl will shuttle to Moncton to start his new railway job as "Coordinator of Linen Services"—the laundering of tablecloths, napkins, sheets, and pillowcases—for the entire Atlantic division of CNR. Carl will now be superior to the Halifax linen depot, though he'd need to acquire *some* French were he to keep the position. (Remembering his mother's ex-career, Carl disputes this necessity: Are germs and dirt, or soap and water, cognizant of languages? A stain is a stain.) But he's certain that he'll continue painting, and now he can use the railway porters to help market his works (wares) to prospective customers as far west as Montreal and as far south as Boston.

In the meantime, tonight, Carl taxis over to a green-painted, three-storey, wooden house on Buckingham Street that he now knows well. He rings a doorbell for the third floor, and the front-door buzzer clatters. The door opens, and he mounts stairs to Liz's capacious digs; indeed, Carl could fit his rooms into her flat and have space left over. (But Belle Aire Terrace is in hard-up North End; Buckingham Street brushes downy South End.)

When Liz opens her door and kisses Carl, he feels the world awake. She takes his coat and sets out red wine. He spills some, by accident, but fingers her name in it on white cotton, and she laughs—contemplative. Her candles splash an obscure yellow on the walls; the effect's a Nativity scene. Carl jugs tender ounces of wine, and Liz plunks into his lap to urge drowsy struggling. Her Fall exams are done; she has the look of an unearthed diamond, instantly imperious amid the surrounding light, tonight.

Liz leads Carl to her clean bed. She strips herself down to the nakedness of a nymph—all turmoil of eyelashes and Coca-Cola mouth and tang of sweat. Carl drinks in her port-hued hair; he caresses Liz's delicate gap. He swells with triumph. Soon, there's a nice, percussive *smack* as he touches bottom, again and again. His outrageous, prodigious loving follows Yma Sumac's rhapsodic aphrodisiac "Ataypura." Their climax is as conclusive as a definition.

Tomorrow, Pablo Neruda will publish privately *Cien sonetos de amor*. What Carl and Liz have just made *live*.

Sunday, January 31

The Year of the Rat, 1960, came in with the same din of spoon-beaten pots and pans that one hears in Halifax. In Moncton, night catches in the pines like black hair in a comb. The wet, sweet scent of black ink images night.

Since January 1, Moncton has been *the* sanctuary of commercial Negro *Art* in the Caucasian-*Art*-market-dominated Maritimes. Carl has become a breakneck, rabid painter, striking, quickly, works that verify his quality and clarify his talent. Simultaneously, he jockeys—maniacally—by train, Moncton-Halifax-Moncton. In Moncton, he works and paints, fulfilling job demands and gratifying painterly inspiration. In Halifax, he has the deliria of Liz and her home and her very uplifting, very elevating "wine cellar."

Also, letters have winged to and fro New York City. Aunt Pretty is able to guarantee Carl's post. He still believes he'll carry Liz along (as *un fait accompli*), flouting his aunt's advice that he arrive unpartnered to Manhattan. Spring—April—can't come too soon!

Good Friday, April 15

"Your son is dying."

Carl was in the Moncton station's Linen and Equipment Room when a co-worker handed him the phone yesterday. The tone of the female speaker was harsh, shrill, and commanding: "You'd best come and see your son before he dies."

That one sentence left Carl shaken, flabbergasted, and anxious. Still, his interlocutor did not allow him time to even wish to hang up. She had much to tell, and she had long delayed in saying it.

His son's birth had been "biblically hard," said the mature female voice. It had been natural, no Caesarean, but extremely painful, and the newborn had been sickly from the start—seemingly prey to every flu. Now he is deathly ill with pneumonia and back in the hospital.

The mother hadn't wanted to call: Carl's son was born in February, but the mother had kept her pregnancy private and Carl's paternity secret, preferring to raise the child within the swaddling embrace of her family home. Once her son was old enough, she had decided, she'd return to college and likely find a proper husband there.

But given the potential mortal illness of the infant, the grandmother had overruled the mother, declaring that Carl should have a chance to see his son before he perished. Carl should be grateful for that grace, though part of him would consider the death of the boy, if he is his son, liberation for the mother—and a painful blessing for himself.

So, yesterday, Carl learned that he's a father—perhaps—though ephemerally—perhaps. Yet, he should wish the child's survival, whoever his sire. He—Carl—has seen more death than most young men who are not soldiers. He should like the tyke to survive, if not thrive.

Today, he leaves Moncton on Liz II (rescued from storage after a visit back to Halifax in March) and motors back to Nova Scotia to see the child—and to verify that he is, in *face*, his very own. After that, and if the boy lives, decisions must be entertained.

Pleasant it is to have thirty-five horses bottled up in the R69's two-cylinder, horizontally opposed, 590 cc engine. It gives Carl the sensation that he's flying. *Flying!* Again. But will his wings be clipped—will he have to crash to earth—if he is no more a single being, but now half the fount of at least one new genealogy?

Cold, sunlit day. Gobs of snow are still clotting ditches and clumped on hillsides. Lots of meltwater, mud, and runoff. The countryside is brown with hints of green: here a patch of grass, there a stand of spruce. Still, Carl notices the imperious Petitcodiac River, its perennial April occupation of adjacent farms and brush, and its dispatching of squads of ice onto the surrounding fields, turning them into plantations of "Arctic cotton." Typical springtime in Nouveau-Brunswick— half-Acadian, half-angler. Carl's mind flashes back to dead Mack and dead Sandy, two once–motorcycle pals, *his*, who can never now know *Paternity*, throughout all of *Eternity*.

Carl roars from Moncton down to Sackville, then back across the Tantramar Marshes and into Nova Scotia. From the border town, Amherst, he has a two-hour drive to Truro, and from there, he meets the Truro-Windsor highway—The Glooscap Trail—a vista of mud flats, Bay of Fundy inlets, one-lane bridges, and timber truck chasing, shadowing, timber truck, the woodlands looking on, askance.

At Windsor, Carl motors to the Memorial Hospital, a kind of bungalow with barracks that crowns a slight hill above the Avon River. His heart is stuck in his lungs: blood wallops through his veins. He half-expects to hear that the infant is dead—and if he is, Carl suspects he'll feel reprieved as much as bereaved.

Carl gives the boy's name (only learned yesterday), and a nurse brings him to look in on a tiny being, brown, and trailing tubes: he is asleep and sucking his thumb. But when he hears Carl's whisper, his eyes—dark brown—suddenly open, and Carl sees himself in his gaze—and he sees himself in the boy's smile.

When Carl sees his son, he feels himself suddenly connected to *Genealogy*—the epic poetry of *Biology*—despite the mistakes of his parents and his own sins. *And his son's mother?*

Carl's heart dissolves. He gasps, "*My* boy . . ." He remembers calling Muriel "my love" at the moment of her miscarriage, nine months ago. Then, Carl must exit the room: tears choke his breath. Still, he asks, "How's Royal Anthony doing? What's the prognosis?"

The nurse warns: "Pneumonia in infants is dangerous, and there may be injury to his organs that's so far invisible, but his heart is strong, and he should pull through." Carl begs her and the doctors to keep his son alive.

Carl has a son, is a father. Must he husband the mother? The boy, should he survive, is the natural consequence of a spring fling, yet he was not wished for. To the mother's credit, she has not tried to trap Carl, but has been eager to leave him free, while she gets on with her own life. Carl thinks, *She's quite the girl—obviously.*

Carl remembers that his own father married his mother under duress, then sailed away, only God knows where. He deposited his seed and signed over his surname. Carl don't want his son to say the same of him, but he also don't want to marry the mother (if she wants him), merely to satisfy *Propriety*. *Fate* has made him a father, but *Necessity* has made him an artist, and trial-and-error (much error) has brought him to Liz and she to Carl. *What is to be done?*

Too, Royal's—Roy's—mom may reject Carlyle: she may feel, rightly, that Carl spurned her by not responding to her November letter mentioning "illness."

At three p.m., Carl drives east on Highway 1, through the rolling countryside of Windsor's Avon River delta. Currently a tan waste, the fields are just commencing to green out of muck and ferment.

After only ten minutes, Carl reaches Green Street and turns right. He jumps over the train tracks, near where Mar's family lives, and continues up a hill on a road that's mud, gravel, and potholes. (This dirt road would drive any driver snaky.)

Carl passes a house with a B/A (British American) Oil Company sign used as decoration (because its initials match those of the home-owner, Boyd Auburn, whose wife left him for a bodybuilder). Opposite sits the now-empty house of Rev. Ohio States. (His son, Washington, married his own pupil, Beulah White [Mar's aunt], but they were never allowed consummation: her father prevented it. So Washington quit teaching, became a railway porter, and remarried. At that point, he was arrested, convicted of bigamy, and jailed. Then, his father died, his sisters wed and moved; thus, the house now sits vacant, evaporating slowly into weeds.)

At the top of the hill is a modest house, a plain affair—two storeys of white-painted wood—but boasting a verandah. It is the largest house on Green Street, with a flower garden beginning to sprout out front beside the lawn, and a tractor and a horse in a field, plus crabapple and pear trees about the property. For a rural dwelling, in a Coloured village, the house boasts *Prosperity*. Carl turns into this driveway, feeling very self-conscious as he rolls to a stop beside a new car and a truck and removes his helmet.

He goes to the back door—the kitchen door—and knocks. At the same time, a mangy, barbed-wire-mean dog roars and growls alarm. The man of the house, Mr. States, meets Carl, "the man of the hour," so to speak, man-to-man. His dog's hullabaloo settles to a series of mutters and yelps once it spies Carl admitted to the household.

Mr. States is gruff but not discourteous in welcoming Carl into his comfy kitchen. It is "his," but the real overlord is Mrs. States, who looks at Carl with a face first sour, then severe. Carl looks away, but now sees, in every nook and cranny, whittled sticks, including a forked one used undoubtedly for "water witching," and even a handmade bow-and-arrow set.

Mr. States wears a plaid shirt and blue denim overalls. He holds a lit pipe in one hand. The handmade moccasins that adorn his feet suit his Micmac heritage: pure copper skin with wavy, sloe-black hair that he wears slicked back straight.

(Laura told Carl last year that her dad had—has—a Casanova reputation, and Carl can see why: he's a fighter, a clear "Indian," with muscles enlarged by the woodwork he does on his substantial land holdings. His history is gypsum quarries and throwing raw punches at big mouths.)

Carl's arrival was anticipated. "Laura called. She's at the hospital with your son. She told us that you'd been to see Royal—we call him Roy—and she figured you'd come up home. Take a seat, Mr. Black."

"I'm sorry that I didn't see her when I was at the hospital."

"You didn't come to see her when she was carryin your child. Why should she make herself available to you now? She stayed in another room until you left."

That rejoinder came from Mrs. States. She spat out the words like hot bullets. Carl had to accept her harshness. His selfishness—if inadvertently harmful—had been harsh.

Moreover, Carl now realizes Laura was already "with child" when she came to see him last August. Thus, she'd brought along the suitcase, and had maybe planned to stay with him, to tell him about their "family situation." But she'd not said a word about her condition, maybe because he'd treated her so cavalierly, so casually, in seeking to sate his own desire. He felt ashamed now.

Carl's seated at the table. Mrs. States's oval face communicates amply her ample disapproval of him, so ample as to seem unending. Still, Carl can't say he blames her.

(She is a very white-looking Coloured woman, and pretty, but Laura takes her beauty from her father. Carl sees again that the few-miles-from-Windsor Three Mile Plains has lots of mixed people: part-Coloured, part-Caucasian, part-Micmac. Some women here are actually English ladies who fell in love with a black or brown man in uniform and a notion of Canada. They came after World War II, from London, to live like frontierswomen here.)

Mrs. States sets a good, solid plate of chicken, potatoes, and stewed carrots in front of Carl, along with a side of bread, butter, and molasses, and a good glass of milk. But she also says, directly, "No one here wants—or expects—anything of you, Mr. Black."

"Please call me Carl."

"Land sakes, Carl," she says (without offering *her* first name), "Laur wants nothing from you; we ask you nothing. I called you over Laura's objections, just because I believe your fatherhood is more important than your once-upon-a-time *friendship* with Laura. She has a right to keep her distance from you, but you have a right, I believe, to know you are a father, seeing how sick Roy is."

Her voice is now a pair of scissors crunching through cardboard. Her glance is corrosive.

Mr. States adds, "We love that boy like our very own."

The phone rings. It's Laura. She says she'll stay at the hospital until Carl leaves. Mrs. States tells her, "The man's come right over from Moncton. You might say hello at least. Anyway, you come home when you want. Your brother will bring you."

Mr. States says, as if Carl is invisible, "Now there's a real man: he made our girl a mom, and now he's come up straight after the phone call. He left everything and came up to see the boy. He has *some* decency."

Mrs. States serves Carl Red Rose tea with Carnation milk. Mr. States tosses a thimble of rum therein but pours himself a generous tumbler. "Son, there's no point in you gettin toxicated. You're the one who's gotta decide things—with Laur. I'm givin you a drop for sociability and me a drippin for my health."

Looking about, Carl sees that the house is right cozy and clean. The Blacks might have a better family name, but the States are clearly better off in wealth. Front and centre in the living room is, poignantly, a crib, stocked with toys and soothers. Given her parents' provision for his son and their love for their daughter, Carl sees that she's not been *undone*. They'd sent her to teachers' college; that she's returned a mother is no diminution of her in their eyes.

Mr. States snaps on the radio: AVR plays Craig Douglas's hit "Pretty Blue Eyes." The melodic song ripples all over the kitchen and washes over Carl's heart. Ricky Valance and his equally emotive song "Tell Laura I Love Her" follows the Douglas tune.

Then the kitchen door swings open and Laura comes in. Carl's eyes fix on her, but she lowers hers. Her skin is cream like handmade paper. She wears a flared skirt. Her little limp now tears at Carl's heart: her slender hips, slightly malformed, had made the delivery of his son excruciatingly difficult for her. Carl rises from his seat and goes to her: "How's Roy Anthony?"

Laura smiles: "Better and better."

Carl asks her how *she* is doing. Laura begins to weep. Mr. and Mrs. States say, "We'll leave you two together a spell." Mr. States pours more rum in Carl's cup and slides it over before he leaves the kitchen. Nicely, the rum clears the warm wash of tea. Carl tells Laura that they'll both take their time.

Lightning as jagged as nerves jangles down Spring Rain Tea:
Love *reminded me of you, but* Love *reminded you of me.*

• • •

A few hours later, Carl picks his way down potholed Green Street toward relatively smooth Highway 1. He's grateful for the effortless, no-shift, speedy ride that Liz II allows as he races to Halifax. He thinks about the motorcycle to keep from fixating on difficult choices. But his actual thinking now, subconsciously, is nostalgic. *Maybe the Triumph Bonneville motorcycle is the fastest production machine of 1960, but my Liz II still yells into the wind. Her engine is frothy, twittering.*

Carl negotiates the good road, the dark road, the Nova Scotia road. Carl makes for the third floor of a house on Buckingham Street. He has to decide things. A reckoning. A rectified account. But where is his—their—pavement leading him now? Might he have *Freedom* and a family? What kind of *Freedom*? Which family?

The future? It possesses the serene silence of clouds—untouchable, unbreakable—a fragility secure in its distance. Wounds—and blessings—remain clandestine.

TERMINATION

You owe me nothing but the truth of your journey.
—CHARLES MINGUS, *BENEATH THE UNDERDOG*

ACKNOWLEDGEMENTS

The Motorcyclist was inked in Vichy, France (July–August 2006); Istanbul, Turkey (December 2006); St. Andrews by-the-Sea, New Brunswick (December 2006); Washington, District of Columbia (January 2007); Rodos, Greece (March 2007); Halifax, Nova Scotia (March 2008); Nantes, France (April–May 2009); Porvoo, Finland (June 2009); Istanbul, Turkey (December 2009); Paris, France (July 2011); Mont-Tremblant, Québec (August 2011); Cable Beach, The Bahamas (May 2012); Puumala, Finland (August 2012); Rönnäs, Finland (July 2013); Ilonojaa, Finland (July 2014); Lunenburg, Nova Scotia (August 2014); Coral Harbour, The Bahamas (August 2014); Bordeaux, France (September 2014); Grotto Bay, Bermuda (December 2014); Fort Lauderdale, Florida (April 2015); Krakow, Poland (May 2015); and Toronto, Ontario (off and on from June 2006 to October 2015). A long, strange odyssey, yes, but 2015 mirrors 1959's calendar.

Thanks—in particular—to Elizabeth Eneroth, Gordon and Marilyn Hamlin, Angus "Sock" Johnson, Gerry Marshall, Joan Mendes, and Reid Kenneth White. They knew the facts—and the stories—that serve as the foundation for this novel. Dear friends (principally Diana Manole, Althea Prince, Robert Edison Sandiford, Mansa Trotman, Riitta Tuohiniemi, and Paul Zemokhol) critiqued, queried, and encouraged. I also thank my excellent editors, Iris Tupholme and Jane Warren, and my patient agent, Denise Bukowski, for their poignant alterations and savvy suggestions. Copy editor Stacey Cameron finessed improvements.

I consulted several works to verify geographical, historical, and psychological details: Bob Beatty, *Florida's Highwaymen: Legendary Landscapes* (2005); Elizabeth Bishop, "First Death in Nova Scotia" (1965); Ted Bishop, *Riding with Rilke: Reflections on Motorcycles and Books* (2005); Michael Boudreau, *City of Order: Crime and Society in Halifax, 1918–1935* (2012); Louis W. Collins, *In Halifax Town* (1975); Dalhousie University, *The Condition of the Negroes of Halifax City, Nova Scotia: A Study* (1962); Fred Kaplan, *1959: The Year Everything Changed* (2009); Clem Kovak, *Casebook: The Interracial Sexualists* (1971); Norman Mailer, *The Presidential Papers* (1964); André Pieyre de Mandiargues, *La Motocyclette* (1963); Bud Masters, *Coed for Hire* (1966); Bill Osgerby, *Biker: Truth and Myth* (2005); Robert M. Pirsig, *Zen and the Art of Motorcycle Maintenance* (1974); Christine Cromwell Simmonds, *The Colour of My Memories* (2006); Larry Tye, *Rising from the Rails: Pullman Porters and the Making of the Black Working Class* (2004); and Tennessee Williams, *The Glass Menagerie* (1944).

Beatty's book (a gift from Denise) was spooky: his chronicle of Afro-Floridians who turned to painting landscapes and seascapes, in the latter 1950s, to escape wage-slavery, is *like* the story of my father, Bill Clarke, in the autumn of 1959. Did he know of the Florida Highwaymen? Did he meet any? Or was his turn to painting an accidental—

and parochial Nova Scotian—decision? Was he the first Africadian, naïf artist?

My peripatetic, authorial style has been supported by Dr. Sonia Labatt, Ph.D., and Victoria University (via the E.J. Pratt Professorship at the University of Toronto), the Pierre Elliott Trudeau Foundation's Fellowship Prize (2005–08), the International Writers' and Translators' Centre of Rhodes (March 2007), and Harvard University's William Lyon Mackenzie King Visiting Professorship in Canadian Studies (2013–14). Irrefutable and unforgettable is my patrons' largesse.

ABOUT THE TYPE

THE BODY TYPE was set in Minion Pro, a typeface designed by Robert Slimbach in 1990. The inspiration for Slimbach's design came from late-Renaissance period classic typefaces in the old serif style. This is most apparent in the lowercase characters of Minion, which use old-style Baroque glyphs.

THE DISPLAY TYPE was set in Bill Clarke Caps, a font named for its designer. It is an elegantly eccentric serif, featuring cuneiform-esque brackets and boldly contrasting strokes. The author remembers his father painting the letters in 1969 and thanks Andrew Steeves (of Gaspereau Press) for digitizing this font in 2011.